My Last Breath
The Space Between the Lines

By
Richard C. McClain II

First Printing: 2018

ISBN-13: 978-0-9994523-0-1
ISBN-10: 0-9994523-0-4

Published By
Richard C. McClain II

Cover design by Brandi Doane McCann

For more information visit: www.richardcmcclain.com

DEDICATION

To my wife Sharon and my five children; Nicholas, Nicola, Nathan, Natalie, and Nadia, if it were not for you, I might have taken up golf instead of storytelling.

My Last Breath

The Space Between the Lines

Inhale

I struggle to lift my head. A thin mist covers my eyes, and I find it difficult to focus though my mind has perfect clarity. I manage a weak smile, but it is not for me that I smile. Surrounding me are the people who have most impacted my life. They carry with them unbelievable despair and anguish. It is impossible for them to disengage from their own disbelief, and downheartedness. I want to help them, to reach out and say it's going to be okay. I can't; their grief is too great.

This time the attack inside my body comes on without warning. My torso rises from the bed. Unbelievable pain shrouds me—every pore filled with the knowledge Death is preparing to snatch me from this world.

I have not asked for the termination of painkillers, because I know I'm not that strong. My request for an abbreviated dose has been honored. I don't want my mind fuzzy before I close my eyes for the final time. Since I entered this world battling, determined to let everyone know that I'd arrived, no way will I exit this life as quietly as a stream that meanders along a grassy bank. If I must, I am going out kicking and screaming.

Another wave of pain assaults me overcoming me with its intensity. I feel my breath exit in vaporous short bursts. Did I misgauge the situation wanting to be strong at the end? This is, by far, the worst I've felt it. Each episode sucks more and more energy from my body. Unlike the Eveready Battery, I cannot keep going. I must admit the truth: I have come to the end of myself.

"Daddy," I cry out pleading for relief that won't come. My voice is less than a whisper. "Hold me." Does he hear? Does he understand?

"I am Princess. I'm holding you as tightly as I can." His rasp vocal chords are raw from many weeks at my bedside praying, bartering, crying, and questioning.

I hear the untethered muses roaming around in his mind as if played on surround-sound speakers. They cannot be anchored. I have seen him sad before even disheartened never this disillusioned. He fights to veil his thoughts. *She'll never get to drive a car or experience true love. She'll never get to hold her children.*

He leans over me. His face is close to mine. I blink eagerly when I feel the butterfly kisses. His lips part and I hone in on a smile that stretches from one side of his face to the other. It is not feigned and expresses unabashed joy reminding me of why I love him as much as I do.

"Allie." His voice is not commanding but gentle, like I'm the only person of importance to him. His warm breath coats my face. My pores absorb his familiar scent and my tense body unknots for a moment. The twinkle in his eyes draws my attention. "Do you remember the Frog question?"

I can't nod. It would mean subjecting myself to mind-altering pain, and I'm out of strength to handle another attack. A flutter of my eyes is my solitary reply. I know the conversation he is referring to extremely well. It's as vivid now as the day he asked it. Though it took time, that question inspirited me to live life differently. I close my eyes and rest, comforted by the story and manage another weak smile.

This time I feel the thundering rumble in my stomach that often precedes an attack. My eyes close tight, and my fingers grip fiercely onto Daddy's hand as a much larger upsurge of agony assaults me. My body lifts from the bed as every muscle inside me contracts.

"Daddy." I cry out.

"Breathe Allie. Breathe. Remember, there's a lifetime between each breath." His tears cascade freely onto my face. Individual warm drops of love wash over me. "Come on honey breath for me."

His voice is louder now, stronger, as if he's calling me out of a deep slumber that wants to claim me. It does not settle on deaf ears. I heed his advice and inhale as deeply as I can.

Twelve Months Ago

Chapter One

Of all the games I've worked this season, this is, by far, the most boring. Up forty-five points over our opponents who supposedly brought their 'A' game. It's embarrassing to watch. At the start of the second quarter Coach Taton sent in the second-string. He told them to play at half-speed to keep the game fair. Even with the considerable adjustments made to the offense and defense, our players shine like seasoned NFL pros.

Now that the first-string is finished for the day, they sit on the sideline engaged in passable to vulgar discussions of food, who has the smelliest fart, cars, weekend plans, and their latest sexual conquests. The talk and odor disgusts me. I move away where I can stand by myself pretending I'm interested in the game.

With 7:54 to go in the fourth quarter, it's second down. Our team needs four yards to get the first down. The center hikes the ball to the quarterback who is standing back in the shotgun. Ray Estrada, the running back, stands to the quarterback's right three yards behind him. Estrada runs up to the line prepared to block. He slides off to the right, passing by a blitzing linebacker and runs seven yards past the first-down marker. The quarterback throws the ball high and Estrada leaps making a spectacular one-handed grab. At the same time, the defense's free safety is airborne and makes an even more outstanding tackle.

CRASH. THUD. SILENCE.

Even from the sideline the impact between the two players sounds more ear-splitting than a shotgun blast. Estrada's head snaps back. He hits the ground defenseless and hard. The linebacker tumbles comfortless onto the natural green turf. His body rolls several times before coming to a stop. He rolls to a sitting position, rustles himself to his feet, and trots to the sideline to blistering cheers from his teammates.

Erin, my boss, mentor, and friend, has been pacing the sidelines on the opposite side of our team's bench. We react as one to the fierce clash. This is the part of the game where we shine. I carry my kit and catch up to her. Purple latex-free gloves cover my small hands.

Estrada is Brescade's only running back. First and second string running backs suffered season ending injuries during the first game of the season. Estrada lies on the ground surrounded by coaches, players, and several referees. It reminds me of a group of obnoxious paparazzi without the jutting cameras and microphones.

Erin pulls out a metal whistle that hangs on two silver Figaro chains around her neck. She blows three times in quick succession. The sharp ear-busting bursts breaks away the testosterone-laden group. They scatter away plugging fingers into their ears.

Estrada's body lies in the fetal position. One arm is pinned with agonizing discomfort underneath his body while the other hangs limp across his right thigh. A quick inspection of his body discloses a laceration underneath his chin. Glistening red blood beads from the wound in large droplets creating a small dark crimson circle on the natural green turf.

Without moving his body, Erin uses great care when unfastening the chinstrap to his helmet. I hold his neck firm as she slips off the protective headgear that failed to protect him. She tosses it aside. The helmet rolls several yards stopping at our opponents forty-five-yard line. I can't be the only person who witnesses the irony.

"Four by fours," Erin says.

I pull three of the sealed sterile packets out of my kit, hold tight onto the bottom of the packets, and rip off the tops. I pull out the large absorbent cotton squares and place them firmly into Erin's open palm. She presses the soft compress firmly onto Estrada's bleeding chin. A brisk wind picks up the empty packets and blows them away before I can retrieve them.

Estrada's blood soaks the dressings in a few seconds. Erin tosses the saturated bandages onto the ground her yellow gloves are ruby. I place more four by fours into her free hand.

Estrada's body tenses as Erin presses the second batch of bandages secure against the gash. I lean over him and apply gentle pressure to his shoulders and head to prevent more sudden movement. I explain to him why he needs to stay still. Within seconds, his rigid body relaxes.

When the bleeding underneath his chin stops I let out a long breath.

What a rush.

I haven't had this much excitement since Mason's anterior cruciate ligament tear and Pepperidge's ruptured Achilles.

"How do you feel?" Erin asks

A dazed Estrada replies. "Like I went one round with the UFC champ and lost."

"You should be used to a few body hits by now," Erin says with a guilty grin.

I'm unamused by the comment. Unbeknownst to Coach Taton, Erin's bandaged Estrada more than once for his off-field clashes. Estrada's needed bandaging for a bruised sternum, stitches in what appeared to be a laceration with a knife, and treatment for a black eye.

Word at school is Estrada's the new leader of FADE, a gang in Brescade that died out ten years ago and has reemerged within the last few weeks. It's only a rumor.

There's no way to prove Estrada's injuries are the result of anything other than bad luck. When you add together the individual incidents, and link it with the gossip, it doesn't take a massive leap to realize he's involved in something idiotic.

I don't approve of gangs, fighting or violence of any kind. Nevertheless, my position as junior sports medical rep doesn't give me license to pass judgment. To help the injured is the only reason I'm here—terrible and terrific alike.

"Do you think you can walk on your own?" I ask.

"Please," Estrada says with a haughty drone. With our help, he sits then rises to his feet as the crowd stands. He waves his hand and they erupt into a round of joyous applause.

Erin and I jog back to the sidelines. Estrada runs in between us maintaining our speed. Coach Taton meets us on the field. His weathered face crinkles into a look of desperation. He holds a tattered cap in one hand and runs the fingers of his other hand through his thinning scalp.

"Bottom line."

"I'm fine Coach," Estrada interjects.

"He'll need half a dozen stitches," Erin exclaims still holding the gauze against Estrada's discolored chin.

"But...," Coach says waiting for the rest of the news.

"Coach, I can play," Estrada says.

"Estrada, I didn't ask you."

"He'll be fine Coach," Erin adds. "The laceration on his chin will heal. I'll use dissolvable stitches. He won't need to see a doctor."

"And..."

"I know you're worried about next week's game. He'll be ready." After what seems like an eternity, Coach breathes a sigh of relief wishing he'd taken Estrada out earlier. "He's through for today," Erin adds with a stern warning.

"That's fine because we've had this thing wrapped up five minutes into the first quarter." Coach turns back to the sideline yelling at one of the defensive players to put on his helmet and take over the running back position.

Erin looks across the field then back at me. "Allie, I'll join you in a second. I want to check on the linebacker and make sure he's not hiding any injuries. You escort Ray to the locker room. Keep the pressure on his chin. I'll meet you there in a few minutes." Estrada tilts his head to the side. I catch a brief facial exchange between the two of them before she rushes to the opponent's sideline.

Chapter Two

"I hope they can get the blood out of your jersey," I say to Estrada back in the locker room trying to make conversation.

For the first time, he notices the white numbers on his jersey smeared with red and pink hues. His auburn face goes pale.

"You're not squeamish over a few drops of blood, are you?"

"Nah, I'm cool," he says with a high pitch voice. To keep from laughing I bite my tongue.

"Un huh, I can see that."

"Just because you want to be doctor…"

"I don't want to be a doctor," I respond with more earnestness than I planned. I'm obliged to pause for a moment. Of late, and without invitation, pieces of my past have come whirling back through my mind like a river during flood season. For a moment, I close my eyes my face in a grimace, my teeth gritted, and then I do what I've always done: force my mind to bury the thoughts of the past. "I want to be a nurse," I add. "That's it, a nurse."

"Same thing."

"Call me when you need brain surgery years from now. You can tell me then if you feel the same."

His laugh is warm, but comes to a premature stop. Something's preoccupying him. "Allie, can I ask you something?"

"Ask," I say, wondering why a boy who's never said please or thank you in his life suddenly needs my permission.

"Allie, you're not seeing anybody are you?" His voice is no more than a whisper and causes my eyebrows to raise.

"You mean going out with somebody?" He nods. "No, I'm not dating anyone," I add with forced bravado.

"What about me?"

"I don't know Estrada. Are you going out with anyone?"

"No, I didn't mean it that way."

"Oh?" I reply. My body tenses fearing the turn the conversation is taking.

"I've been watching you, you know, since you started working with the team. You're a cool person. You're focused, skilled, driven and," he pauses, "hot."

A brief smile crosses my lips. It's not something I see when I stare into the mirror. I wave away the comment.

The following pause teems with tension.

"I've given this a lot of thought. You and me together…could be a cool merge don't you think?"

"I—"

"Go out with me Allie."

Estrada's invitation reminds me of a contractual arrangement between business partners. Behind his words is something he's afraid to utter. I reject any genuineness in his question. At least as I stand behind him holding the gauze against his chin, he can't see the nerves in my face pounding against my cheeks both heated and red.

Nevertheless, I'm not sure how to tell him he doesn't interest me. I shake my head in bewilderment. Estrada's not a bad looking guy. His burnished complexion, muscular build, long ebony hair, and shrewd eyes, make him stand out amongst the football jocks. Pitted against the males in school, I'm sure he'd score in the top one percentile.

It never occurred to me Estrada enjoyed a life of singleness. I assumed, overhearing some of the discussion on the sidelines, he had a girlfriend. Doesn't every girl in school want to be his significant other? Then why ask me? Other than joining the football team this season to aid with sports injuries, we share nothing in common.

The blood from his laceration which reopened when we entered the locker room has finally coagulated. My thoughts are numerous and self-deprecating: *Don't reopen the wound. The first words out of Erin's mouth will be, "what did you do?" Remember your training.* With the prudence of a surgeon, I peel the gauze from his chin.

"I'll be right back," I say.

I walk towards the counter to retrieve a red contamination bag from the pack. It's medical protocol to dispose of bloods and fluids in this manner and gives me time to think. Air penetrates the bag once I give it a frantic shake. I toss the rubbish and my gloves inside grateful to extend an uncomfortable moment till I can figure out a way to tell him—.

"You okay Allie?"

Erin's sudden appearance at my side startles me. A powerful shock runs from my lower-back to the top of my shoulders as if a stingray is sliding up my spine. In the past, when a sensation of this magnitude came over me, something terrible always followed.

"Huh, what did you say?" I ask with obvious awkwardness.

"I asked if you're okay." Erin moves closer crowding into my personal space.

"The bleeding's stopped."

"I can see that Allie. My question was if *you* were okay." After sanitizing my hands and putting on a new pair of gloves, I turn to face Erin. I do my best not to betray what's going on in my mind. Her knowing stare makes me shudder inside. "He asked you out, didn't he?"

I'm in utter shock as Erin pinpoints with precision what occurred between Estrada and me. My tongue becomes heavier than a hundred-pound weight. I nod.

"Geez, I told him to wait till next week, and to let me talk to you first," she says very straightforward.

Her wicked smile scares me and suddenly I want to take a shower to clean myself. I shake my head in disbelief.

"Boys, what can I say?"

For the last five weeks since I joined the team, Erin and I have worked closely together. There are things I've confided in her few others know. In my desire to be transparent, she's taken advantage and betrayed me.

"I don't get it," I lash out. "Give me a reason Estrada wants *you* to talk to *me* about going out with *him*?" Erin doesn't blink or take a breath before responding.

"He trusts me." Pause. "Same as you trust me Allie," she says too sugary. Erin slides her arm around my shoulders. I'm trapped by her firm grip. "You do trust me don't you Allie?"

Erin is a medical student who volunteers to help at sports events since the county school budget couldn't afford any more funding for staff medical representatives to attend games. After an eight-week summer sports medical workshop which I attended, Erin and I hooked up. We hit it off right away. Now I wonder if she played me since the beginning?

I fear what Erin's reaction might be if I refuse to answer. "I trust you," I spew out at last.

"Then you should consider Ray's proposal." My mouth closes after swallowing massive gulps of air. Erin's hold around me tightens. I want to pull from her grip, but I can't. I stand there speechless and afraid. "Ray's a great catch Allie. He's got everything a girl wants in a guy: looks, brains, dubious charm and soon he'll be one of the most powerful people in Brescade. You'd be wise to consider his proposal."

I've felt fear this overpowering once in my life. It was when I was seven. I was with Daddy playing in the park. I'd jumped to the ground after climbing the monkey bars when a dog broke loose from his owner's grip and tore a path straight my direction. Daddy was at the picnic table watching me when the attack occurred.

"Climb back up the bars Allie," he screams at me with a ferociousness in his voice that is foreign.

I barely reach the fourth rung when the dog arrives. He jumps up missing my Reebok's by millimeters. Loud vicious barks make my heart beat fast. The look on the dog's face is pure evil. Thick saliva drips from its mouth as leaky as the faucet in the laundry room.

Daddy's wearing shorts and a tee-shirt. The only weapon at his disposal is a medium-size drink cooler. He picks up the red container by the plastic handle and runs towards the monkey bars. The dog turns its attention towards Daddy.

"Go on. Get out of here." Daddy growls. The dog responds by leaping at Daddy. Next, Daddy takes the lemonade-filled drink cooler and swings it at the dog connecting with its jaw. The dog yelps and falls to the ground as his thick body takes the brunt of the hit. He's up in seconds preparing to attack again. The owner rushes to the scene and secures the beastly animal. A heated exchange takes place between Daddy and the owner of the dog. The deafening sound of my pounding heart drowns out their words.

That same booming fills my ears now. The metal doors clang open smacking against the walls as players from the Brescade football team barge into the locker room victorious. At this rate they'll enjoy another undefeated season. Erin releases her hold and I escape. Neither Estrada nor Erin makes a move towards me. In their eyes, I see the expression of the evil dog.

Chapter Three

The moment I step through the front door of my house I race up the stairs two at a time. Like the skin of a Tamworth pig found frolicking in the mud, the pungent stench of manipulation coats me. I strip off my clothes and step into the shower turning the water on as hot as I can stand it. Ten minutes of scalding jet sprays pelting my body does nothing to cleanse me.

Cass stops by the house as she often does after the completion of a football game. She and I are what I term as 'tolerable friends.' We've known each other since the third grade. She bullied me through the primary school years. I incurred no physical abuse at her hands. Her words, meant to hurt me, stung and scarred me terribly.

By the time we attended high school, she grew out of the bullying phase. Forgiveness, for me, I've learned, is a lengthy process. Certain wounds take longer to heal than others. I wonder if we'll ever be real friends. Our tolerable friendship is evolving. Into what, I cannot say.

"Did we win?" asks Cass jumping onto my bed.

"What do you care? You hate sports."

"Ray was playing."

Cass's unhealthy fascination with Estrada is another thing that keeps our relationship fragile. We don't see Brescade High School's newest heartthrob the same way.

"We won," I said. "Estrada scored three touchdowns."

Excitement refuses to contain itself within Cass. "He's amazing, isn't he?"

"Spoken like a true football supporter."

"That's what I've heard, at least."

"He's in a class by himself when the football touches his hands. I dare say, he was born to play football."

"See."

"Unfortunately, he got hurt today." Cass's face turns pale.

"Is he okay?"

For a moment, I consider garnishing payback for the bullying by withholding the news and letting her sweat. Born with a congenial nature, shaped for the most part by Daddy's influence, I stop myself from suppressing the good that is within my power to give.

"He suffered a laceration underneath his chin." Her eyes widen in fright. "A cut for Pete's sake," I add for clarification. She breathes a sigh of relief.

"Then he'll be okay to play next week?" I nod. "That's good."

Thus, goes the typical conversation between Cass and me.

She rises from the bed preoccupying herself with the volumes of books neatly stacked on my bookshelf. I detect a tickle in her voice as she fights back a cough. I ask her if she's contracted a cold. Cass exhibits a politician's poise by changing the subject.

"You know Tre, the guy in my third period class?" She turns to face me when I don't answer. I shrug my shoulders. "The one that shaves his head." Now I nod. "He says Ray is the new leader of FADE."

After my confrontation with Estrada and Erin earlier, I believe Cass's words.

"So?"

"So, FADE is making a name for themselves Allie. You know those gas station robberies last week?" she asks. I can see the excitement bubbling inside her.

"Yeah."

"Tre told me it was FADE."

"The damage they caused was severe considering the owner didn't put up a fight. It will cost thousands to get her business up and running again."

"That's why business owners are required to have insurance," Cass replies. Callous remarks, typical of this nature, are another thing that keeps are relationship tenuous.

"Maybe Tre's wrong," I say.

Cass jumps in, "One of his friends on the football team bragged about it at a party last weekend."

Most of the conversations Cass and I have had of late have focused around Estrada and his association with FADE. Though she's never come right out and said it, I believe Cass is hot for Brescade's alleged bad boy.

More stunning than any person I can name, Cass's beauty can be attributed to a mom who was once a Swedish model and a father who played rugby for the Samoa national rugby union team. Her figure takes after her mother. With a complexion somewhere between sand and honey beige, Cass displays perfect skin.

Cass is the only girl I know who doesn't wear makeup and looks just as attractive without it. Her chestnut brown hair reaches below her shoulders, and she always wears it up covering it with a printed satin headscarf. Her glasses are relics from the nineties making her look older. She always dresses in dowdy jeans and boys' t-shirts that are a size too big. I think it's intentional. Maybe a mandate by her protective father.

I do wish the right guy would come along and sweep Cass off her feet. Underneath her brash exterior exists a nice girl. It disturbs me she's unconcerned by rumors of Estrada's affiliation with FADE and, rather, appears turned on by it.

Comparison wise, Cass is way better-looking than me which doesn't explain why Estrada hasn't latched onto her yet. It's possible he's too busy with school, sports and his *extracurricular* off-field activities or his spooky infatuation with me to even take notice. Cass refuses to attend sporting events because of the gladiatorial violence they promote. It's possible their paths have never crossed. Whatever the reason they haven't met, I'm glad.

I refuse to share with Cass what happened in the locker room. She'd tell me I'm being a prude uncovering wounds I prefer to leave buried.

From the little I know of FADE, they're a gang formed in Brescade years ago. They went underground for ten years, then reemerged, on my sixteenth birthday a few weeks back. FADE vandalized several buildings including a few trucks and busses leaving unpretentious graffiti reminding the public of their presence. Their symbol is simple yet glamorous; the word "fade" in all-caps using a calligraphy script with the next letter lighter than the letter before it. Quite awesome if you're a graffiti artist.

$$\mathcal{F} \mathcal{A} \mathcal{D}$$

Brescade is not a large community and is a good hour and a half past the suburbs of Spokane. Even with its rural location, we're not considered ignorant country folk. However, too many of these 'country folk' bury their heads in the sand when involved in discussions of gangs, drugs, and violence. "They won't reach us way out here in Brescade," they say.

Too late.

"A-a-a-choo." Cass's sneeze leaves her mouth at breakneck speed.

My focus shifts in a flash.

"You're sick."

"Allie, it's a sneeze."

"Cass."

With reluctance, Cass stands and lifts her arms raising them above her head. She knows better than to fight me on this. If she's sick, I'll hound her until she gets well. After rubbing my hands together to make sure my touch isn't cold, I put them underneath her neck. I probe the skin feeling for any swelling in her lymph nodes. Next, I examine underneath her jaw, behind her ears and behind the back of her head.

"And Doctor?" she asks waiting for my findings.

I pull my hands to my side. "You're coming down with something, I know that much." My comment is not an accusation.

"Look Allie, just because I've had a runny nose for a few days—"

"A few days and I'm only finding out now?" Some might call me overly dramatic. I don't think I'm overreacting, because if her runny nose is accompanied by an infection she must see a doctor to get antibiotics. I watch as Cass's body jiggles. "And you have a cough?"

Cass shakes her head several times to prove me wrong. I wait and wait until her face changes to the color of a beetroot. She fights the tickle in her throat willing herself not to cough. I watch with amusement as tears drip from her eyes. Several times her stomach buckles as if she is on the verge of vomiting. She is determined. I'll give her that.

I laugh. "You're going to blow."

Afraid to move, Cass remains frozen. I wait until she reaches the breaking point and hand her a fistful of tissues. When the sneeze bursts from her lips she unleashes a mini tornado.

I race to my medicine cabinet. It doesn't contain any prescription drugs. Inside, sits a collection of herbs and vitamins to help combat colds and flu. After grabbing small amounts of licorice root, thyme, and garlic tablets, I place the natural remedies on my desk.

"You know I hate tea Allie."

I ignore her.

"Drink one cup a day as hot as you can stand it. Chew on the roots when you're at home. And take two garlic tablets each day." I place the remedies in a brown paper bag and fold it before handing it to her. "Trust me, you'll feel better."

"I don't want to smell like an Italian restaurant."

"For Pete's sake. You won't stink. It's your choice if you want to stay sick."

"Fine." She snatches the bag from me. Pedantic when it comes to medical matters, I fiddle with her sweater trying to button it up for her.

Flailing arms at Cass's sides come close to striking me in the face. "Allie, will you stop? You're worse than your mother." One hand shoots to cover Cass's mouth. "Allie, I'm sorry." With the other, she reaches to retrieve short-tempered words. Regrettably, her ineffectual attempt incites fresh injury to unhealed emotional wounds festering with anger and hate.

Chapter Four

Sensing my unease, Cass excuses herself right away. The second she leaves the house, I grab my tablet from off my desk and tap on the Diary App. I attach the keyboard and within seconds blank pages appear. Fingers wild with fury pound hard on the keys.

Page after page adds up until at the thirty-minute mark I've typed a total of seven—a record for me even when my emotions are soaring. Replete with pain-filled imagery and honest critique, my brain is, at last, emptied of frustration.

I'm not sure where this desire to pen thoughts to paper originated. If you perused my bookshelf, you'd notice a dozen journals thick and ready to burst. A decorative rubber band closes over each one to keep the pages from looking disheveled or becoming misplaced. I suppose in the future I'll want to reminisce about my childhood, although I can't imagine why.

On my birthday, Daddy gave me my own tablet. A godsend. I type much faster than write. In this fashion, my journal entries these days are quite extensive.

Each day I'm deliberate and spend thirty minutes or more voicing my thoughts. This mental workout allows me to vent frustration, subdue anxiety, and attack, on paper, the demons who desire to conquer my once tranquil soul. Sometimes I discover my writing can be a profound religious experience. Now and then when I'm writing, I talk out loud to God sharing my dreams, fears, and struggles. He listens. And on occasion, I sense him talking back.

When I put the journal away, often, a measure of peace settles into my spirit. The following day I'm much calmer and better equipped to handle the curve balls life loves to pitch my direction.

Please don't let my words mislead. I'm no saint. I lose it from time to time and can become an unbearable person to be around. It doesn't happen often. When it does, watch out.

I take tonight's run-in with Cass and place it in a mental box which I lock away. No one needs to tell me this method of concealing my feelings won't force them to dwindle or die. Like a witch's cauldron, they bubble underneath the surface of my mind needing room to expand. Eventually an explosion of catastrophic proportions will take place. Can't concern myself with that now.

Of all people, Cass knows better than to drop my mom's name in a conversation. Even the word mother makes me break out in hives. What ticks me off more than anything is Cass's underscoring of an issue that has stolen sleep from me since my birthday. I'm bombarded by frightful impressions of this woman I barely remember.

No matter how many times I try to incinerate the past it rises from the ashes.

A fierce storm is on the horizon. I sense it coming.

I walk downstairs. Daddy is in the lounge room stretching out on the automatic recliner. He holds the handle of a cup of steaming hot apple cider and is letting it sit on the arm rest. A brown stick of cinnamon bobbles in the hot liquid. The entire room relaxes with the permeating smells of autumn my favorite season.

His eyes are closed; yet I know he isn't sleeping. The first clue is the mug of cider with a continuous cloud of white vapor swirling towards the ceiling. The other is the wiggling lips of a smile he struggles to contain.

"Hi Princess," Daddy says unable to hold-out any longer and rewards me with a large grin.

"Hey Daddy."

"Everything okay with you and Cass?"

"Fine." The word exits at supersonic speed from my mouth.

He pauses. I think he's contemplating whether to pursue the line of questioning. He decides against it. "What's on your mind?"

"Who says there's something on mind?" I reply with artificial indignation. "Maybe I was passing through the lounge room on my way to the kitchen to get something to drink and by chance I saw you sitting on your chair and rather than ignoring you and retrieving a glass from the cabinet and filling it with water to satisfy my thirst and traipsing back upstairs to my room where I will shut my door and not retreat downstairs for the rest of the evening because I have work to do which will keep me occupied, I decided to come in here and say hello." I take in a needed breath.

Daddy smiles again. His chest rattles into a laugh as his eyes open.

"All that for a hello. How can I resist? Hello."

"I need to talk."

"Hmm."

He sets the mug on the small wooden table next to his chair. He presses a button with the thumb of his right hand and I watch his legs lower on the recliner and his body straighten into an upright position.

"I'm listening Allie?"

"I've been considering college."

"And you've come to tell me you've decided on a school?" He reaches over and picks up the cup and takes a long sip. His face shows no signs of surprise. He's lived with me my whole life and knows me better than anyone.

"Yes. I'm interested in two schools. Columbia University School of Nursing," I see surprise in his eyes, "... and Duquesne University School of Nursing."

"Those are the top two nursing schools in the country," comments Daddy.

"I'm leaning towards Columbia not for any other reason than I love New York and I'm not a fan of Pittsburgh. They both offer Bachelors, Masters, and PhD's in nursing."

"Then you're serious about becoming a doctor of nursing?" It sounds strange when he says it.

"Totally."

Daddy gets up from his seat and joins me on the couch. I snuggle into him. His body is as warm as the cider. The lingering silence lasts for a full minute.

"Allie, you know you have my support, whatever you decide." He pauses. "You have something else on your mind?"

I sit up straight focused on what I want to say.

"I was thinking if I went to summer school over the next two years, I could graduate early and that way I could start nursing school sooner."

"Will that put undue pressure upon you?"

"What do you mean?"

"If your summers are full, and we both know how jammed pack your schedule already is, when are you going to have time for yourself? I don't want you getting ill again because you pushed yourself too hard."

"I'll be fine," I say grazed by Daddy's words.

When I was six, I contracted the rotavirus. At nine I suffered from pneumonia. Two years ago, I spent three weeks at home when I developed mononucleosis. And last year I suffered a bout of exhaustion. My lips flutter as I blow out air. My foot taps without control. I cross my arms. Daddy knows my signs of frustration.

"I'm not saying you can't or shouldn't finish high school in two years Allie. Remember, if you're not well, it doesn't matter how fast you get your high school diploma."

Most people who know me call me driven. No doubt excessively so. One reason I'm this determined is because of something Daddy says. *Whatever purpose God has for our lives we don't want to get to the end of our lives and realize we've missed it. Nor do we want to waste the days we have with frivolous activities that detract us from our role as human beings to love and serve one another.*

This drumbeat forms the foundation for my life. Daddy instilled this into me at a young age. *My mind, heart, and spirit need alignment. Otherwise, that metal ball that bangs back and forth in a pinball machine will be me.*

Since I can remember, I have always wanted to impact the world. I want to accomplish something great. One day when I'm dead and gone I want people to remember me, and if not me at least the accomplishments I made during my time on earth.

I suppose this explains my hectic schedule. While most kids my age pad their time with countless hours of Xbox and Facebook, I saturate my mind with knowledge and information that supports my life choices.

I spend bouts of time reading medical books and journals and watch the medical network having watched tons of operations. When I share with someone my love for medicine and my wish to be a nurse, invariably I'm asked why I don't become a doctor. More than once well-meaning people have told me I'm shortchanging myself by not becoming a physician. I don't see it that way.

True, doctors are awesome at what they do. However, it's the love and strength of a nurse that nurtures a patient back to health. It's his or her compassion for the hurting that drives what they do: the long hours, the repetitive work, the suitable pay. It takes a special person to be a nurse.

I guess that's why I don't spend loads of time vegging out in front of mindless television. Time is too short to waste. I have a lot I want to accomplish before I die. Also, I need to heed Daddy's words. If I exhaust myself again, I'll be no good to anyone.

Chapter Five

At four o'clock, I stand at the front door anxious for Ian to arrive. Every Saturday afternoon he stops by to see me. Mostly, it's to hang out. Sometimes his visits are purposeful. Today, for example, he's bringing me my birthday gift. This has me pacing back and forth in the hallway.

"He won't get here any faster by patrolling the doorway," says Daddy sticking his head out of the kitchen. Daddy's making quesadillas for dinner. His black apron is too amazingly clean considering the tortillas are being made from scratch.

"He's already a few minutes late," I say looking at my watch. "He should be here by now."

Daddy pulls out the cell from his apron pocket and touches the screen. "Your watch is fast Princess. He'll be here at four. I've never known Ian to be late not when it means having time to spend with you."

Daddy's words offer me no comfort. I lean up against the hallway wall and continue to wait. Sure enough, when my watch is three minutes past the hour the doorbell rings. I fumble for the doorknob and open the door. On the other side stands my best friend.

Dressed in his customary blue jeans, black t-shirt, and Chuck Taylor's, Ian enters. Tucked behind his ear is a small yellow number one pencil. A thin pad sticks out of his back pocket in case he's bitten by the creativity bug. His strictly-for-vision glasses feature him as geeky. I don't mind the look.

"Hey Allie," he says with a cavern smile that shows his snow-white teeth.

"Hi Ian." I smile back.

I won't lie when I say I like Ian because I do. Since the third grade, he and I have been friends Everybody needs a friend as loyal and kind as Ian. If I'm honest, sometimes, I let my mind wonder. I fantasize about things that will never eventuate. Ian's interest is in one thing and that's painting.

At the age of five he 'kind of' borrowed 'kind of' stole a sketch book from school. A year later each page introduced a sketch or drawing he'd made. When he was eight his parents bought him an easel with a vast complement of blank canvasses, paints, and brushes. I saw none of his paintings until last year. Deriving a synonym to describe the awesomeness of his paintings is impossible. Is he in league with the masters? Can't say for sure. What I do know, I'm in awe of how much talent exists in one person.

In his hands, he carries a large black leather case which holds the painting. I know he does it to protect the canvas. This isn't his only reason. He uses the method to annoy me. Unable to view his painting until he, *the artist*, is ready to unveil his masterpiece, drives me crazy.

"Daddy, Ian and I are going upstairs to the lounge room."

Daddy sticks his head out of the kitchen. He's holding a plate of freshly made chocolate chip cookies. He is quite the culinary virtuoso.

"How are you Ian?"

"I'm fine Mr. Alexander." Ian's calm reply exposes no nervousness. He's been coming to my house for years. Two years older than me, and a senior at a private school, none of this discourages Daddy's trust. Ian's down-to-earth nature endears him to everyone. Daddy loves him to death and has told me that on more than one occasion.

I take the plate. "Thanks Daddy."

Ian waits for me to walk upstairs first and then follows. After I put the plate on the coffee table, I retrieve an easel from the corner.

I wait as he places the painting on the stand facing away from me. At once, he drapes a large black cloth over it, turns the tripod around, and sits next to me. I decide not to get sucked into this juvenile game of bait and hook.

"So, tell me how it felt to get out there on the field? I heard you stitched Estrada's chin yesterday," Ian says.

I've blocked the events of last night from my mind. For a moment, I shudder. The fear is real and fresh.

"Nothing as exciting as that. I handed Erin a few swabs and escorted him to the locker room. Erin took care of the stitches after I left."

"How many did it take?"

"Nine." When an injury occurs during a game, no matter how minor, if Erin or my services are required, a record of it is logged on a special account set up at the school for the Principal's use. While online, I viewed Erin's detailed report. "Do you mind if we change the subject?" I ask, trying to keep an even composure.

"Sure."

Ian doesn't comment on my unwillingness to discuss the details. Like clockwork, he stands and walks to the window. Out past our backyard is a massive lake. Daffodils, azaleas and wild flowers from our backyard line the path to an empty boat dock. During the summer, fishing vessels, yachts, waterski boats, and wave runners churn up the water reminding me of a blueberry shake topped with whipped cream. Every time Ian visits he leaves the couch to go stare through the window as if he's looking for something he's lost.

He passes by the painting again on his way back and grabs two warm cookies before sitting. In an instant, my focus is back to the easel. Five minutes, and I've exhausted my reserve of willpower.

"I give already. Will you *please* show me the painting?"

Two months ago, Ian made me wait till after dinner before letting me see his creation. Well worth the wait. Still...

The same thrill I get from patching up someone's wound Ian gets from painting. Our canvasses are different. Mine are actual people who find themselves in need of medical attention. His is a blank sheet of parchment waiting for transformation as a kaleidoscope of colors and brush strokes attack it.

As perfect as Ian is, his life is not without complications. His parents have it in their mind that he should concentrate less on art and more on school work. Their ultimate expectation for him is to gain entrance into a top medical school where he can study to become a cardiovascular, orthopedic or transplant surgeon—three of the top paying positions in the medical field.

Money is important to Ian's parents. They live in a fancy house in a neighborhood fifteen minutes away. They own four cars, foreign models, and very expensive. In view of this fact, they harp at him constantly regarding his educational and financial future. I wonder, if before graduation, Ian will give in to them rather than follow his dream of becoming an artist.

This is a great sense of frustration for Ian and discouragement for me. Of late, his parents have begun to resemble the enemy. Ian can do whatever he sets his mind to. He'll find no joy in becoming a doctor, of this I'm certain. Often, we discuss our passions. One of the things that makes our relationship gratifying is that Ian supports me in what I do, and I back him no matter what exploits he might encounter. This explains why he's become more than a friend to me. Still, this matter of him leaving painting to become a doctor unsettles me.

"Dinner's ready," Daddy yells upstairs.

Ian rises from the couch.

"Don't you dare."

He looks at me with his piercing brown eyes and breaches my often-rigid exterior. The desperation written on my face is genuine. This time he chooses not to ignore it. After taking a long breath, he pulls back the cover that has been causing me disquiet for the last half an hour. Amazed and powerless to move, I realize I'm the subject of my birthday painting. This throws me off-balance.

There I am on the canvass seated bareback on a dark stallion. The horse is cantering through the shallow waves of the ocean. The sun is low over the horizon and the sky a tangerine orange. The horse moves towards an unknown destination. I hold onto the stirrups with both hands relaxed with the horse's stride.

"Ian, it's breathtaking." I'm incapable of manufacturing more words.

Though hard to make out, I detect a smile on my face. The horse's breath leaves his body in large puffs of vapor. Whatever their destination, neither the horse nor girl will arrive before the setting of the sun.

The painting is both emotional and compelling and leaves me feeling more than a little melancholy. I can't explain the emotions welling up inside me as I study it. I'm aware the girl is me. At the same time, I know I don't want to be the girl on the canvass. Something about this ride troubles me.

Chapter Six

September 8, 2016

Dear Diary

 Daddy and I attended church this morning. The preacher continued part two of his series on death and dying and our need to prepare for the inevitable. His focal point, obviously, centered on our need to establish a right relationship with God prior to death. He also stressed the importance of making sure we do our best to reconcile any strained or damaged relationships we have, and instead of waiting, to start now while we have time.

 It was a good message as far as sermons go. The subject matter unnerved me. Death is not something I want to think about. Two weeks and five days ago I turned sixteen. With a full life before me and much to accomplish, I'm too busy to die. Spared from seeing death, I can think of no one personally who's died. Today, I considered how Daddy's death might affect me. The handling of such pain—I see myself crumbling in a heap and dying alongside him.

 I realize life goes on because when someone on the news dies or something catastrophic happens around the globe the world doesn't stop. The earth rotates on its axis, people fall in love, get married, babies are born, banks foreclose on housing loans, crime continues, and war-torn countries suffer vast devastation,

 Even if this is the way life is supposed to be, isn't it selfish to go on when a loved one dies? Or, is it more selfish not to go on? It's a toss-up for me.

 I've been thinking a lot about Ian's painting. Of all the paintings I've seen, this is by far his finest work. Yet, it has caused me to wonder. Why am I riding a horse? Ian knows I have no interest in horses. What is the horse's destination? Perhaps, and most importantly, why do I cry each time I pass by the painting?

On a more chilling note, a convenience store was broken into last night. Fortunately, no one was hurt. Reports say the perpetrators got away with a significant amount of the store's product.

There is no doubt FADE is responsible. Their symbol was painted on the walls and on the front door. Surveillance videos picked up the images. The thieves wore dark hooded clothing concealing their sex and identities. I stared at the news footage trying to determine if Estrada was one of the perpetrators.

In my gut, I know he's responsible. How could he be involved in apparent lawless behavior then casually ask me to be his girlfriend as if he's ordering burgers at the drive thru? He has no idea what kind of person I am. He's crazy if he thinks I'm okay with robbery. It sickens me to think about it and kept me up most of the night

It makes sense, considering Erin's behavior on Friday night, she's probably mixed up with FADE. None of this makes any sense. She's a medical student studying to be a Gastroenterologist for Pete's sake. What does she gain by joining a gang?

I love the job I do at the football games. After the incident in the locker-room, I question my further involvement. Not that he wouldn't listen, understand, and offer wise counsel, but I need to talk to someone about this other than Daddy. Spilling my guts to him regarding what happened in the locker room could lead to Estrada's disembodiment. Just kidding.

Diary, some things won't stay buried no matter how hard you try. How do you continue to hold onto a secret you know is a lie? The tingling in my spine, with each day, increases in intensity.

Chapter Seven

I love Mondays.

When the school bell rings after third period indicating the start of lunch, the halls teem with craziness. The menu of lukewarm chicken nuggets and stale oven-cooked French fries is not what draws the herds to the cafeteria. Each week on Monday, one of the bands in our schools gets to play a twenty-minute set.

Normal restrictions, loosed on this day, allow students to dance and sing along if they want without reproach or repercussion from teachers or staff. Almost every student in the school attends to support the talent. A few nerd types abscond preferring to hang out in the computer lab.

DREY, a soft rock band, composed of three guys; Dez, Ric, Emory, and the lone female, Yana, have been playing together for three years having formed their band back in middle school. Yana, the lead singer, has the best voice of anyone in school. I think she and I could have been friends. She's one of those people blessed with a magnetic personality. Her popularity has made her almost untouchable. Still, I love to hear her sing.

As rowdy as our school can be at pep rallies and football games they understand the need for quiet as DREY plays. A group of girls dance at the front. Enormous cheers fill the cafeteria after each song. I can't sing or dance and I can't play an instrument. This doesn't mean I don't have a great love for music. At home behind the locked doors in my room, I turn up my speaker to full volume and sing along with Taylor Swift, Forget Tomorrow, and One Direction allowing the artist's voices to drown out mine.

After their third song *Stand Straight,* my favorite, and seconds before they sing their final number, the commotion turns me backward. A quick forming crowd circles around the incident. I rush over—something's wrong, I can feel it.

I push through the throng of bodies and notice Damien Federoff, a sophomore exchange student from Russia who is in several of my classes, lying on the floor. Purple coloration around his lips suggests oxygen deprivation. Both hands grip his throat as if he's choking himself.

I wiggle my arms out of my purple backpack and ignore it as it drops hard to the floor and slide next to Damien's body. The weather outside has been uncharacteristically warm and today I happen to be wearing a pair of shorts that come to above the knee. They aren't lengthy enough and the skin on my shin bunches up underneath my leg causing an excruciating burning sensation. I ignore the pain.

I listen for a heartbeat. It's faint. After opening his mouth, I peer inside. I'm sure I know what's wrong. Placing one arm underneath Damien's left arm pit and the other underneath his right, I tug at his body. Proper lifting requires extensive use of the leg muscles. Mine almost go into spasms. Once he's seated, my legs maneuver around his waist until I sit behind him.

The surrounding crowd steps back to give me space, barely. It bothers me to see the numbers of students with their phones out recording the incident. Generation Z, my peers, knows nothing of tact. We record every kind of misfortune convincing ourselves of its importance. The more undignified the event; the more we're drawn to it. Recordings of this, no doubt, will be uploaded to YouTube before lunch is over. I can't concern myself with that.

I pull Damien towards me his back against my chest. His head flops onto my shoulder. I wrap both of my arms tight around his mid-section and grab my wrists. I pull my hands firm into his sternum. It takes two attempts to dislodge a full-sized chicken nugget from his throat. The quiet crowd erupts with anxious chatter.

Damien sits up on his own. His cough tapers to a simple rasp.

More phones flash making his and my eyes flicker.

"Are you okay?" I ask.

He dips his head. I can understand his reluctance to answer with the boisterous crowd gathered close capturing his image and every word.

"Break it up. Break it up." Principal Jorgenson who comes to the cafeteria only on Mondays paces around the circle eyeballing students. They begin to back off and head to class before the fourth period bell sounds.

"Are you okay Damien?" she asks.

He nods. She motions to one of the male teachers to help Damien. The teacher whose name I don't know assists Damien to his feet. They shuffle off together to the nurse's office. As Damien reaches the door, he turns and raises his hand. I acknowledge his thanks with a smile. Principal Jorgenson casts an uncharitable glance at me then leaves.

Something about that woman creeps me out.

HOMEWORK IS THE only thing on my agenda when I reach the house. French leads the list followed by science then math. Two hours later I close my books and stuff them into my backpack. The smell of dinner wafts up the stairs and settles in my room. I can taste it now. Before heading downstairs, I decide to check the web. Sure enough, four videos of me performing the Heimlich maneuver on Damien were uploaded to YouTube. It takes no willpower to ignore the links.

IN THE MORNING, I wake earlier than usual because the phone in the hallway destroys the silence with its clamorous tone. Daddy has promised to get rid of the landline. Sentimental attachment for the retro device means it maintains its place in the hallway. Since anyone of importance calls me on my cell, I turn over and let Daddy answer the phone. Maybe now he'll see why we need to rid ourselves of the nuisance.

When my eyes finally crack open, I stumble into the shower shaking off the remains of an interrupted sleep. I let the hot water needle my body until a real person emerges from the shower.

After dressing, I grab my backpack and head downstairs for breakfast that Daddy makes most weekday mornings. It's just the two of us. Since the loss of Karla ten years ago, he has assumed the role of father and mother.

"Morning Princess," he says kissing me on the cheek. "I've made your favorite: lemon ricotta pancakes with warm cranberry compote."

"Yum, I'm starving."

He plates a separate dish with two pancakes and a second plate with one egg over hard tucked next to a duo of chicken patties. After filling his plate, he sits. We bow our heads.

"God, thanks for the provisions you've given us. Bless it to the nourishment of our bodies. Let us live today honoring you with our thoughts, our words, and our actions. Amen."

"Amen," I add.

"The phone hasn't stopped ringing all morning," he says between bites.

"I thought it a bit strange for a school morning. Was it work related?"

"No, yet I found the interruptions gratifyingly profound."

"What are you talking about?"

"You didn't tell me you saved a boy's life yesterday."

"Damien needed help. I helped him. That simple." Nonchalant as my answer may be, I hold to its veracity. Had it been anyone in need of medical treatment, I would have given them the same attention. My actions weren't motivated by the resultant praise.

"The *FOX Morning Show, The Brescade Chronicle,* and a few other radio stations called because they're interested in interviewing you. You know, high school girl saves high school boy or something of that order."

"You've got to be kidding me," I say looking up from my plate. "It was the Heimlich maneuver for Pete's sake. Everybody knows how to do it."

"If that were the case," says Daddy pushing a piece of pancake into the prongs of his fork, "why the interest from the press?"

I say, "I suppose," shrugging my shoulders.

He swirls the light pastry around in the cranberry compote. "What should I tell the gaggle of reporters?"

My fork drops onto my plate emphasizing my frustration.

"Are you saying I have to do the interviews?"

"No, Allie." Daddy stabs a tiny piece of the sausage and holds off sticking it into his mouth. "This could be a great opportunity to reinforce to the public why it's important to learn this simple technique. It doesn't cost you anything, and who knows maybe you save someone's life down the road."

I consider his words, and, this time, place my fork and knife in the middle of my plate parallel to one another and push it toward the center of the table.

"Aren't you the girl who wants nothing more than to impact her world?" Daddy asks.

"Yes, I'm that girl."

"This seems like a big deal to me."

After a long pause, I respond. "I'll do one interview."

"Which one?"

"You said FOX called?" Daddy nods his head. "The guy on the Morning Show is cute.

"That settles it," says Daddy laughing.

After we clear the table and load the dishes into the dishwasher Daddy gently grabs my shoulders and faces me towards him. "Allie, I hope you don't think I'm pushing you to do something you don't want to do. I respect your right to say no."

"No Daddy, you're right. If an interview could help other kids my age save a life, it's totally worth it. I'm worried this might create more negative publicity for Damien. The kids at school are ruthless and will take great pleasure in ridiculing him over this. He's only here till June. I don't want him going back to Russia with a sour taste of Americans. At last count, seven clips are on YouTube. It's not like he can escape this even if he wanted."

"Do you have Damien's number?"

"Yes."

"Why don't you call him and discuss it. If he says no, then you have your answer."

It's a brilliant idea I should have come up with on my own.

"Okay Daddy."

Later, as I'm ready to leave the house to catch the bus Daddy says, "Allie, I'm very proud of you." He starts to add something, but hesitates.

"What were you going to say?" I ask selfishly anxious for another compliment.

"Nothing. It's nothing. Go, you're going to be late."

"Daddy we promised never to keep secrets from one another." He hesitates. "I'm not going to school if you don't tell me." My threat is empty and he knows this.

He laughs. It's nothing more than playacting and far from jovial. "I was going to say how much you remind me of Karla before she..." He doesn't finish the statement.

My stomach rocks back and forth as it does when I ride one of those rickety wooden rollercoasters at Six Flags. I regret pressing him to share.

Chapter Eight

The moment I step outside the front door a young female reporter dressed in an Oxford blue business suit accosts me. She holds a microphone with a red top and shoves it into my face while asking me a bunch of questions, none of which I can understand. Her colleague, an older man in his fifties, holds a camera over his shoulders pointing it towards me. There are more cameras and reporters exiting vans and moving this direction.

Mr. Reynolds, the bus driver, snakes around five vehicles and double the number of pedestrians until he can come to a safe stop. I want to bolt. Bodies block my path. Seeing my dilemma, he leans on the horn creating a loud off-key brass tone forcing the small crowd to turn. I seize the opportunity and spring forward weaving through the crowd and into the open doors of the bus. Mr. Reynolds pulls off the moment I'm seated.

"Thanks."

"The least I can do for Brescade's newest celebrity."

"Not you too."

"No offence Allie, you're headline news. What you did to save that young boy's life yesterday was nothing short of amazing."

I don't respond to his comment. At the next stop, Cass boards the bus alone. After wishing Mr. Reynolds good morning pleasantries, she sits next to me. Puzzled by Cass's actions, I watch with interest as she reaches into her bag and pulls out a pen and a book with blank pages. She shoves it into my lap

"What's this?"

"Can I have your autograph?" Unamused, I grab both items and slam them onto her lap.

"It's not funny Cass."

"Don't hate me. You're the one on the news making Daniel vomit."

I almost hit her again. "You think they'd have more important stories to report than this."

Cass leans in with her head crooned against my shoulder. "When you're rich and famous don't forget the little people." I jolt her with my shoulder forcing her off the seat onto the aisle.

"Hey."

"Keep it up Cass. There's more where that came from."

"Alright, alright."

"I'm serious Cass," I say with a mild laugh. The two of us reel with laughter.

"I heard there were tons of reporters at your house."

"Who told you?"

"I have my sources."

"If it weren't for Mr. Reynolds, those vultures would've surrounded me. Anyway, I'm only going to do one interview."

"One?" asks Cass tugging at my arm. "The world needs to meet the Florence Nightingale of Brescade." If I didn't know better, I'd say Cass is disappointed. "Which one?"

"What's it to you?" I can't pull from her hold.

"Which one Allie?"

"The Morning Show on FOX News. Are you happy now?" She lets go of my arm and sits back. "What's gotten into you?"

"Nothing," she says with a touch of coyness in her voice. "Rye Adler's talked about you for the entire morning show."

"Who is Rye Adler?"

Cass turns towards me her face inches from mine. "You're kidding me. Rye, the good-looking guy on the Morning Show."

"Oh, that Rye."

Cass is right. Rye Adler is the hottest guys on television. He's young, vibrant, passionate, and without your awareness, draws you deep into his stories. And then sometimes he'll ask that one question that changes the entire direction of the interview or takes it even deeper. If I do happen to turn the television on during a week morning, I try to catch his show.

"What did he say?" I ask.

"Oh, so now you're interested in what the reporters think?"

"Tell me Cass."

She laughs refusing to answer me.

"I guess you'll find out." She giggles to herself.

"Daddy's going to arrange the interview. It'll be sometime tomorrow I'm assuming."

At every stop until the bus reaches the school, students board the bus and stare. It's terribly unnerving.

Later than usual, the bus arrives at school.

"Have fun," says Cass leaving me to sit in my seat while the others file past me refusing to let me break up their caterpillar line.

"Fun?" I shove away the comment chalking it up to Cass acting crazy.

I avoid contact with the countless eyes peering my direction as I enter the school. When the first period bell rings the masses in hallway scatter creating chaos in the halls. I slam my locker door shut and head to class. The short beep on my phone indicates a text. Late for class, I ignore it.

I enter class oblivious to the bodies and noise around me and take my seat. After reaching into my backpack and retrieving the textbook and a spiral notebook, I focus my attention towards the front of the classroom expecting to eyeball the teacher.

That's when I see Rye Adler, his cameraman, several other school personnel, and the rest of the class staring at me. This explains Cass's earlier odd behavior.

Am I the only one without a clue?

The lights attached to the camera flick on and blind me. Nerves I didn't know I had stand erect ready to sprint.

"Hi Allie."

The words come from the only man who could make me rise early to watch the morning news. His camel-colored suit, compliments his bronze complexion. The dappled blue shirt without a tie makes him appear charming. I've never swooned over a guy before, and with countless numbers of people watching the show, I don't need to create another media frenzy by fainting in from of the most beautiful man I have ever seen.

Rye doesn't wait for me to answer or acknowledge him.

"The world is talking about the amazing thing you did yesterday saving the life of one of your fellow students." Rye sits on stool less than two feet from me. "How is it Allie that you were able to act with such single-mindedness with pandemonium going on around you yesterday?"

"Someone needed help. I happened to be there. So, I helped."

"We interviewed one of the students standing next to you. She said you perceived the problem even before it became clear there was one."

"I'm not clairvoyant. I heard a commotion behind me. Anytime a crowd forms, you've got to figure something's happening. You watch the body language, listen to the voices. Every action and reaction is an indicator to what might be happening. I happened to be in the right place."

"And at the right time. Your principal and teachers tell me you are planning to attend nursing school when you graduate from Brescade High School." I watch as both the Principal and Vice Principal's faces beam with pride as another camera captures their responses. Something in the way Principal Jorgenson smiles makes me think she's faking it.

"That's my hope," I reply with my best natural smile.

"Is that because your mother, Karla Alexander a.k.a. Mag Steel the current lead singer of the heavy metal Asian Band *Fear and Death Express* once worked in the ER at Brescade Memorial?"

In an instant, my heart liquefies. I pray for a hole in the floor to swallow me whole. Perhaps God would consider rapturing me to avoid the chasm of worms Rye has just unearthed. Unanswered prayer makes this the worst news to ever air on live television and the worst day of my life. How did he uncover the truth? Whatever my previous infatuation with Rye, it's ancient history now.

After ten years of virtual silence, and in less than a minute into the interview, Rye has unraveled the flimsy thread that has kept my secret history knit together. It's not that Daddy and I were being untruthful when it came to Karla. Extenuating circumstances kept us from disclosing the truth.

"I've grown up learning life is more than about me. An entire world of people lives outside these school walls. It's my privilege to serve them. The love I have for nursing is nothing more than a desire to help others."

"Am I right in saying Mag Steel *wasn't* an influence in your decision?"

The lights from the camera are hot and make my face flush. The crowd of people in my class and those peering through the outside windows only add to the muggy heat. Rye's question regarding Karla's influence brings me to boiling point. If he's such a cool guy and concerned with how compassionate I am, he should stay on the subject.

"No Mr. Adler that's not what I'm saying. Every one of us is shaped and influenced by those around us no matter how much or little contact we may have had with them."

I take a deep breath hoping the viewers see only a confident teenager on screen and not a whiny brat. I can tell Rye's eager to ask the logical follow-up question. He senses my apprehension and once again does the unexpected returning to the original line of questioning.

When the interview is over and the lights and cameras no longer cast brilliant light my direction, Rye Adler approaches me. He asks me to join him outside. We leave the classroom and enter the hallway.

"I didn't mean to upset you Allie," he says. His voice maintains calm.

"Yes, you did. You wanted me to look stupid on National television to increase your ratings. And here I imagined you were a different kind of reporter. You're like the rest of them." He stops in his tracks and faces me.

He doesn't debate the issue.

"I'm a reporter."

"Is that the line you use to justify your actions?"

"It works great when I'm trying to get a date." I don't smile. Rye walks closer to me. "News is news Allie. People want to hear it. The more fantastic or outlandish the more they eat it up."

Here it comes.

"I've got to ask, 'How come you and your father allowed everyone in Brescade to believe Karla was dead?'" This was the question he chose not to ask earlier.

"It's a private matter."

"Not anymore."

"You made sure of that."

"If I hadn't broken the story…" He doesn't finish the statement.

"Confronting a sixteen-year-old on live television happened to be your first choice?"

"Your dad agreed to the interview."

"Yeah, I guess he did." I start to walk away.

"There's more Allie," says Rye leaning against the lockers.

"What do you mean there's more?" I retrace my steps and face him.

"I got a call from one of my sources."

"And?" My impatience mounts.

"It's better if I show you."

He retrieves his phone from his inside jacket pocket and after a few seconds of tapping and swiping the screen, he hands it to me. I don't take notice of the sender. Even so, the lead-in sentence grabs my attention while at the same time arresting my heart.

Karla Alexander, better known as Mag Steel, the lead singer of the heavy metal group Fear and Death Express, was questioned by police in Bangkok after authorities discovered a kilo of heroin hidden inside of one of the band's guitar cases. In 2007, Karla is purported to have died from a drug overdose overseas. Mrs. Alexander is the wife of renowned chef, restaurateur, and food critic Jack Alexander and daughter Allie who currently reside in Brescade, Washington.

Chapter Nine

I'm baffled Rye's source forwarded a superabundance of detailed information about Karla on his Android. He didn't gather this information by making a phone call or surfing the net. This comprehensive research took time piecing together. To collect this quantity and quality of information it's as if he'd gotten it firsthand long before the story broke.

Unlike the opening two sentences, the sender catalogues the next section of Karla's life history into sequential bullet points. There's much about Karla I didn't know.

Karla Gayle Alexander

- *Born April 18, 1975 to Mark and Gloria Brackenridge natives of Brescade, Washington.*
- *Parents died in an automobile accident on her sixth birthday.*
- *Social Services takes control of Karla and places her into a foster home.*
- *During a two-year period, Karla lived in six different foster homes.*
- *Karla struggled with reading, writing, and comprehension. She repeated the first grade twice.*
- *Started bullying kids during the third grade. In the fifth grade, she terrorized a classmate to the point the parents moved their child to another grade school.*
- *During grade four, Karla became involved in fights with her classmates both female and male. She punched a student who wore glasses. The principal suspended Karla following this incident.*
- *Placed with Jon and Jinni Jefferson where she resided until high school graduation.*

- ➤ *Jinni Jefferson quits her job to home-school Karla for the rest of grade school.*
- ➤ *On her tenth birthday, Karla receives a guitar. She becomes a quick self-learner. After a year, Mr. and Mrs. Jefferson provide guitar lessons for her.*
- ➤ *Karla attends Yakima Middle School and becomes involved in the school band.*
- ➤ *Karla settles down from sixth to tenth grade.*

Karla had a hard life. My reluctance to manufacture empathy for her results from a heart she nailed shut years ago.

Embarrassment trips my mind. The whole world realizes the truth: Daddy and I lied. Open for the world to see is the dysfunctionality of our family. If it's true the apple doesn't fall far from the tree, what will become of me?

I continue to read.

Somewhere during grade eleven, Karla meets Dizzy Bufano, a transfer student from Los Angeles. They hook up and Karla's life spirals downwards. Allegedly she and Dizzy got involved in petty crimes such as defacing school property. Breaking windows, trashing classrooms, and a break-in at the nurse's office containing limited amounts of medications were attributed to the duo. Nothing ever traced back to them.

This destruction branched out from schools to the community. Brescade incurred a rise in thefts, shoplifting, and vandalism to cars and homes. When Karla and Dizzy graduated into pilfering drugstores and stealing large amounts of pharmaceutical drugs, the police took more than an avid interest in the couple.

Uniformed and plain-clothes officers tailed them from time to time. When other break-ins occurred during the surveillance it led police to think that this two-person destruction team had grown into a much larger more skillful gang.

During senior year, Dizzy got arrested for drug possession and felonious assault. Less than a month from turning eighteen, the court tried him as an adult and Dizzy spent time in jail. The judge gave him the maximum sentence.

After that, Karla decided to reform her ways and joined a church that Daddy attended. The two of them spent a great deal of time together in a Young Adult Group and became very fond of one another.

Karla focused on school and graduated with a four-year scholarship to the Columbia University School of Nursing. This I didn't know. *A month after Karla graduated from college she returned to Brescade where she and Daddy married several months later. Two years later I came along.*

Brescade Memorial Hospital offered her a job, and she became the top emergency room nurse.

I remember Daddy telling me he and Karla enjoyed happiness for a while. Upon Dizzy's release, he sought out Karla. A few months later she packed up her stuff and left Daddy and me. Before leaving, she performed a classic Karla raiding the one account shared by her and Daddy and emptying it of twenty thousand dollars.

She and Dizzy moved to Thailand where they bought a dilapidated Pho restaurant and formed a band with other dysfunctional American musicians. She changed her name to Mag Steel and six months later they formed the band *Fear and Death Express*. They traveled throughout Asia with a few stints in Europe.

Her exploits after she left America were difficult to trace. At eight years of age, Daddy left me with Aunt Cinnamon, his sister, and travelled to Asia. It took a week for him to find Karla. She and the band were playing in a rundown dive in Thailand. After the gig finished, Daddy met with Karla backstage to plead with her to return home. Too drunk and drugged out to care about us, Daddy returned a few days later telling me Karla had died. He shared the news with a neighbor knowing her inclination towards gossip. The entire city of Brescade soon learned of Karla's death and released a collective breath.

At ten, I went through a phase where I missed having a mom. While on Daddy's computer, and purely by accident, I discovered a picture of *Fear and Death Express*. There on the screen, in the middle of the other men, I saw Karla. She looked different than I remembered. Nevertheless, the eyes of my mother stared back at me. I knew it in my heart. Dated after the date Daddy told me she died meant one thing.

I cried for an hour when I realized Karla was alive. I wept for another hour knowing she lived overseas. And then an hour after that my mood turned to disgust as I counted the years she'd kept herself away from me. By the passing of the fourth hour, anger won out.

Daddy and I stayed up half the night discussing the reasons for lying. His deception went beyond the two of us extending to the inhabitants of Brescade. It took several weeks before I resolved it in my mind. We weren't lying to protect ourselves I understood. Those around us needed to believe she passed.

Time healed the rift between Daddy and me. We promised one another from that day forward to always tell each other the truth. Since the inhabitants of Brescade relaxed in thinking Karla dead, we allowed them to believe the lie.

I hand the phone back to Rye. My numbness doesn't surprise him. "Allie, I'm sorry. You're going to have to weather the storm that's coming, and I promise you it's going to be a nasty one. From what I've gathered, your shoulders are broad and strong. You'll be able to handle it. Unfortunately, this story is going to be on the midday news. It will be the lead-in for the five, six and ten o'clock broadcasts."

I'm too stunned to reply.

Chapter Ten

No longer jovial, Cass's attitude on the bus ride home leans towards cool and starchy. Stilted expresses the other student's demeanors. Karla caused a lot of havoc in Brescade when she lived here. People rejoiced upon her exit, and reticent to admit it in public, were even happier when they believed she'd died. News that she's alive has already changed the climate in Brescade, that I'm sure of.

Sad, most students don't have a clue who Karla is and have no interest in the new development. They are, nonetheless, children of parents who lived through her reign of terror. Cass is one of those learning the *truth*. She slides her fingers multiple times across the screen reading page after page. When the eyes blur and her mind reaches overload, the screen goes black. Cass stuffs the Android into her back pocket.

"I can't believe you lied to me Allie," she says three miles from my stop. "You told me your mother died." Cass doesn't look at me as she's speaking.

"She is dead to me Cass."

"Don't even." Cass waves her hand as if swatting a nuisance wasp. "You let me believe she died in a horrible overseas accident. What kind of friend does that?"

I'm facing a moment of crisis. Cass and my tolerable relationship teeter-totters towards collapse. Desperate to save it, I face the window to conjure a reason Cass will believe, one that will allow me to save face.

"I was scared to tell you."

"You afraid of me?" Our eyes meet. She scans them trying to read my mind. "That makes no sense. What have I ever done to make you afraid of me?"

Momentarily stumped by her pleading, I mull over our past. Our relationship didn't solidify during a joint climb up Everest or braving the Amazon jungle together. She bullied me for years and one day decided to stop. The relationship evolved to what we currently have. We tolerate one another, and yet, I don't want the relationship to end.

"Because Karla's a liar and will do anything to support her drug habit. She lived overseas because the city of Brescade hated her, because Daddy and I weren't enough to hold her attention, because she's the last person I want to discuss with anyone. Is that what you want to hear? She hurt me Cass, you know that."

A touch on the shoulder, a kind word letting me know it's okay; neither enters Cass's mind.

"We've been friends a long time, maybe not best friends. You could have trusted me with the truth."

Desperate breaths flee from an open mouth. What little friendship I have left I see slipping away.

"I do trust you Cass, I swear I do." Taking an oath is my last resort.

"Do you? Do you really Allie?" Cass's stop is not for another mile yet when Mr. Reynolds slows the bus to let off another student, she steps off without saying goodbye.

"Cass I'm sorry," I whisper.

I consider running after her as the doors shut. More important matters await me at home; my concern shifts to Daddy. How is he handling this? I retrieve my phone to send a text and realize I have an unopened message from him. *Rye Adler has agreed to conduct the interview today at your school during first period. Have fun. I'm proud of you Allie.*

A large cluster of reporters stands outside our home hoping for tidbits of seedy information on Karla and Daddy's relationship. If that means gleaning the information from me so be it. Pleas with Mr. Reynolds to keep driving and to let me off at the next stop land on deaf ears. His disposition towards me has changed a hundred and eighty degrees since this morning.

"Please Mr. Reynolds," I beg for the hundredth time.

Akin to the wolf in the story of *The Three Pigs*, he huffs and puffs reluctantly agreeing to my request.

At the stop, I tread from my seat to the door feeling dozens of eyes burn holes through my skull. In less than twenty-four hours, my celebrity status, once bright and promising, burns more rapidly than a meteorite entering the earth's atmosphere.

Chilled air pushes against me when I step onto the sidewalk. Unable to fight the cold and the storm of reporters crowding our driveway, I drop my head and forge home. Two houses before I reach mine, I skirt through the pristine backyards of our neighbors and enter through the back door evading the slew of reporters.

"Daddy. Daddy."

"In here Princess." His voice is calm.

I rush to the lounge room and find him reclined on his Lazy Boy eyes closed. I kneel next to him and place my head on his chest.

"What are we going to do?"

"Nothing we can do Princess."

"Tons of reporters are camped outside our front yard." He doesn't respond. "Yeah, I guess you know that. We're not going to do anything?"

"What do you want me to tell them Allie? Nothing I say is going to change their impression of Karla, me or you. Sensationalism is what drives news these days. You should know that."

Hesitant to reflect on the events of the morning, I recall how Rye, for the sake of tabloid-journalism, exposed the story of Karla being alive.

"Yeah."

"They'll want to know why we lied and why I haven't filed for divorce.

Daddy's aged since I saw him this morning. After ten years, he hasn't given up hope the three of us will one day be reunited. With the immense hurt Karla's caused us, I don't know how he can still love her. My feelings border on hate.

Around eleven thirty, after their live feeds for their respective evening news programs, the reporters pack up. By midnight, red lights from the last van fade into the darkness. I go to bed. For the first night in ten years, I have no wish to write in my diary.

At six fifty-eight my phone alarm vibrates in my hands. Since I haven't slept a wink, I silence it and turn on the FOX Morning Show. Rye Adler comes on with Dana Banks, his cohost. Karla commands the top story if you can believe it.

The package of heroin discovered by the police belonged to Dizzy and not Karla. They arrested him for possession with intent to distribute. According to Bangkok drug laws he could spend the rest of his life in jail or even face the death penalty. I sigh grateful the arrest didn't include Karla while in the same breath I wish she'd died ten years ago.

GOOD MORNING PLEASANTRIES, somewhat difficult to articulate to Mr. Reynolds go unacknowledged. When the bus arrives at Cass's stop I'm openmouthed as are the rest of the occupants. Cass is wearing a thermal baseball gray sweater shirt with sleeves that are maroon, a pair of too-tight black jeans, and a pair of black leather boots that reach up to her knees.

Her hair rests against her shoulders. Glasses no longer hide a makeup-covered face. Instead of her regular seat, I receive the cold shoulder. A student on the back seat moves his backpack out of the way to allow her to sit.

Before the first period bell rings, I see Cass again. To my amazement and dismay, she huddles closely with three football players including Estrada, the suspected leader of FADE.

Chapter Eleven

On Saturday, ten minutes before four o'clock, I stand at the door waiting for Ian. With the hoopla of this week still in full-force, he and I haven't spoken. My choice, not his.

"I'm making Ian's favorite for dinner," he says with a smile.

"He loves your Saltimbocca."

"And the veal is fresh."

"Good, because I've ignored him. I hope he's not angry."

"When have you seen that young man lose his cool?" Daddy asks.

"Never, now that you mention it."

"Ian is one of the most down-to-earth people I've come across in my life."

"I'll start with a plea for forgiveness."

The doorbell rings. Daddy steps back into the hallway. "He's early."

"That's good news," I say.

As I open the door, the harsh glare of the afternoon sun blinds me. I shade my eyes. A dark silhouette with an oppressive odor of sweat and tobacco barges in like a whirlwind pushing Daddy and me back to opposite walls of the entryway. Mouths ajar, he and I shake our heads in utter astonishment as Karla plods past us.

Short blasts of a horn severs our attention. Daddy grabs his wallet and pays the cabbie who has unloaded Karla's luggage and awaits payment. From the number of bags in her possession, I gather this visit is more than a weekend trip.

Daddy carries her luggage into the house and sets the worn cases next to one another. The downstairs room where she used to sit and play her guitar in the evenings after coming home from the hospital remains unchanged. I haven't stepped in the room since her departure.

I count my lucky stars none of the media was about to capture her unsavory entrance. From opposing directions, two police cars slow in front of our house coming to a stop at the driveway. Windows ease down and the officers appear to be chatting on the brisk October day. Five minutes later they ease away without the pageantry of sirens or lights.

Keen on avoiding the inevitable, I scramble onto the porch swing to consider these new events. I realize I have nothing to say to the woman who abandoned me a decade ago. Vapor from my breath exits in staccato puffs when Ian turns the corner. Not once have I ever been to his house. Still, he must live nearby if he's walking. My heart beats faster as he approaches.

A trench coat is the only addition to his normal attire. His hair is cobalt black and cropped military style. It creates a notable contrast against his maple colored complexion. He is one of the few teenagers I know blessed with acne-free skin.

Ian's features are not sharp and blend in a favorable way with one another. His face is smooth almost satiny to the touch. Sincere almond-shaped eyes captivate my frequent glances. Slender lips, a medium-sized nose and evenly matched ears are, to use a Mary Poppinsism, "Perfect in every way." His black-rimmed glasses are a ploy to keep away the number of women vying for his attention Ian snubs their advances. They don't understand him the way I do. He's driven by one thing, his passion for painting.

Oblivious to my location, I call out, "Want to swing?" before he rings the bell. He smiles surprised to see me sitting there.

"Sure."

Ian walks to the swing and sidles next to me. The swing is not wide. Heat from his body warms me. My breath slips in awkward puffs and I open my mouth wider to take in more air.

Together our feet push at the ground creating pendulum motion.

"This is a first."

"Karla's here."

His feet grab at the ground and the swing stops in mid-motion at the apex.

"When did she get back?"

"Ten minutes before you showed."

"Wow. Sorry Allie. You've had a tough week." I never told Daddy I'd shared the truth about Karla with Ian. "Are you okay?" Ian says putting his arm around me. This is not the first time he's held me this close, today somehow, I experience a difference in his touch. My body fights for oxygen while longing for more of his touch.

Ian's arm squeezes me harder. I could sit with him this way forever. Before enjoying forever and a day on a porch swing with my best friend, I have an important question to ask.

"Ian, there's something weird going on with the painting you gave me last week. I can't pass by it without crying or feeling a wave of despair creep up over me. Is there a story behind it I should know?"

Ian stands and places his back on the outside of the porch. We stare at one another for a moment before his eyes shift upward. I observe him pull the flaps of his collar open then thrust his hands into the pockets. The move serves two purposes I think: For warmth and for something to do.

"Have you ever done something for no other reason than you're driven to do it?" My expression stays blank. "It's hard to explain." He lifts his right foot and places it against the house's exterior. "Six weeks ago, I came home from school. Throughout the day, these random ideas entered my mind. I couldn't control their frequency or intensity. Unable to put them into words, I grabbed a blank canvass and started painting without any idea what my hands and brushes might create. A week later I finished…you saw the completed project."

"It's beautiful."

"I almost didn't give it to you."

"Why?"

"It's a moody picture. I understand what you mean when you say you're enveloped by sorrow."

My face is aghast. "Don't say that. I'm glad you showed me. It's the most breathtaking painting I've ever seen." I pause before continuing. "Tell me why I'm riding a horse? You know I hate horses." My jittery laugh does little to lighten the moment.

"That's what makes it crazy. I lost control of what appeared on the canvass. It's like—"

"Someone guided your hand."

"You nailed it." His eyes widen. "My mind, my hand, and even my color selection deferred to someone else's supervision. Never happened to me before."

Ian joins me on the swing and puts his arm around me again. I lean back into his body as we commence eternity together. For a long time, we sit clinging to each other braving the gale-force winds swirling through Brescade.

"Are you going to stay for dinner?"

"Maybe with your mom back home... I shouldn't."

"Daddy made Saltimbocca."

"That settles it," Ian says pulling me closer.

DADDY, IAN AND I sit waiting at the table for Karla to join us. After five minutes, she arrives. Her hair is long and mangled reminding me of a bird's nest ruffled by the wind. Since I last saw her at age six, she's aged a century. Dressed in gray sweats, top and bottom, with pink fluffy house shoes that resemble two overgrown disfigured mice, I want to vomit.

Karla sits at the table without offering an apology for her tardiness. Daddy bows his head. Ian and I join him. Karla picks up the fork and starts hoeing into the food on her plate as if she hasn't eaten once in her ten-year absence. When she raises her head the three of us are studying her.

"What?" she asks with a full mouth.

Anger ignites an unquenchable fire in me. I can't sit here any longer without making a comment.

"Maybe in your ten-year absence you forgot what manners are. At this table, we say grace before we eat."

My eyes don't blink. When she sets her utensil on the table, Daddy prays. During his prayer, I lift my head and open my eyes. Karla is staring at me with poisonous arrow eyes. If looks could, kill I'd be dead. I murder her back.

Conversation is light during dinner. Despite my wanting him to stay, Ian excuses himself and heads home early. Karla roams the house familiarizing herself with her past our present.

I stay in the lounge room with Daddy not wanting to be alone with the woman who calls herself my mom.

"You've gotten new bedroom furniture," she blurts out as she enters the lounge. She chooses a seat away from me.

"Yeah, that happens when you get older. Funny, huh?" She ignores my crack.

"It looks nice." Karla's voice is sandpaper rough and grates on my nerves.

I don't comment.

"You don't want me here do you Allie?"

For a second, I consider not answering, then the appreciation of this gift anchors my thinking. If someone hands you a stick and says, "Hit me," it would be downright impolite not to oblige and take at least one swing.

"Karla." She looks surprised that I called her by her first name. "I wish you stayed in Europe, Asia or wherever the heck you call home because honestly I don't want you here."

"You mean to tell me you weren't a little excited when I walked through those doors earlier?"

"If you mean sick to the stomach then yeah."

"I tried to make your birthday a few weeks back. Stuff came up."

"Yeah, the whole world knows about *your stuff.*"

"I brought a gift back for you. I know you're going to love it."

Daddy's Lazy Boy moves to a normal sitting position. He's said little. This move, I'm guessing, is preparation for the fireworks doomed to explode between Karla and me any moment.

"Karla," I censure, "I can promise you, there's nothing in this world you could offer that would hold my interest."

"Not even a baby sister?"

Chapter Twelve

I can say, with decisiveness, I've never seen Daddy lose his temper. As I sit on the couch listening to Karla drop the bombshell, I imagine he's close to blowing a gasket. His rigid body, hands gripped tightly onto one another, and clenched jaw are my first clues. Eyes, for the most part, intentional on making anyone nearby feel at ease avoid interaction. Does he envision, I wonder, his world is about to come crashing down around him?

During their ten years apart, I never saw Daddy bring another woman into our home, go out on a date or even spend a casual night somewhere else. Observant of his vows, he remained faithful. Since the breakup of *Fear and Death Express* days ago, stories inundate the internet telling of Mag Steel's infamous "parties of perversion" they called them. I wonder if Daddy's image of Karla can ever be the same. The picture I have of Karla in my mind makes my insides quiver. It's an image I'll never share with anyone else, ever, not even Ian. I can't see her anything more than a slut. How awful that must sound.

Hey, I want you to meet Karla, my mom. She's the hoe from Pho.

As an alternative to unleashing years of pent-up anger upon the woman he continues to call his wife, he retreats in quietness to his bedroom. Karla shakes her head in utter disgust blaming me for Daddy's passive reaction. She ought to be glad he didn't punch her in the nose. It's what I would've done.

Karla leaves in a huff. I hear her go outside the house and return a few minutes later. Of the moral laws she's broken, and that covers pretty much the entire list, I'm surprised she still adheres to Daddy's rule of no smoking in the house.

Am I the only one concerned about the baby?

Dishes from the evening meal clutter the dining table. I grab a plastic tub placing the dishes inside resembling a busboy at a cheap diner. Once I fill the dishwasher and set the washing mode, I exit through the lounge room, I walk past Karla's room to head upstairs. Her voice fills the lighted room. I hear her talking on the antique phone. The long cord hunkers underneath the thin space emitting a dull orange glow. I stop outside her door to eavesdrop on the conversation.

"It's only been a day. I haven't made contact yet. Give me time."

As she moves towards the door I tiptoe away. I hear the door open. Karla peeks out waiting for the intruder to reveal themselves. The door shuts. I wait, making sure to keep very still. A minute later, the door opens and she returns to her room. Muffled tones from within, her room make it impossible to decipher the conversation. When I'm sure the coast is clear, I walk upstairs and fill ten pages in my diary before turning off the light and going to bed.

The moment my head touches the pillow I'm asleep. My mind must be delirious. For I dream of our house being invaded by police and Karla being arrested and taken away in police custody. Only, it's not a dream.

Around midnight I'm awakened by loud banging and screaming coming from downstairs. A horde of police bust through our front door invading our home. In less than twenty-four hours, Karla has not managed only to tick us off, she's brought the police into our house. In the hallway at the top of the stairs, I see an image that will stay with me the rest of my life. Karla is kicking and screaming while four police officers try to subdue her. One of the policeman pulls a Taser from its holster and tags her. She yells out and crumples to the ground without further struggle.

Two officers grab her by the arms and drag her out of the front door. Daddy is in the hallway still dressed. I don't think he's been to bed. He grabs his keys from the table in the hallway as if he's making a run to the grocery store. I assume he's going to the police station to bail Karla out from whatever troubles she's in this time. He glances at me. Neither of us has the words to say what we're feeling.

Brilliant blue and red lights cast a purple glow over our house. Seemingly, no one else in the neighborhood can sleep. Neighbors peer through windows, stand outside their front doors and in their driveways dressed in robes and slippers observing the spectacle happening at 9773 Brighton Drive. I shut the front door leaving the group of snoopy gossipers outside to fabricate their own stories.

I plan to sit on the couch and wait up till Daddy returns. His hand on my shoulder tells me different.

"What time is it?" I ask my voice slurring.

"A little after three."

"What happened?" I ask feeling my mind coming into focus.

"They let her go. They got a tip that she'd picked up drugs somewhere between the airport and the house."

"And?" I ask expecting the worse.

"They didn't find drugs. I'm not even sure that's the real reason they came otherwise the entire house should've been searched."

"Where is she now?"

"In her room. I'm going to bed. I need sleep if we're going to make church in a few hours."

"Goodnight Daddy."

"Goodnight Princess," he says walking away.

Back in my room, I slip between the sheets. Sleep evades me. Early light glares through my window evoking a toddler-like tantrum. I bang the bed over and over with my legs and fists—one more thing Karla's stolen away from me.

Several hours later Daddy and I, dog-tired, prepare to attend church. He waits for me on the second-floor landing. His drawn face is the canvass for the dark circles around his eyes and defined lines at the corners of his mouth. We pass by Karla's closed door. If the noise awakened her, she doesn't come out to acknowledge us.

Several hours later we return. Her bedroom door is still shut. I know she's awake because she's taken an old coffee mug and used it as an ashtray. As we came in, I could see faint wafts of smoke emanating from a burning cigarette.

After changing my clothes, I come downstairs to make a sandwich. On the weekends, I generally fend for myself in the kitchen which I don't mind. There are always leftovers. I pull out a piece of meatloaf stuffed with goat cheese and spinach wrapped in plastic, and place it in the microwave to heat.

While the meal is warming, I decide to empty the dishwasher only to discover someone's already completed the task. Cleaned benches emit the lemony scent of bacterial cleanser. During my quick venture through the other downstairs rooms, I discover polished wood furniture, Windexed glass tables, mopped tile floors and vacuumed carpets. Karla's playing housemaid to get back in Daddy's good graces. Nice move. Calculated, but smooth.

My mind reverts to last night's surprise of a baby sister and I want to vomit. Three abbreviated beeps indicate the microwave has stopped. I remove the steaming meatloaf from the microwave and toss it in the bin. I turn to see Karla standing there. She startles me. I refuse to show it. Rudeness is not one of my usual character traits. Time to activate it. I walk away as if she isn't even there.

"I'm back for good Allie. You need to know that."

If her words are meant to make me rejoice, I can't. If they're meant to make me feel sorry for her, I'm not. If she's made this statement to worm her way back into my life, not going to happen.

I continue to walk.

"Whatever you may think of me it's not going to change the fact that I'm your mother, you're my daughter, and we *are* going to be a family again."

I turn at her words as if she's accosted me on a street corner. My first instinct is to walk up to her and put my hands around her neck and squeeze. When that image subsides, it's replaced with several other images similarly gruesome. Once those images disappear, I'm left with one horrible picture.

I close my hand and turn my body to gain momentum. For a moment, I struggle against the impulse to hurt her. Fury takes over and I strike her against the cheek. The full hit sends her flying over the kitchen table. Her body slides across the slick wood and she knocks over a plastic bowl filled with autumn fruits. Karla falls to the floor landing on the chairs that tumble alongside her.

My heart beats at a trillion miles a second. A single swing. Still, I'm out of breath.

Karla stands, shocked by my actions. I resist the urge to help her. It goes against everything inside me. I open the freezer, pull out the ice container, reach into a drawer, retrieve two plastic bags, fill them with ice, and seal them. One I toss at Karla. She catches it and places it against the fresh bruising flesh on her left cheek. The other I press onto the hand I used to punch her.

Daddy enters not long after. The sound of crashing must have stirred him. His quick assessment of the situation is correct. He asks one question. "Is everyone okay?"

"I'm fine," I say heading upstairs.

"I slipped and fell. Allie tried to help me and we both got tangled. Nothing more than a silly accident."

The lie drips off Karla's tongue like an expert skier on a fresh blanket of snow—smooth and effortless. Does Karla think she can win me over by lying for me? I turn back.

"Daddy."

He turns to face me. "Yes Princess."

"This whole thing is my fault. I punched Karla in the face when she told me I had to accept her as my mom and back into this family." Karla's surprised I own up to my misconduct. "I've done fine without a mom for over a decade, I sure as heck am not starting now," I say out loud.

MONDAY MORNING, AND running late, I rush downstairs. Daddy has breakfast ready for me most mornings. Today he isn't in the kitchen. I open the cabinet and grab a multigrain breakfast bar. I yell goodbye, but he doesn't respond. Mr. Reynolds pulls up with the bus the moment I shut the door. I wish him a good morning. He grunts back.

When the bus arrives at Cass's stop Mr. Reynolds waits for thirty seconds. He even sounds the horn several times. Cass never ventures from the house. I figure she must be sick. He drives off heading towards the next stop.

On the way to first period, I do a double take to confirm the person I'm staring at is Cass. Her clothing is pure black. She wears a Lycra mini dress with a lace top. Black sheer stockings cover her long legs and extend two inches past her knees. The four-inch heel black platform boots make her one of the tallest girls in school.

Her luscious russet hair is Stygian black. The oval area around her eyes is inky and reminds me of the football players at school who paint black lines underneath their eyes. Black lipstick and fingernails even out her outfit.

As she passes by me her nose is pointed upwards. I'm a peon she's loathed to acknowledge.

"What's gotten into you?" I ask.

Cass doesn't hear or chooses to ignore me. Either way, she continues walking. Her platforms fill the hallway with their clanging. At the end of the hall, Estrada and two other Brescade football players, Deke, the cornerback, and Koreil, the defensive tackle join her. Each is dressed in Goth attire. I'm surprised to see Cass slip her slender fingers into Estrada's strong hand.

I don't care what anyone says, people don't change overnight, not to this extreme.

At lunchtime when the Brescade Jazz Band plays their set, Cass, Estrada, Deke, and Koreil huddle at a table in the corner. Two other girls I don't know have joined them. Leaning into together, they ignore the music, noise, and people around them.

I'm not the only concerned person. Students and teachers alike cast glances towards the group—nothing further happens. I worry if nothing is done to help Cass and the others, trouble will soon find them.

ELECTRONIC GONGS SOUND the final bell for the day. I rush with the masses towards my locker grabbing needed books to complete homework. Normally, I stay after for practice, but Monday is the day the football team works in the weight room and does cardio in the gym. Erin has me skip these non-practice days. Since the locker room incident, we haven't spoken.

I rush for the bus that comes close to leaving without me.

As I exit the bus ten minutes later, I notice the missing mug of cigarette butts and ashes. Daddy must have dumped the debris and taken the cup inside to disinfect it.

Daddy rushes out of Karla's room when I enter the front door. I catch his deer-hypnotized-by-headlights gaze. This can't be right. My quick judgment of the situation sparks me to full-fledged anger. I cross my arms over my chest and stomp out an aimless rhythm.

How could you?

I turn even more irate as I watch him rush back into her room carrying a tray with a bowl of fresh soup with two slices of warm ciabatta, a bottle of purified water and a cup of hot tea with honey drops skirted around the small plate. He exits her room again and returns with a blanket seconds later. I'm still standing at the front door aghast when he exits her room.

"Try to rest Karla. I'll check on you later," he says closing the door.

"Daddy," I say keeping my voice low, "I can't believe you."

"It's not what you think Princess," he says his face glum.

"Then explain it to me," I demand.

He fumbles for words. I want to throw up. I turn away disgusted by the whole episode. His words catch me four stairs up. "Karla lost the baby."

My legs freeze. No matter how much I will them to move forward they're stuck. Daddy's words arrest my mind and I can think of nothing else. Uncontrollable shakes assault my body. Legs give out and I sink to the floor in horror clearly remembering the events of yesterday. I'm the one who killed her baby my half-sister.

Chapter Thirteen

Consumed by rage.
How could something this terrible happen?
Bedeviled by the truth.
I don't deserve to live.
Trapped between two worlds.
I detest Karla. Who can free me from this iniquity?

From toddler-hood till now, I've prided myself in being able to maintain self-control in any situation no matter how terrible or erratic things around me might become. This time however, I lost total control. It felt as if someone inside me thought and acted on behalf of my dark side without my consent. There's no justification for what I've done. And now a living being, created in God's image, has died. This burden is too heavy to bear.

I collapse; every part of me stops. For two-and-a-half days, I cannot will myself to get out of bed. I'm overwhelmed with sorrow and dread. Sleep is my only comfort. Grief sticks to my sheets and becomes my skin. I can't consume food. I fight chills and aches and pains I believe to be psychosomatic and allow them to cripple me.

Outside my door, the clinking of dishes captures my attention. I fight to reposition my body so I'm facing the opposite way and struggle to pull the covers up to my neck. I close my eyes. Even a momentary glimpse of Daddy's face might send me over the edge. I can't begin to fathom how disillusioned he must be with me not to mention infuriated. Even with the scrambled history between him and Karla, raising the child as his very own is a joy Daddy would've embraced.

The doorknob twists open and he enters carrying a tray of food. The smell of chili mixed with white cocoa butter wafts towards me. It's one of my favorite meals and smells out-of-this-world amazing. Daddy knows this. The potent aroma entices me to fight through my slump and get up out of bed. Surfaced thoughts of killing a baby instantly subjugates any willpower.

"Allie."

Daddy's deep voice resonates around the room with the robustness of a baritone. For a moment, I feel better. The feeling vanishes all too quickly. The image of a dead baby girl bereft of life hovers over me— hungry vultures seek to attack me for her death.

I listen to the soft sound of metal hitting wood as Daddy sets the tray on my desk. Minutes or maybe hours pass as I lay here. My ears are attuned to the slightest noise and movement within the room. I don't remember retreating footsteps or the door opening and closing, Daddy is still in the room.

I must have fallen asleep because the light coming through my window has softened from a heavy auburn to a dusky gray. I turn to shift positions and discover Daddy sitting in my chair staring my direction. The moment our eyes connect I start blubbering unable to control the release of tears and mucus. My guilt intensifies.

Daddy picks up the box of tissues from my dresser and places them on the bed. He curls his strong hand around my shoulders. I can't see the tears on his face. Soft splashes of saltwater touch my pajamas. I wipe my face, blow my nose, and continue to lie motionless.

"Daddy," I say between heavy sorrowful sobs, "I'm sorry." My voice cracks reminiscent of a young boy in the throes of puberty. "I never meant to…" the words choke in my throat

His hand stiffens on my back. He turns me towards him. I'm right. He has been crying. Two thin sparkling streams run across his cheeks collecting at the bottom of his chin.

"Karla faked the pregnancy," he whispers.

Amid the cheerless anguish, his voice launches a beacon and I see through the debilitating storm. My rigid body relaxes a touch.

"What?" I ask.

"Karla was never pregnant."

"Really?" My sobs progress into full throbbed hiccups.

It takes a long while before I fully understand the gravity of his words. When I do, I let go a gladsome sigh. I sit and life rushes through my arteries and veins again. All the while, my newfound sense of peace is blitzed on every side by a battalion of irritation. I fight to keep it at bay "Why did she lie? I spit.

"To gain sympathy from me." Daddy shakes his head. "And to make you look bad."

"What?" I ask dumbfounded.

"Karla's afraid of you."

I laugh. It's not a funny ha-ha burst. "My own mother afraid of me?"

"You have to remember Karla hasn't been part of our family for a long time. When the band split up prior to Dizzy's arrest, Karla had nowhere else to go; she came here. She lived under the delusion she could waltz in here and pick up where she left off. Your no-fear attitude frightened her the other night. She expected weakness and helplessness. You surprised her."

"I feel sorry for her."

"You may not want to say that to her face," Daddy chuckles his voice forlorn.

"Why not?"

"After her parents died, and she became part of the foster system, Karla became pitied by everyone who came into her life. She hated the consoling and fought hard against it."

It's difficult processing this new information because a huge piece of our family story has never been resolved to my satisfaction.

"Daddy, I need to ask you something?" I've never posed this question, and I'm nervous about asking it. Whatever his answer, it's not going to change the stableness of our relationship. It might give me deeper insight as to why he allows Karla to manipulate him.

"What is it Princess?"

"When you went to Bangkok and saw first-hand everything Karla was doing, you must've felt betrayed. Why didn't you leave her?" The words exit my mouth as hardened bits of clay.

"You mean divorce Karla?" I nod. My question hasn't taken him by surprise. He may be wondering why I haven't asked before now. "I've contemplated pulling up stakes and starting afresh many times. The truth won't make sense to you Allie," He pauses, "I love Karla, and I can't give her up."

"She gave you up," I reply defending his honor. He reveals no signs of being bushwhacked by my follow-up comment.

"That's true. In life, we must learn to leave the past where it belongs. It's the only way to true healing."

Can Karla change her spots? Look at the mayhem she's caused in less than a week.

"How 'bout dinner?" Daddy asks changing the subject.

I push off the covers and follow him downstairs.

"Please tell me you have chili left?"

Chapter Fourteen

Recharged, innocent, free.

It's Thursday morning and Daddy drives me to school after the bus fails to show up to the house. He parks in one of the available visitor's spaces and together we walk unhurried toward the entrance. My upbeat mood is challenged the moment we pass through the front doors. The hallways are alive with energy: The hustle and bustle of students getting ready for classes, lockers opening and slamming shut, the mad search for homework, final reviews before a test, couples walking hand in hand together or kissing one another goodbye till next period, and discussions of the football game tomorrow night.

One of the students I recognize as being in my first period class observes me. I'm a germ underneath the powerful lens of a microscope at its greatest magnification. Students remain frozen until the first period bell rings. On their way to class, they tread, with care, past Daddy and me giving us a wide birth as if we've contracted Anthrax.

While Daddy heads to the attendance office to take care of my absences, I race to my locker not wanting to be late for class. When I get there, I stop dead in my tracks. On the locker door written in perfect calligraphy with purple spray paint, is the phrase;

Mag Steel is a $.#&%

My mind floods with an array of feelings. One, I don't disagree with the statement. In a fit of rage, I might use the same word to express my own feelings. Two, whatever Karla's past may have been it shouldn't reflect on me. Three, this hatred for Karla, a.k.a. Mag Steel, isn't being fueled by kids in my generation. Those from Daddy's era are the guilty ones. Until the news broke a week ago, none of the high school kids knew of Mag Steel. Whatever Karla did before she fled to Malaysia, they have been unable or unwilling to forgive even after a ten-year absence.

Four, what bothers me most is that the perpetrator or perpetrators painted the phrase in purple. I know I carry a purple backpack and dress in purple whenever I can. This act of vandalism is personal. They could have used any of the primary colors or a host of subsidiary shades to make their statement. Why purple? Because the person who did this knew how I'd receive the message in purple. Thus, someone I know wrote this, someone close.

My mind sifts through the short list of people who know of my affinity for purple. Five people make the list; Daddy, Karla, Ian, Erin, and Cass. I mentally cross off the first four names.

In the hallway before lunchtime, I hear the harsh clanging of heels as they traverse the hallway. I'm in my locker unloading my backpack of stuff I won't need for the second half of the school day. The sound stops. I slam the locker door and turn crashing into Cass who is standing in my path with a defiant posture.

My breathing turns heavy and rivers of molten lava rush through my veins at breakneck speed. I haven't seen Cass for several days, her appearance, if possible, is even more eerie. She stares at me without speaking. Her black ringed eyes signify evil behind them. Her face is blank. Our tolerable friendship threatens to crumble.

"Watch it $.#&%."

"You're the one who graffitied my locker?" I attack.

"Is that a question?" she asks. I see the hate for me in her eyes increasing. She pushes through me knocking me back against the metal enclosures. It takes me everything not to follow her and deck her like I did Karla.

After school, I arrive at my bus departure area in time to see Mr. Reynolds drive away. I run after the bus yelling. He can't hear me and my screaming only serves to draw more unwanted attention from the other students. I chalk up the mishap to poor communication. It's possible Reynolds didn't know I attended school today. It's an inconvenience; I let it go. With no other choice, I return to my locker and put on my Reebok's for the long walk home.

The forecast today is for colder weather. Clear skies and acute heat make the prediction an untruth. It might as well be a summer afternoon. After ten minutes of brisk aerobic activity, my breathing is heavy and rapid. The temperature of my body has increased by one degree. Frequent easterly breezes do little to cool me. Moistness gathers underneath my arm pits, around my neck, temples, and forehead.

Halfway home I'm glad I decided to walk. I need the break from thinking. I reach the start of our block in less than twenty minutes which means my pace is excellent. As I approach home, I can tell something about the yard is different. A lake of white surrounds the house. I can't decode the illusion until I reach the neighbor's yard two houses from us.

Numerous wooden stakes, four feet in length, have been pounded into the front yard. Stapled or nailed to them are white signs with very foul verbiage painted on them. Each one has something hostile and unfriendly to say about Mag Steel.

Running to the yard, I angrily toss my backpack to the sidewalk and pull out the stakes. I don't want to read the words. As I come near each sign to yank it from the ground my eyes linger. I'm more hurt that Daddy and I have now become official targets of the 'Mag Steel' hate campaign than the actual words on the signs.

A splinter works its way into the proximal phalanx of the ring finger in my right hand. My teeth grab at the coarse toothpick-sized piece and tug until the fragment hangs from my lips. I spit it from my mouth. My pain tolerance isn't high; my anger is. I suck the excretion of blood and spit it on the ground.

After I've grabbed as many of the signs as I can, I take them around to the back of the house and toss them into the fire pit. On my return to the front yard, Daddy pulls into the driveway. Karla's in the car with him. I watch as she extricates herself from the car committing to memory the language of the signs. Her hands draw out the deeply rooted signs with colossal strength and speed. Daddy and I acknowledge one another with a nod as he joins in the removal.

The pile in the backyard is a small mountain of wooden planks—the perfect bonfire. Without consultation, I grab a can of gasoline from the garage and give the wood a dense coating. I back up twenty feet before lighting a birthday candle and tossing it onto the mound. Erupting flames and spontaneous heat forces me farther away.

The orange glow of the flickering flames equals the foul mood in my spirit. From separate windows, eyes peer to glimpse the roaring flames. Neither Daddy nor Karla is concerned by the backyard fire. Karla's eyes and mine connect for the first time since she told me about the pregnancy. It bothers me that my hatred of her has grown in increments. She must sense it because she pulls away from the window. The curtain drapes back into position.

Daddy leaves forty-five minutes later to review a new restaurant in Fairview, an hour and a half drive away, leaving Karla and me alone. I don't relish being left alone with her alone for that long.

Dinner, made by Daddy before leaving, cools on the kitchen counter. Rumbles in my stomach are hard to ignore. I'm not anxious to go downstairs. Not because I fear Karla, I'm just not sure I'll be able control myself. I've already shown my tolerance level isn't very high.

Downstairs in the kitchen, I'm careful not to make a sound. Two plates covered with foil sit on the counter. I grab one and put it into the microwave careful to heat it per Daddy's instructions. I take the plum sauce and place it on the table. The toaster oven buzzes. I reach inside and pull out one packet of thin pancakes.

I glance outside the window. Faint orange embers indicate the death of the fire. The vileness within me, I realize, didn't disappear with the blazing inferno.

The bell on the microwave sounds. Karla enters the kitchen as I open the door. I can't explain my next actions. With deft politeness, I hand her the heated meal. I take the warm foil packet and place it on the plate. She thanks me and sits at the table.

"Go ahead and eat," I say watching as she waits for me.

In a hundred and nine seconds, the microwave dings again. I retrieve the plate, pull out the last packet from the oven, and grab a fork and knife from the drawer on my way to the table. The seat I take is my normal place. It happens to face her.

"I forgot how awesome Jack's moo shu pork is."

"Yep." I pull out the thin Chinese pastry and swirl a thin layer of plum sauce over it. After placing the shredded pork, wood ear mushrooms, scallions, garlic and ginger onto the pancake, I fold it burrito-style and take a humongous bite. It bothers me that Karla and I can agree on anything. She's right. The meal is great.

I load up my second pancake when Karla breaks the weighty silence.

"The signs in the yard, Allie? I'm sorry you had to see them."

"It's not as if you put them there," I reply my voice cold.

Karla takes a deep breath.

"And making you think I was pregnant."

"Forget it," I say interrupting. "Daddy explained your reasons for lying." I see her look up from her plate and make sure to keep my eyes focused downward.

"It's not that simple Allie."

"You either tell the truth or you lie. No gray area."

"Is that how you see it?"

I want to scream *of course*. "It's how Daddy raised me."

"You don't have much tolerance for people who operate outside the boundaries of truth?"

"If you're trying to tell me you had a good reason for lying to me, I can't buy it."

"I'm sorry you feel that way," she says almost satirically.

"What should my reaction be Karla?" I push the plate aside and wipe my hands using the napkin in my lap and toss it onto the plate. "Tell me how I should feel when you were deliberate in lying to both Daddy and me? I'm interested in hearing your explanation, really I am." I place my elbows on the table with my fingers interlocked underneath my chin and wait.

"Forget it."

Karla gets up from the table and exits.

"That's right Karla, run. It's what you do best."

Chapter Fifteen

Razor-sharp winds, slice through my chilled-to-the-bone body. Winter's raucous voice shrieks with laughter unsympathetic to my wardrobe of woolen socks, boots, heavy sweater, and a long jacket treating me as if I'm clothed in gossamer. Yesterday's freak summer, no longer an ally, leaves me alone to suffer the unending assault of artic blasts.

Hidden behind the wooden mailbox, my only shelter, I wait for the bus to arrive. My usual practice is to hold-up inside the house till the yellow streak stops at the end of the driveway. The reason for leaving the house early is twofold: In case Mr. Reynolds didn't receive the news I'm no longer ill, I want to make sure he has a visual of me. The second reason? To avoid any interaction with Karla.

Ear-piercing squeaks from the bus's brakes raise hope within me as the wind continues its assault. Dashed even more quickly as Mr. Reynolds avoids my street altogether are my hopes of getting to school on time. Now I'm faced with a dilemma. Daddy won't return for another hour and I don't have a license to drive. If I walk, I'll be late and arrive a frozen block of flesh and bone. As much as it pains me, Karla's the only one who can get me to school on time.

Two-faced diplomacy is what's needed. I walk back into the house preparing to turn my frown upside down and offer my estranged mom a pleasant morning. Karla is holding a cluster of keys while donning her winter jacket. I wonder where she's headed. Our eyes connect and I opt for brooding over tactfulness. I'll wait for Daddy to return.

"Come on," Karla says. "You're going to be late." Laced with anger, her voice seizes my attention. I figure her mood is a result of last night's conversation. "The nerve of refusing to pick you up." The seething in her voice is not directed at me. I breathe a sigh of relief. "I have half a mind to…" Her words trail off into quiet.

On the ride to school, Karla's unable to let go of my mistreatment. I surmise she's thinking of the signs in the yard over the bus driver's inconsideration. She stops in front of the school parking in the bus zone. I plan to exit the car quickly. Gulps of saliva coat my throat when she unleashes her seatbelt and opens her door to step out. It's embarrassing enough she's returned to Brescade, I don't want to incur more humiliation because of something she might say or do.

A swell of students cut across the frozen grounds. None averts their eyes. Karla is dressed in a sweat suit; the same one she wore on her first day back home. I'm glad she's wearing Reeboks and not mouse shoes. Her scraggly hair lifts from her shoulders as the wind rises.

Gawkers of the infamous Mag Steel linger in quiet. The wrong type of pride swells in my heart. My uneasiness grows as I consider what everyone must be thinking.

"I'll pick you up after school and we'll go shopping," she says. Making a beeline for the entrance, I walk without responding. Karla follows me up the steps. Her mention of mall hopping is either because she needs new clothing or thinks I do. "Just us girls, okay Allie?" she says almost catching up with me.

My feet hold as Principal Jorgenson walks towards us. One of the students informed her Mag Steel was on her way into the school? Karla continues to walk until her path is blocked by Principal Jorgenson.

"Is this how you treat your students?" she asks of a woman similar in age. "My daughter missed the bus because Reynolds, that scum sucking pig, refused to pick her up."

I'm struck by three things from Karla's statement: How does she know the name of my bus driver? Is her anger directed to him or someone else? This is the first time I can remember Karla ever calling me her daughter.

The proper pride surfaces in my heart, its feelings without a doubt temporary.

"Hello Karla," says the woman I've revered since the first day I attended high school.

"Kamren," Karla replies.

The two of you know each other?

"It's been a long time."

"Ten years," replies Karla. "Not long enough."

"What do you want?" For the first time, Principal Jorgenson acts out of character, a real person with real feelings. Is it Karla's proficiency in drawing the worst out in a person or something else?

"I expected more from a highly respected Principal of a high school than to join with the rest of the community and wear her bias on her sleeve."

"I don't control the busses," Principal Jorgensen replies.

"Cut the crap Kamren." Karla raises her hand as if asking a question. "There isn't anything that goes on around here you're not aware of or have your filthy fingers in. Don't stand there and play me for a fool."

The crowd of students burgeons into a mass congregation. Principal Jorgenson eyeballs the students. Without a word, they disperse. She speaks again when the steps are empty

"I won't have you addressing me that way in front of my students."

"Then you better treat my daughter with the respect she deserves. The same respect you give every other student who passes through the doors of this school. Don't forget Kamren I know enough to make you rot a long time."

At this, Principal Jorgenson's face turns flush pink and transitions to blood red. If we weren't on the steps and in a boxing ring, I'd venture to say the two women were preparing to square off and whack each other.

"If you want the past to stay in the past, leave Allie out of this."

"Get off the school property."

"Or what? I might have feared you ten years ago Kamren. I'm not afraid any longer You know where to find me when you want to settle this."

I hear the screeching of brakes and turn to see four squad cars arrive on the parking lot below. Behind them a speeding tow truck pulls up in front of Daddy's second car and backs up until he's inches from the front bumper. From the lead car, two officers exit. Dressed in their blues they take the time to reposition their caps before approaching and ascending the steps.

One of them is a tall man with large muscles that bulge through his shirt sleeves. His face is rectangular with a chin that tappers into a triangle. He is clean shaven except for a small dark patch underneath the middle of his bottom lip and commands the space as he moves towards us.

The officer next to him is a woman barely five feet four inches tall. Next to the six-foot four Goliath, she doesn't look menacing until you study her face which has strong lines that come from having lived a hard life or from the things she sees daily. Her long brown hair is cropped into a tight ponytail.

Neither of the police officers smile as they approach.

Who called them?

"I'm Officer Wiles," says the tall man, "and this is my partner Officer Dominguez." His voice is as deep as the earth's core with tones that make me want to confess crimes I haven't committed. "Is there a problem here?"

I expect Karla to back down and walk away, instead, she descends several steps until she's the same height as the man speaking to her.

"The problem is this town. None of you is innocent," she says. "You're all guilty."

Guilty of what?

Karla sounds like a raving lunatic.

"Ma'am, do you have a complaint to make?" says Wiles ignoring Karla while projecting his question to Principal Jorgenson

"This woman is making a scene and has disrupted my school. Please remove her from the premises. I'll file the necessary paperwork to ban her from showing up on school grounds in the future."

Conflicting feelings tear at me. I balk at Principal Jorgenson's statement. The police believe her over Karla because Officer Dominguez unsnaps her holster and touches her handgun. Except for Officer Wiles the other officers imitate her action. I'm more nervous than I've ever been. Karla's done nothing for the police to exhibit this kind of force.

"Ma'am, I'm going to have to ask you to come with me," says Wiles. The morning sun covers the bottom half of his face while clouds shadow the top half. As he moves toward her his entire face becomes engulfed by sunlight. From his belt, he unclips a pair of handcuffs.

"You don't think I can see what you're doing Kamren? This won't be the end of it, I promise. You'll regret the day you made me an enemy."

Karla turns around and places her hands, in a practiced move, behind her back unembarrassed. Students and teachers watch the spectacle. I hear the clicking of the cuffs as they secure her hands. It sounds harsher than gunshots.

"I'm sorry we can't go shopping Allie," Karla says as she's being led away to the squad car.

As if that's the most important thing to worry about.

The driver of the tow truck finishes hooking up the car and pulls away not long after the police leave. This won't win her any brownie points with Daddy. I turn my gaze away from the empty drive path and pass by a seething Principal Jorgenson.

Chapter Sixteen

Shouts, yells, and hyperactivity fill the medium-sized locker room comparable to the sweat and body odor that permeates the space. I'm the only one who takes notice of the pungent air. Animated players jump, stretch out, pace back and forth, and perform weekly rituals for good luck. Others pray as they pump themselves up for the biggest game of the season. Lego blocks of adrenaline build within their bodies.

The moment I finish taping the last player I receive a text from Erin. Her message indicates she's sending someone tonight to fill in for her. I'm glad because things have been awkward enough today. The person she sends could be a toddler for all I care.

I recheck the gear in my kit to make sure I've the necessary complement of supplies for the game.

Coach Taton walks in with his small entourage of assistant coaches. He stands tall amongst the youthful players. After he graduated from the University of Miami, the Dallas Cowboys drafted him in the third round as a middle linebacker. His career came to a halt thirteen years later when he incurred ligament damage to his knee or in colloquial terms, blew out his knee. Passion for football and his beautiful wife is what led him to the Northwest, and, in specific, to the town of Brescade.

His record at Brescade High School over the seven years he's coached at our school is sixty-three wins and four losses. Each year he's taken the team to the championship having lost once coincidentally last season to the team we're playing tonight, the George Washington Battlers. Their coach is also a former NFL player who played for the Cincinnati Bengals. The purple and gold uniforms of George Washington in contrast to our own black and orange will cause a psychedelic display of color out on the field tonight.

I listen as Coach Taton motivates his team. He's an inspirational speaker of the highest caliber. Though I'm not a huge football fan, I might have enjoyed watching Coach Taton tackle ball carriers. Before he sends the players out onto the field, they gather together and stretch their arms out putting their hands into the middle of a cockeyed circle. After a few seconds of bantering, hype, and even more yelling, the large huddle screams for a final time before disbanding. Players and coaches trot out onto the field with justifiable swagger.

I wonder if the Warriors exude this same confidence.

To my surprise, Cass shows up on the sideline. She is in a tamer outfit dressed in fashionable sweats and wearing a stylish pair of Nikes. The muffler around her neck and earmuffs match her shoes. She carries a similar kit to mine. After taking a closer inspection, I realize the kit is Erin's. I glare at her in disbelief.

"What are you doing here?" I ask. I could not be any more perturbed than I am right this moment.

"You got the message?"

"What message?" My reply is brisker than the wind.

"Erin's not going to be here, I'm her replacement." I'm sick to the stomach and want to puke. "If a player gets injured during the game, it's your job to fix whatever is wrong."

I almost scream. The boisterous noise on the field prevents anyone from overhearing our conversation. "And what happens if one of the players suffers a broken tibia or a torn Achilles Cass? What then?"

Cass's response is classic.

"Wrap a bandage around their arm and call 911." I shake my head in disgust.

"The tibia and the Achilles are in the leg and foot you idiot."

Cass's expression is vintage; arms folded across her chest reminiscent of the eighties valley girl.

"Whatever."

"That's your response, whatever? Cass you're dealing with real lives out there. If one of the players gets hurt, their life is in your hands."

"No Allie, that's where you're wrong. Their life is in your hands and don't screw up or it'll be your—

"I'm not doing this." Cass takes her finger and jabs it into my chest forcing me backwards. "Once Coach Taton hears you're on the sidelines, he'll rip you a new ear hole."

"I don't think so." I hear the voice and experience the strong fingers of Estrada squeezing my arm at the bend below the humerus. His tight grip makes me want to cry.

"You're hurting me." Estrada crushes me harder. "Cass, he's hurting me." Tears well up in my eyes.

"I guess maybe now you understand we mean business."

"You do understand now don't you Allie?" I can't believe the boy who wanted me to be his girlfriend two weeks ago can inflict such heavy-handed pain.

I nod in agreement. Estrada doesn't abandon his grip.

"Let her go Ray." At her request, he releases my arm, and the blood starts flowing again. I can't see through my long-sleeved pullover. I'm certain a major hematoma is developing underneath my skin.

"Listen up Allie. Do your job tonight and there won't be any problems. Cross me again and I swear I'll make Ray hurt you worse."

I believe her.

THE BRESCADE WARRIORS traipse onto the field from the locker room after halftime followed by their archenemies the George Washington Battlers who are ahead 16 to 9. Our team is less enthused than at pregame. I've never seen Coach Taton this concerned. For the first time in two years, the Warriors are trailing at halftime.

The fierce play of the first half continues during the second half with hard fast blocking and even harsher hits and tackles. Neither team gives an inch. As far as my services go the night has been quiet. I haven't re-taped or attended to a single player. Cass sits on the bench at the opposite end. On occasion, she'll give me the evil stare.

Three minutes remain in the fourth quarter and the score hasn't changed. On fourth down, the Battlers are on their own forty-five-yard line. The center snaps the ball over the head of the punter and the defense hunts the pigskin akin to hounds tracking a fox at an English hunt. After the scrum is pulled apart, Sadler, one of our defensive linemen, comes up with the ball. Our school's sideline and the Warrior fans erupt with jubilee releasing a shared outcry.

Now the offense takes the field pumped up following the turnover. Covering his mouth with the play sheet, Coach Taton whispers the play to the wide receiver who races to the huddle. On both sides of the field, expectant fans stand stomping to bring warmth to their feet. Everyone realizes the shift in the momentum. Maybe it'll be enough to equal the score. That's if time permits.

Estrada, who plays in the backfield most of the time, is on the line of scrimmage in the wide receiver position to the left of the ball. The wide receiver on the opposite side jogs towards the quarterback. When the quarterback takes the snap, he pitches the ball to the wide receiver. The defense moves to their right to tackle him. Next, the wide receiver tosses the ball to Estrada who races down the right sideline until tackled in-bounds at the sixteen-and-a-half-yard line.

It takes three downs to get the ball to the six-yard line. No timeouts and twenty-three seconds remaining in the game means the team needs to score now. On the next play, the quarterback fakes the ball to Estrada who blocks the safety coming on the blitz. Backing up, the quarterback finds himself under pressure with a defensive end having broken through the line. The defensive end puts one of his paws on the quarterback's shoulders. With a show of determination and finesse, the quarterback spins around and scrambles away from him avoiding the sack. Estrada slides off the safety's block and runs toward the middle of the end zone. There are no Battler's jerseys in sight. The quarterback shuttle-passes the ball to Estrada who walks in untouched for a touchdown.

The city of Brescade goes crazy.

Coach Taton faces a tough a decision. Will he kick the extra point to tie the game and go into overtime or will he opt to go for the two points to seal the win? After a few seconds of deliberation with the special teams and the offensive line coaches, He settles on the latter. The kicker, who has already trotted out onto the field, and practiced his leg-swings, lopes back to the sideline with a dejected sigh and disappointed look.

Estrada is the sole back. Referees have placed the ball on the two-yard line. The bunched up offensive line pulsates like an enlarged heart. Linebackers and safeties move forward and backward and slide positions on the line making instant adjustments while trying to rattle the offense to commit a false start. Everyone watching the game, including me, is expecting a run. As the center hikes the ball he and the right guard pull to the right. The quarterback drops back and fakes the handoff to Estrada who is to his right. Estrada dashes left while the quarterback breaks to the right. He passes the ball over the head of the fast approaching bodies. The divergent stomping of the crowd creates a thunderous noise. Despite the earlier events of the evening I find myself joining them. Even Cass who hates sports watches with total engagement. Estrada catches the ball and follows his two lead blockers. He holds the ball under his right arm and zeroes in on the goal line. The ball crosses the plane...

My kit is in my hands. "Cass." I don't know if she's heard me. "Cass," I yell again, "we've got to go." I run onto the field. The only one who isn't silent in the stadium is Estrada who writhes on the field in pain. His vocal grimaces silence the onlookers on both sides of the field. As I race to the end zone, I pull out my phone and tap the red emergency button. My headset activated.

"Nine one one. What's the standing emergency?

"This is Allie Alexander from Brescade High School. We need an ambulance at the football stadium."

"Ma'am, are you okay? Have you been injured?"

"It's not me. I'm running across the field to the injured player."

"What are the injuries?"

"Give me a second." I reach Estrada and pull on my gloves. I can tell by the way Estrada's ankle twisted that he's sustained a fracture.

"Estrada, can you hear me?" His groans return to my ears. "I need to look at your ankle." He grimaces to give me the okay. As gently as I can I touch his leg and slide my hands to his ankle to inspect the swollen mass. Estrada winces at my touch.

"Ma'am, I'm a junior sports rep and I can't be positive, I believe he's suffered a trimalleolar fracture of the right ankle."

"The ambulance is dispatched. Do you want me to stay on the line until the paramedics get there?"

"No need. I'm going to leave him where he is, elevate his legs as best I can without causing him anymore pain, and keep him warm." The scarlet lights of the ambulance flash in the distance. *"I can see the ambulance now. Thank you."*

Signals from the refs indicate a successful two-point try. The coaches and players rush onto the field where I am in a non-celebratory mood. Stunned observers shuffle on their feet anxious to know the plight of Ray Estrada, running back extraordinaire. The refs ask me if I need any help and I inform them the ambulance is on its way.

Cass remains on the sideline frozen in fear. She hasn't moved a muscle since Estrada's accident.

"Coach!" I yell as he gets closer, "He's going into shock." Unzipping my jacket, I place it over Estrada. "Do you have blankets?" Coach relays the orders. Several of the players pull away from the crowd and run to the sideline.

"Allie, how is he?" I shake my head to indicate a severe injury. "Do you know what's wrong?"

"Coach, you saw the way his ankle bent when the two hundred and eighty-pound defensive lineman rolled up on his leg. I think he's suffered a trimalleolar fracture to his right ankle."

"His ankle's broken?" Removing his hat Coach holds it with reverence and bows his head hoping against hope my assessment is wrong.

When the blankets arrive, I roll one up, and, with Coaches help, I lift Estrada's legs and place the makeshift pillow underneath his feet.

"It's okay Estrada," I say as he groans. I take the two remaining blankets and place them over his body to keep him warm.

The sirens are silent as the ambulance approaches. Two EMTs exit the vehicle. One comes toward me with his kit and the other opens the back door and pulls the gurney out.

"What's his name?" asks the EMT.

"Estrada, Ray Estrada," I reply.

"Ray, I'm Gabe. I'm going to check out your ankle okay?" His inspection is more thorough than the one I performed and a touch more painful.

"I can't be sure, but I think it's a trimalleolar fracture," he says out loud. He, his partner, and several other football players lift Estrada onto the gurney. They secure and roll him into the back of the square looking truck. The ambulance takes off with flashing lights and no siren.

By now, many of the fans have vanished; a few diehards remain. Our score topped the Battlers. A win? None of the warriors is a winner tonight. Estrada's injury is going to require surgery and a long recovery period that includes months and months of rehab. His absence will alter the dynamics of the team.

At the sidelines, I grab the rest of my gear. Cass is standing in the same position shivering. I grab her jacket from the bench and place it over her shoulders. She's too stunned to acknowledge me. I put the kit in the backpack and carry it over my right shoulder and carry the foldup table with my right hand. I put my left arm around Cass's waist and walk her towards the locker room.

Chapter Seventeen

Two major stories on page one of today's *Brescade Herald* capture my attention. The most prominent article is titled:

Is the Brescade Warriors' Winning Streak in Jeopardy?

I'm much more interested in the second article.

FADE break-in at the Rundstedt Pharmacy totals over $50,000

October 4, 2016 | Reggie Shortwater

Police are investigating the robbery of the Rundstedt Pharmacy where thieves purportedly got away with over fifty thousand dollars' worth of pharmaceuticals, including both narcotics and depressants. The robbery occurred around 10:15 p.m. Friday night shortly after closing in the 1200 block of Montevideo Street.

Pharmaceutical representatives from Rundstedt Pharmacy say the thieves possessed pinpoint information on what they stole. They took Oxycontin, Vicodin, and Codeine, considered narcotics, and stole two types of depressants; Xanax and Valium.

The security cameras captured five individuals wearing large black hooded jackets and black masks. They're described as males or females ranging in heights from five feet five to six foot two. Members of Brescade's reemerging gang FADE are being sought for questioning. So far, no one has claimed responsibility for the theft. Up to now, FADE has concentrated on mostly gas stations and convenience stores.

Surprising is the fact the name FADE, written in calligraphy, always marking the scene of a robbery could not be found. Despite this occurrence, police believe FADE is responsible.

Police consider their break-in at the pharmacy as part of an escalation phase. Years ago, when the original FADE appeared in Brescade they started with small robberies and break-ins then graduated into pharmaceutical theft. Police have alerted the local pharmacies promising to step up security around these establishments.

None of the FADE members, thus far, has been identified. The highly organized and extremely knowledgeable group is adept at disabling security systems without alerting the authorities. Police do not have any leads.

An award of ten thousand dollars is being offered to anyone with information leading to the arrest of any FADE member and or the recovery of any of the missing drugs. Police have set up a hotline number. They're asking members of the public to call with any news no matter how insignificant. The police promise anonymity to the callers. The number is, 1-877-438-3233 or 1-877-GET-FADE.

Whatever suspicions I may have had about Ray being involved in the thefts I'm forced to table them. He isn't responsible for last night's break-in because I attended to his injuries before the thefts occurred.

"Anything good in the news?" asks Daddy entering the kitchen. He pours the pot of coffee I brewed only moments ago into one of two large mugs I set out. The hot liquid swirls around the bottom of the cup dousing a single sugar cube.

"If you can find it, let me know."

Daddy's mood is despondent, uncharacteristic of the most positive person I know. I pass him the paper. He takes it and places it on the counter while glancing at me sideways.

"What's up?" I ask concerned about his concern. I get up from my stool and stand at the counter next to him.

A slight pause.

"Principal Jorgenson called last night."

"I bet. You should have seen the way she and Karla went at it yesterday in front of the whole school. Karla must have dirt on her because I've never seen Principal Jorgenson scared of anyone. Police arriving on the scene calmed her. Did she call to apologize for her inappropriate outburst?"

Another pause.

"Not in so many words."

"What did she want?"

"Maybe you should sit."

"Why should I sit?" I ask sensing something's not right.

A long pause.

"Principal Jorgenson called to say Brescade High School is no longer in need of the services of a junior sports rep."

"What?" I say tugging at Daddy's arm and turning his body to face me. "You're kidding, right?" Bright eyes betray the pensiveness in his face. "You've got to be kidding me."

Daddy could have said any number of things; "You're flunking French," "school bands won't be playing on Mondays anymore," or "they're getting rid of the salad bowls in the cafeteria," and none of them could devastate me the way these words do. I can't prevent the tears from welling up in my eyes nor can I hold back the onslaught.

"Did she give you a reason?" I ask sniffling.

"She didn't. I assume it must have something to do with the altercation that occurred between her and Karla. Parents complained, and the school followed through on a restraining order forbidding Karla from coming within 100 yards of the high school. Principal Jorgenson believes it to be in the school's best interest if you give up your responsibilities as the team's medical rep."

I stand to attention. "You can't be serious. The team needs me."

"I'm sorry Allie, I tried to reason with her. No budging."

"Who refused to budge?" Karla asks entering the room.

I want to rip the mouse slippers off her feet and feed them to her in fleecy bite-size pieces.

Daddy interjects. "Principal Jorgenson called last night and informed me Allie can no longer work with the football team."

"Kamren did what?" Karla's face turns as red as Principal Jorgenson's did yesterday. I can feel the heat radiating from her crimson cheeks. "As if restricting me from coming to school didn't go too far. This is how she wants to play it? I'm going to call her right now and give her a piece of my mind."

"Don't." My raised voice seizes the attention of both parents. "I don't need your help Karla. Daddy taught me to fight my own battles."

My comment isn't meant to be a slap in the face. She takes it as such folding her arms across her chest and turning to leave the room.

"What is it with you?"

"What?" Karla asks stopping in her tracks and facing me.

"Every time something doesn't go your way, you bolt. What is that? You told me the other day you wanted to be my mom. How do you see that happening if you walk away when things don't go your way?"

"Allie, I…"

"Please don't think I'm saying I want you back in my life. But, if you leave every time there's friction, nothing gets solved. After all these years, I can't imagine you haven't learned that lesson."

"That isn't fair Allie."

"What's not fair Karla is you walking out of our lives for no good reason."

"You don't have the facts."

"I understand everything I need to. Drugs, rock-n-roll and sex. How am I doing?" Karla kills me with one of her looks. "Because Daddy and I weren't enough for you, you left to pursue your music, find yourself, and, in the meantime, sow your wild oats."

"Now hold on there a second." A fiery retort is more fight than I've seen from her since she arrived. "You can make any accusations you want. That—"

"Doesn't mean they're true? I figured that'd be your comeback. That's why I brought proof." I reach into the cabinet near me and pull out the pictures I downloaded years ago. "Here's one where you took your shirt off while the band's playing." I toss it at her. I watch it land at her feet. "And here's another where, oh yeah, you're drunk standing on one of the customer's table. Oh, you'll love this one. Here you are backstage smoking a joint. And there are lots more." I toss the remaining photos at her feet surrounding her with kindling for a fire.

"Allie." By the volume of Daddy's voice, I've gone too far. He'll give me the speech saying I need to forgive Karla for the hurt she's caused me.

Hurt? If only it were that easy. Karla's leaving isn't a pimple zit-cream removes. Her walking out of my life left a hole the size of a crater in my heart, and my entire life has never been the same. I've tried to fill it with a busy schedule; working hard at my studies, pursuing nursing, helping the football team. Now I realize now how fruitless these activities have become.

"Allie," Daddy says again.

"What is it?" My reply is heated as I wait for the deserved berating.

"Why is Cass standing outside hiding behind the tree in our front yard?"

Chapter Eighteen

Cass darts to a bush and crouches like a hunter afraid of giving away her position to a prey she's been stalking for hours. I stare in amazement as she repeats the move several times. The weather outside is bitter-cold and Cass isn't wearing a coat. I leave Daddy and Karla alone in the lounge room grateful for the distraction.

Cass stands at the doorway with her arms wrapped around her body. She sports red raw eyes. I imagine they come from crying most of the night. On her face is a look of real terror. Her eyes dart back and forth over her shoulders anxious to get out of the open.

"Can I come in?"

"Of course," I say. She walks inside shutting the door before I have a chance. While leaning up against the hallway wall she exhales a long breath. I wonder if something terrible might have happened to her last night. After the game, on our way back to the locker-room, a guy I'd never seen before intercepted us. Cass knew him. He grabbed her by the arm and told me to keep walking and to mind my own business.

Subconsciously, I begin rubbing my arm. Cass notices. "Let me see." I slowly pull the sleeve of my shirt up to reveal a massive bruise that is larger than Ray's hand having stretched almost as far as my shoulder and not quite down to the wrist. "Ray did that to you?"

"Cass, why did you let him hurt me?"

"Allie, I didn't mean for it to happen. It shouldn't have gone down that way. Ray went overboard. He didn't mean too Cass honest he didn't. He's been under a lot of pressure."

I don't understand what kind of pressure makes someone hurt another person. Cass's voice is frantic and loud and I don't want our conversation being detected by Karla or Daddy. I walk her to the lounge room on the lower level. Intense yet warm flames spill out from the fireplace drawing Cass closer.

"Last night…" Uttering words seems a struggle, "… wasn't an accident."

"What are you saying?"

"Ray's ankle."

I saw the break along with several hundred other people. No foul called, no flag thrown, and no obvious intent on the defensive lineman's part to cause bodily injury. An unfortunate event.

"Then explain it to my satisfaction." Cass closes her eyes. Everything about her demeanor suggests fear. "Come on Cass, talk to me."

"A warning."

"A warning from whom?"

"From K, the leader of FADE."

"What?" Now I'm confused. Who's K? "You told me Estrada was the leader of FADE."

"He is, I mean he was until K showed up a few days ago to reclaim the old position."

None of this makes sense.

"You're telling me this new leader deliberately had Estrada's ankle broken to show you what, how powerful he is?"

"Something like that."

"Estrada may never play football again." I let the words sink in. Her nonreaction disarms me. Possibly it's because she already knows this. Or it's something else altogether. Now, I realize, may be as good a time as any to fleece her for information about FADE. "Cass, tell me why Estrada resurrected FADE?"

"His home life," she replies almost immediately.

"What do you mean?"

"Ray comes from a poor family. It's only him, his mom, and his little brother. His dad died a year ago and left them without anything. She's forced to work two jobs and barely keeps the roof over their heads. He'd been thinking about a way he could make money to help out at home."

I don't buy it.

"A lot of people in Brescade are poor Cass. They're not starting gangs and robbing gas stations."

"Ray came across an old article online. It mentioned a gang that created havoc in Brescade for a brief period and fizzled out ten years ago. That motivated Ray, I guess, to revive it."

There must be more she's not telling me. Cass is satisfied to toss me bits and pieces.

"What happened?"

"At first, it started with a couple of us. We'd rob a few gas stations and stuff..." She stops mid-sentence.

"Then K appeared," I say. Cass remains silent. "Are you guys being forced against your will?"

"I'm not sure what you mean," she says. Stiff movements, glances over the shoulder, while inside my house, lay bare her deception. Random pieces struggle to find binding. The picture is unfinished. It's vital I probe more deeply.

"The pharmaceutical robberies."

"What about them?" Her sharp response suggests surprise. Quivers around the mouth could be contrived.

"Nothing." I pause to formulate my thoughts. "I get the feeling you don't have a choice in the matter." Another careless glance and she confirms my suspicion. "K found out Estrada resurrected FADE, came out of hiding, and pushed Estrada out."

Crackling pops, the type made by someone stomping on plastic bubbled sheets, sound from the fire. Cass moves next to the flames and sits. After a few moments, she turns to face me. Heat from the fireplace is strong. I worry about her sitting so close and receiving second-degree burns, she appears unaffected.

"Cass, who is the leader of FADE?"

I expect more passion and resistance from her. She composes herself and says, "I can't tell you that Allie."

"I've gathered you, Estrada, Erin, Deke, Koreil, those two girls you've been hanging around, the guy who grabbed you last night are all part of FADE. Those are the only ones I'm sure of except for the guy who broke Estrada's ankle. Since you substituted for Erin during the game last night, I'm guessing she participated in last night's robbery. And I'm betting the reason you showed up to the game is because K didn't give you a choice." Cass doesn't deny it. "I'm not sure how putting you in a situation where you were out of your depth made sense unless…"

"Unless what?"

"K knew of my passion for nursing and expected me to attend to Estrada's injury professionally and appropriately."

It scares Cass that my formulation of the events is accurate. For the many years I've known Cass, she's never struck me as the following type. Ironic, the bully is now being bullied. Justice? Joy makes no entrance into my heart. Though they've angered me, I hurt for Cass and Estrada.

While Cass has been sitting by the fire her body has slumped. The dominant almost defiant attitude she displayed over me recently has become a fizzling fuse with no explosive attached. What remains is an impotent outlook of hope.

"You and Estrada can't leave, can you?"

"We've been told if we walk we become permanent scenery at the bottom of the lake." I glance the direction of the hallway. Because of my position in the house I'm unable to see outside. Later today, Ian is going to stop by. No doubt he'll stand at the window and stare into the only lake within ten miles of Brescade.

"Who told you?" Cass's face lifts and her eyes force themselves into mine. A brazen look of fear molds her fire-warmed face.

"Tell me who the leader of FADE is." My voice is firm and commanding. I feel she's at the breaking point and pray she'll let something significant drop from her lips.

"After what I told you, you still have the nerve to ask me that? If I tell you, I'm as good as dead." A wave of terror travels through her body causing it to shake. Clammy hands take hold of mine. "Allie, I have no idea what I'm going to do."

Interrupted by the soothing tones of Daddy's voice, and before excusing myself, I take Cass's hands, hold them together for a long moment, then place them in her lap. A quick promise to return and I leave the room. Daddy stands in the hallway holding a tray with two mugs of apple cider. Each holds a long twig of cinnamon.

"Thanks Daddy."

"Everything okay?" Daddy whispers.

"I'll talk to you later." I worry of leaving Cass alone by herself.

"Okay, Princess."

Cass looks up at me with droopy dog eyes as I enter the room. I smile back maintaining a cheerful disposition and offer her one of the steaming mugs of cider. She takes it into her hands and doesn't reel from the heated ceramic. I set mine on the table next to me. Cass brings the cup to her mouth resting her lips on the rim and blows for a few seconds before taking a sip. Eyes retreat into her sockets, and she gulps as the hot liquid burns her lips and tongue. She blows again, harder this time and takes another sip swallowing without incident.

Cass twirls the thin stick of cinnamon creating a whirlwind of brown liquid. The small ripples hypnotize her for an entire minute. I assume she's trying to recall how she got into this mess—the feeling of being a trapped animal.

"Cass," I say gently, "can I ask how you got involved?"

"It's your fault," she says withdrawing from her daze.

"What?" I reply. My defenses soar to high alert.

"I don't mean it that way. K instructed Ray to ask you out—"

"You can't be serious?"

"For days, he tried to build up the nerve. When he finally spoke to you it was a colossal disaster. He asked me next."

"Why you?" I ask exasperated.

"Because of our friendship I might be able to influence you to..."

"Influence me to do what?" I ask.

Karla's abrupt entrance into the lounge despite the raging fire drops the temperature until the room is icier than outdoors. The cup in Cass's hand shakes uncontrollably and apple cider spills onto the carpet. I place my hands around the mug and take it from her and place it on the end table.

"I have to go," she says rising quickly. I watch as she steals a look at Karla. Something is exchanged between them. "I'll see you later." She doesn't wait for me to lead her to the door and runs down the hall shutting the front door quietly behind her.

"Odd, don't you think?" says Karla with a puzzled expression.

"You did something," I say.

"What on earth are you talking about?"

"Cass and I were having a heart to heart for the first time in a long time and the moment you walk in suddenly she's got to go. Tell me what's going on right now."

Karla walks into the lounge room and sits next to me. She grabs me by the elbow that is already incredibly sore.

"There are things in life that you don't need to concern yourself with. It's important for your survival, if you catch my drift?"

I nod quickly as the pain in my arm increases. Karla releases her grip. I pull away from her and stand in front of the fire facing her. She stands and moves towards me.

"Say anything to your father about this..."

She doesn't need to finish.

When she walks out of the room I find myself shaking from a vicious chill traveling through my bloodstream. What did Karla do to Cass? Then I realize Karla's got to be involved. I'm standing in front of the fire when Daddy enters several minutes later.

"You alright?" he asks.

"Fine," I reply instantly faking a smile I hope he'll believe.

"What did Cass want?"

"Daddy, do you mind if we don't talk about that now? There's something else I need to ask you."

He reaches for my hand; I offer it willingly. We walk to the couch together, sit, and stare at the fire a while.

"Daddy, this whole mess with the town hating Karla can't be because she did some terrible things during her youth, became the depraved Mag Steel or on the grounds she didn't die eight years ago. There's more you haven't told me. Can you explain her involvement with FADE?"

Deep breathing, averted eyes.

"Allie, I'm not sure…" he mumbles, "if now is the time…"

"I'm so tired of everyone thinking I'm too young to understand. When do I get to learn the truth about what happened back then?"

Daddy gets up from the couch and now it's his turn to stand in front of the fire of confession. Instead of turning, he faces it, and speaks softly.

"The day Karla left Brescade to go to Asia someone discovered a dead body at the lake."

"Murdered?"

"Yes."

My eyes widen in panic. "The police were never able to prove who killed him," he interjects quickly. "There were more than a few of the townspeople who believed Karla responsible."

I take a breath. That explains the terror in Cass's eyes.

Chapter Nineteen

Thrown off schedule due to the earlier commotion, when the doorbell rings at four o'clock on-the-dot, instead of standing ready in the hallway to greet Ian, I'm in the bathroom bushing my teeth and hair. With my phone in the bedroom and the ringer turned down, by the time I realize how late it is, Ian has been waiting outside in the cold for five minutes. Overcome by guilt when I see him stomping his feet to keep warm, I apologize profusely. His warm smile tells me he's not upset.

I hope Ian's being here will cheer me up; I can use a heavy dose of bolstering. Though he's not as upbeat as normal, his expression is nowhere as sour as the attitude I carry. I invite him in. Karla left earlier and Daddy not long after, so no fresh chocolate chip cookies to take upstairs to the lounge room.

Ian's roving eyes, wiping his hands on his pants, and the jittering of his leg tells me he's distracted. Too much of a gentleman to unload his stuff on me right away, we spend a few minutes talking chit chat before moving onto the deeper stuff.

When he asks me how things are going, I spill my guts telling him everything that's happened since we were last together. When I'm done spouting Ian doesn't say a word. He's processing the conversation. I don't ask for advice and he is careful not to offer any. Still, he shoots me a pleasant smile.

Now that an hour has passed I ask Ian how the trip with his father went. Ian's father took him to visit The University of Washington's School of Medicine. Future monthly trips will take them across the country until they've had an opportunity to visit the top five medical schools in the nation. Ian tells me his father is expecting him to approach these outings with courage and an open mind. At the end of this school year, he'll be expected to attend one of these schools.

"What are you going to do?" I ask sympathetic to Ian's dilemma.

"I don't know Allie." He shrugs his shoulders with indifference. "Neither of my parents is giving me much of a choice."

"You can't give into them Ian, you can't." My cheeks are as flush as the imaginary red flag being waved in front of me. "You're meant to be a painter. I know it. You know it. I don't know why your parents close themselves off to the idea."

Silence is one of Ian's strong suits. When he's quiet, it's because he's thinking critically over what I've said or forming a question to ask or even preparing to answer me. I think I may have said too much. I shut up waiting for a response. When he's quiet after a long period, I start worrying.

"You're not upset with me are you Ian?"

"Never," he says turning to me. "I was considering life as a surgeon."

"You can't be serious." Fumes steam from my nostrils.

"You want to become a nurse." Turning the tables on me is a new tactic.

"Because I don't want to do anything except nursing."

"You're wrong Allie." His statement is unsettling. "A nurse is only part of what you want to do. Deep down, you want to do something huge with your life. That is what drives you not becoming a nurse."

Irritated at Ian for not standing up to his parents, he's dead-on when it comes to my motives. I can't wait to be a nurse that's true, yet it's only the tip of the iceberg.

"My desire to be a nurse and your contemplation of becoming a surgeon are two different scenarios."

"They're the same thing."

"No, they're not," I say my voice raised. "For one, you don't have any wish to enter medicine. And second, you're at your best behind an easel with a blank canvass and a paintbrush in your hand." Ian starts to interrupt. "And third," I jump in silencing him, "I don't want you to enter the field of medicine.

"You don't want me to become a doctor?"

"No, I don't."

"Is that because you don't believe I could, do it?"

"I didn't say that." Ian's sly smile lets me know I'm overreacting again. "Okay, maybe I'm a little vocal," another smile, "too vocal. You and I both feel the same way about this."

"Feelings won't keep your parents off your back." Ian stands. I wonder if he's mad. In my estimation, it's a good thing. He needs to get angry for a change and tell his parents what they can do with their position.

Every time Ian visits, he walks to the window. His body relaxes as he takes in the wide view of the lake for the millionth time. This time I decide to join him to discover what captivates his focus. We stand together for several minutes.

"What are you looking at?" I ask observing tiny ripples invade the calm water.

"That clump of trees over there across the lake." He points with his finger to show me. I follow his line of sight. It takes me a few seconds before I locate the cluster. I nod when I find it. "Now, move your eyes straight up three-inches."

My eyes settle on the white house that resembles a mini castle. I've drooled over it many times.

"Does a politician or movie star live there?" I ask.

"Not exactly."

From my peripheral vision, I capture his guilty grin.

"Tell me that's not your house." Ian says nothing. "You're kidding me. That's your home?" I exclaim realizing what I've discovered. "Is that what you look at every time you go to the window?" With a mannerism I've not observed in Ian before, he turns so he's facing away from me. Red-faced with puffed cheeks evokes a picture of two balloons on the verge of bursting. "How come you never told me you lived on the lake?"

"The subject never came up." Evasive responses from Ian trouble me.

"Now it has." I turn and face the lake. After a few word stumbles, uncharacteristic of Ian since he's been speaking complete sentences since the age of two, he continues.

"It's not my house I'm thinking about..." His voice stops mid-sentence. Moments later his right hand reaches over and brushes the top of mine. I don't jump at his startling touch. My heart beats more rapidly and I feel lightheaded. Placing my right hand on the window ledge steadies my wobbling knees.

Now I understand.

The backs of our hands continue to touch. Neither of us wants to be the first to sever the connection. Our fingers wiggle together until entwined. I glance to see what's causing the warm flutters in my heart. It's impossible to tell where Ian's fingers begin and mine end. A single mold of flesh greets my eyes.

Ian and I have been friends for a long time, I care for him a lot. Never have I considered anything more, especially when his art comes first. When he reaches over and turns me to face him, my heart needs resuscitating. Our eyes stare a long time into each other's, until the dream unfolds between us.

Distinct to the vision of dancing sugar-plums, my fantasy has flesh, and warmth, and strength attached to it. Ian, my prince, summons me. I accept his willing invitation.

Ian leans towards me. With the passion of an artist and the proficiency of a surgeon, he places his lips on mine. Tremors in the earth's core or in my percolating heart, I can't tell which, shake my world until liquid love races through my veins where blood once ran. Its light speed flow dizzies me and my knees lose their rigidity. Ian's arm slides around me holding me close.

No one ever told me paradise could be found in the casual brush of two hands or rhapsody revealed when those two hands, his and mine, intermingle. This moment of ecstasy blazes when his mouth touches mine.

Ian pulls back slowly, I think to gauge my reaction. Afraid he might mistake the incalculable number of stars cascading through my eyes as glaring indignation, I lean in and return his kiss. The tangle of our lips is not a call to war nor is it a signal of retreat. We are content to allow the power of passion to hold us in its grasp.

The noise from the steps startles us. We turn to find Karla standing at the top of the stairs arms folded, foot tapping, and staring. I'm the first to withdraw from the grip.

"Isn't this nice," she says with a sneer that sends a stingray shiver throughout my spine.

"Your father told me the two of you were just friends."

"We are friends," I spit back releasing my fingers from Ian's grip.

"Friends don't do what you were doing."

"You're overreacting Karla."

"I don't think so, and I'm sure your father wouldn't approve even if it's with a good friend you've known all your life."

"Where do you get off telling me who I can be with? It's none of your business." Her eyes shift upwards to the side showing disdain for my snappy retort.

"I'm still your mother whether you accept it or not Allie. By right, I get to rule over certain aspects of your life."

"The blood running through my body might be the same as yours. That is as close as you and I will ever be. I won't listen to you and you can't make me." Immediately, I want to swallow my juvenile remark. Karla pounces on it right away.

"You're such a child. There is a world of untrustworthy and unsavory men out there…" Her voice comes to an abrupt stop.

I pounce.

"And I'm sure you've been with every one of them."

My remark is meant to wound. Target acquired, Karla steps onto the landing and walks my direction. In front of Ian, she slaps me across the face. I stand in shock as if an alien vessel has landed and a green woman exited the ship to assault me. Karla's strike sends me to the ground. Ian reaches down to lift me up and walks me to the couch.

"I'll wait here with you until your dad returns," he says.

"No, Ian, you'll be leaving now or I'm going to call the police."

"And tell them what?" I say.

"There's a boy taking advantage of my daughter."

"You wouldn't."

Karla slips her hand into her pocket and retrieves her cell. She looks at me prior to punching in the three most recognized numbers in the country. Crossed arms accentuate my defiance. With the speaker feature on, the crisp voice on the end confirms her threat.

"Nine-one-one, what is your emergency?"

Karla gives me a foul scowl.

Ian stands. "It might be better if I leave."

"Is someone there?"

"Sorry," Karla says, "wrong number." She swipes the screen to end the call.

"I'll talk to you later," says Ian leaving me to walk downstairs.

Karla keeps herself stationary making Ian walk around her. My heart breaks as he descends the stairs. A few seconds later the door closes. In a huff, I walk to my room.

"Don't turn your back on me, we're not finished here."

Ticked, angry, and hormonal, I place my face inches from her.

"This mother daughter fairytale you live in is over. I never want to see you again Karla. Pack your things and get out of this house or else."

"Or else what?" I hold my tongue. "I'm not going anywhere Allie." She steps half an inch closer. "Jack's never stopped loving me even after all these years. You of all people know that." Her smile sickens me. "The three of us *are* going to have that family I've always wanted.

Daddy's keys jingle as he walks through the kitchen. I wait till he is almost at the steps.

"Stop it!" I lift Karla's hand from her side and whack it into the side of my head before she can react. The firecracker explosion reverberates throughout the house. "Ow." Daddy's halfway up the steps when I fall to the ground.

"What are you doing?" he asks Karla.

"Jack," she laughs, "it's not what it looks like."

My writhing on the floor and the added moans should elicit a nomination for an Oscar-worthy performance. My acting moves Daddy to action.

"Karla," he says, "I'm really sorry, this isn't working out the way either of us hoped. Allie is my number one responsibility. I can't have you treating her..." He chooses not to end the sentence. "You're going to have to leave and I mean tonight." He walks downstairs waiting for her to join him.

Of course, when I need my phone camera to record, for posterity, Karla's astonished reaction, I don't have one. That woman had no idea how devious this daughter of hers could be.

"You want help packing?" I ask.

Chapter Twenty

On Sunday morning, I awaken with a massive headache. I've known it was coming for a few days and should have addressed it immediately. With the franticness going on in my life, the result of Karla's interference, I neglected to address it. The moment I'm out of bed I start stretching. This is a natural remedy I've used a few times in the past. Fifteen-minutes of exercise later, still no relief. I go to the kitchen and wrap a dish towel around a frozen can of juice and place it against my temple. Relief doesn't come at once. Over time, it dissipates enough to where the throbbing doesn't feel as if a quarterback is firing footballs into my temple every few seconds.

The door to Karla's room is open. Reaching over, I pull it shut. I have nary an ounce of remorse for my actions. Daddy hasn't commented, and I refuse to bring up the subject of Karla. I'm hoping we've gotten rid of her once and for all.

I hit the shower in preparation to attend church with Daddy. While inspecting the hematoma I realize it's increased in size and discoloration. More shades of blue appear to have joined the diversity of colors on my arm. Other bruises spot my body: one on my opposite arm and the other on my calf. I make a mental note to research medical reasons later.

When church is over Daddy takes me to lunch for fusion cuisine at Legends, an upscale reservation only establishment that opened outside Spokane a month ago. Chef and owner Ron O'Keeffe is a good friend of Daddy's. When we arrive, a gently spoken *Maître d'* escorts us to the best table in the establishment and after being seated, he offers us a menu and an extensive wine list. I notice the menu is not as comprehensive as I've come to deplore from the mediocre franchises and find it uncomplicated to read. Score for Ron. Scan a menu; read a book. That's my philosophy. I count twelve entrée items on the menu, a generous smattering of choice salads, soups, and a dessert list to die for.

Following the scrumptious meal, we push back from the table stuffed. Ron waves the check partly because Daddy is reviewing the restaurant for the paper and the other because they're such good friends. Nonetheless, Daddy leaves a hefty tip for the waiter. While Daddy and Ron catch up on old times, I inspect the décor. It's modern and yet very warm and cozy, close to being one of those steakhouses without the grunginess of peanut shells covering the floor.

As I scan the walls, I notice many paintings. None of them imprisons my senses as the ones Ian paints.

I'm struck with a crazy idea.

As the conversation between Daddy and Ron ends, I pose a question regarding the paintings. I ask Ron if he has any interest in looking at the work of a painter I know. Ron tells me of his passion for supporting artists and that each painting on Legends' walls was created by a local painter. This allows artists exposure to their work they might not get elsewhere. In addition, Ron sells the paintings in his restaurant. I notice the small white price tags for the first time. Three of the paintings are priced for over a thousand dollars. With Daddy's permission, I promise to return later that evening with a trio of paintings for Ron to place on his walls.

On the ride home, Daddy asks an unnerving question. "You're not sticking your nose somewhere it doesn't belong are you Allie?"

"Ian's paintings are as good as the ones at Legends."

"I'm not arguing that point. You know his parents' position."

"Ian isn't interested in medicine."

"Maybe not. In my experience, underhanded acts, like the one you're considering, have a way of backfiring. You don't want to alienate Ian or his parents. Remember, Ian's loyalty is to them first, not you."

"Daddy, I'm only giving him a venue where people can evaluate his work."

"Uh huh."

"What do you mean by that?"

"Allie, I've known you for sixteen years. I know how you think. You tend to exceed the established limits."

"Sometimes you need to step out of the boat and walk on water. I'm giving him exposure. That's all. What Ian does with it after that is his choice not mine."

"Okay, Princess. Don't say I didn't warn you."

It takes me the bulk of the afternoon to develop the courage to call Ian. When I place the call, I reason to myself I'm only telling him a tiny white untruth. I tell him Daddy wants to use the paintings at one of his restaurants and wondered if we couldn't display three of them. Ian's happy to accommodate us. I ask Daddy to drive me to his house. We pick up the paintings—his best works, other than the piece with me riding bareback on a stallion which I refuse to give away.

Before the restaurant closes, Daddy and I show up with the paintings. Straightaway, Ian's work impresses Ron. I'm surprised when he chooses to replace the entry paintings with Ian's. He pulls out a checkbook and asks me who to make the check out to. I question his actions. Ron tells me he loves Ian's work and, on the spot, purchases two of the paintings for himself. For now, he'll leave them on the wall to generate interest. He tells me if Ian has more work, he'd love to examine those pieces as well. Ron sets the price for the paintings right there. I'm crazy excited for Ian and tell Ron to make the check out to Ian McPhetridge. I steal a look at the amount. Ron's check is for eighteen hundred dollars.

When I get home, I put the check in an envelope and include a small note.

Congratulations Ian you're going places.
This is the first step.
Allie

Chapter Twenty-One

Stout-hearted as I await the busses arrival, my toes feel the effects of winter's wrath as it turns my tiny appendages into iced chicken nuggets. I stand up on my tiptoes and repeat the move to keep the blood circulating.

Reynold's refusal to pick me up means Daddy must once again drive me to school. He promises that he'll talk to the office and get this sorted out. I know people are angry with Daddy and me. Reynolds is obviously one of them. Does that give him the right to shirk his responsibilities? He's a county employee for Pete's sake.

My headache's back. I've done everything I can to eradicate it; nothing's working. After a fierce internal quarrel, I ingest two acetaminophen tablets before exiting the car. This should take the edge off the gnawing pain. Missing classes, with the educational goals I've set for myself, is unacceptable.

I approach my locker with hesitancy. Thank God, a custodial worker removed the vile phrasing. While I have my head poked into the locker, I hear the sharp clanging of heels echo in the hallway. Cass is walking towards me dressed in her now traditional Goth attire. This time as she passes me I notice a horrified grimace and bruises on her face that weren't there on Saturday. I want to reach out and say something to her to help her if I can. Her eyes shoot me a message warning me to stay back.

Less than five feet behind her, Deke and Koreil stalk her steps. If she's in fear of her life, these are the guys who are making sure she stays scared. They eyeball me as they pass by, I stare back unafraid at first. Their stares are pure evil. I'm glad when they're turned the corner.

Four hours later, going against the drug company's recommendations, I take several more acetaminophen. I've succumbed to a few minor illnesses here and there, normally, I'm not the person who gets sick. In fact, I pride myself on being one of the healthiest people I know. This is one of the reasons why I prefer homeopathic remedies over prescriptive drug usage. However, my penchant for natural medicines is doing nothing to deter my debilitating headache.

At lunchtime when Fume, an alternative rock group plays their set, I exit the cafeteria because the noise is too abrasive shattering my ear drums. I find refuge in the tranquility of the library. In the back, I find a small table where I can work unbothered. This will give me an opportunity to complete my homework early.

By chance, one of the assignments I have requires actual physical library research. This is the first time I've spent any time in the school's library since attending the school. Most of my research I get off the web. While I'm stooping between rows of books looking for the biography on Harriet Tubman *The Road to Freedom* by Catherine Clinton, I notice Deke and Koreil sidle into the row catty-corner to mine. I keep low to stay out of view and eavesdrop on their conversation.

"K says this weekend it's going to take every one of us to handle the break-in at Memorial." This voice I recognize as Deke's. His high-pitched voice screeches when he talks. Thus, the nickname, "Squeak."

"I'm not sure we can count on Cass." Koreil adds.

"Not even after what Campo did to Estrada?"

"K called me to rough her up last night for talking to Allie. That stubborn streak of hers is going to get her hurt a lot worse."

Anger mounts within me comparable to a jockey clambering onto a thoroughbred. I want to take a book and hurl it at Koreil's head. When it comes to baseball my curve ball mirrors a straight line. The act might cause them to readjust their focus. I don't want that.

"The only leverage we have is to go after Estrada," Deke says. There is a long uncomfortable silence.

"When you say, 'go after him,'" Koreil's voice shakes uncontrolled.

"Stop your whining Koreil. We knew when we joined FADE someone might get hurt or worse." My heart skips a beat.

"Yeah, Squeak, I know. Estrada's no longer boss. Now he's a peon like the rest of us. No way am I going to kill him because K asks me too."

"Keep your voice down," Deke demands.

"Dude, I'm looking at a full ride at Syracuse next year. I can't jeopardize my football scholarship."

"You jeopardized it by joining FADE you moron."

Deke is the shorter of the two defensive players. It sounds as if Koreil, the giant, is reconsidering his involvement and Squeaky Deke has few scruples.

"Look Koreil, the gang didn't call itself Fear and Death Express for nothing. Make waves and K will see to it you end up with a few broken bones or worse, at the bottom of the lake."

My breathing stops when I hear the words Fear and Death Express. I don't know why it never clicked before now. It stared me right in the face the entire time, hidden in plain sight. Since Cass's visit, I've been trying to figure out the identity of K. Now I know. Karla is the old/new leader and is targeting Estrada for death.

I stand and back out of the aisle. My backpack makes contact with the bookshelf knocking several books to the floor causing a slamming noise.

"Did you hear that?" Squeaky asks.

Both boys race to the end of the aisle and scout for the intruder. I've hidden myself in an alcove. That doesn't halt their investigation and they continue to scour each row. They are only a few feet from me when the bell rings for fourth period. They keep in their stance hoping the eavesdropper will come out prematurely. I wait until I see them exit the library. I wait even longer in case one or both are stationed in the hallway waiting for me to appear. It makes me tardy for class.

Halfway through last period I can't take the throbbing in my head. Unable to take more acetaminophen for another few hours, I don't welcome the discomfort I'll suffer until I can pop more tablets. Securing a pass from my teacher, and on my way to the nurse's office, I stop at the women's restroom.

My fingers grab a wad of paper towels and turn the water on at the sink letting it run until the water cools. After I place the paper under the water, I squeeze the towels to get rid of the excess water and dab them against my temples and on my face. This belligerent headache refuses to subside. I toss the wet towels in the trashcan and grab more paper towels to wipe off the remaining moisture. A toilet flushes in the farthest stall and I'm surprised to see Cass exit. Her face is a heavy pink and her eyes red and puffy which tells me she's been crying.

"What are you doing here?" Cass asks making me feel I belong in the men's bathroom.

"I'm on my way to the nurse's office. What are you doing here?" I ask reacting to her verbal lashing.

"Nothing." Cass lets the faucet run. Her hands never touch the water. I sidle up next to her and put my arm around her. "Allie, it's awful. K sent Koreil over yesterday."

"He hit you?" I ask with mounting anger.

"Yes."

I inspect her face and can see the slap marks. "Cass, when you go home put a warm compress on it. Then an hour before you go to bed I want you mix Cayenne Pepper and melted Vaseline together—a five to one ration. Put it on the swelling. Don't get any in your eye. Okay?" I know it will work because I've used the formula.

"Okay."

"Why did Koreil hit you?" I ask.

"Because they don't want me hanging around you. You're *persona non grata.*"

"Off limits. What the heck does that mean?"

"What do you think it means Allie? No one is to talk to you or contact you in any way. K has special plans for you."

"What, plans to hurt me?"

"Allie, I've said too much." She walks away; I step in her path.

"Un uh, you're not running away this time. Now tell me why K wants to hurt me Cass?"

Another stall flushes. Cass's and my eyes both widen in fear to see who's going to exit. We wait for a good minute. The toilet flushes again and we wait. The person in the stall refuses to come out. I motion to Cass to leave the bathroom and wait outside. I tiptoe towards the back of the bathroom and wait. The whooshing sound of the toilet sounds again. This time I hold my position. With caution, I approach the stall. I take a deep breath before pushing in the door.

The door swings forward then back. An empty stall. I'm baffled by the event. As I turn to leave it flushes again. I rush to find Cass. She's nowhere in sight.

Chapter Twenty-Two

Tuesday morning arrives. I've tried everything I can to relieve this blasted headache. Bad news, nothing's working. I'm familiar enough with the workings of my body to know these reactions are the result of an antipathetic interaction. On top of the headache, I have been vomiting for two straight days. Everything I ingest makes its way back within minutes. I've perused the medical journals I have on my shelves, yet I'm nowhere near to diagnosing my illness. I keep reminding myself I'm not a doctor, and, in this case, I need to see one.

On the whole, Daddy is not a worrier. His concern is impossible to hide. He drives me to the emergency room less than fifteen minutes later. The nurse at the front desk asks me my reason for the emergency visit. Daddy steps back intrigued as I engage in stimulating medical exchange. The nurse's surprise at my prowess for medical terminology shows and she types in fastidious notes. Following our talk, she takes my temperature and blood pressure. Both register as normal.

Twenty minutes after we've been ushered into a small examination room a female doctor enters. She asks me to re-explain my reason for the hospital visit. Daddy steps out of the room while she examines me. She relays information to the nurse standing next to her. I know I'm being prescribed medication for the headache. The vomiting, she thinks, could be a reaction to the debilitating headaches. Subsequent blood tests will be run to rule that out.

"I notice you have a massive bruise on your arm Allie."

"The hematoma is three days old."

The doctor moves closer and whispers. "Is your father responsible for this? Because if he is…"

While I'm appalled by her allegation, I understand her need to voice the question. Domestic violence, which is at epic proportions, I classify as nothing more than an abominable act of today's coward.

"No Dr. Seville." I shake my head in disgust. "A guy at school trying to get my attention grabbed me."

She shakes her head in disgust.

"If that's what guys are doing today to meet girls, what's this world coming too? You don't seem the type of woman to waste your time with an immature adolescent."

"Not for a second," I say. "I'm with a nice guy who knows how to treat a lady." She smiles and pulls the curtain back to allow Daddy entrance.

"Mr. Alexander, I want to keep Allie overnight for observation."

"Do you have any idea what's causing the headaches?"

"It's too early to tell at this stage. That's one of the reasons admittance makes sense. I'm going to have several tests run to rule out certain disorders. She tells me the headaches are debilitating. We're going to administer a shot that will ease Allie's pain." Right on cue a nurse enters carrying a syringe and vial. Daddy steps out again this time the doctor accompanies him.

I've watched the procedure many times. This time, it's with active interest that I observe the nurse insert the syringe into the lid of the vial. The needle pierces it with ease, and she draws out a clear liquid. She pushes on the plunger expelling every bit of air from the syringe. Thin lines of fluid shoot out into space. The nurse asks me to loosen my pants and to turn over. After ripping open an alcohol wipe and wiping the cold swab over my skin, the sharp thin metal shard penetrates my buttock. It doesn't take very long before the effects of the drug take place.

I'm running on a path. I'm not alone. Someone jogs alongside me. It's not till I steal a look at my running mate I realize she is a young woman my age. Void of hair, I can't stop myself from staring at her shaved scalp.

Dogs with fierce barks dash towards us from the rear. The fear I feel, I see in her eyes—our terrors unite. A fun run this isn't. We increase our speed and traverse sharp bends and turns, through thick bush and worn trails until we reach the edge of a cliff. We lean over, hands touching the ground, exhausted while trying to catch our breath. Hanging from the tree is a rope that swings from one side of the cliff to the other. Unfortunately, the rope can only hold one person at a time leaving time for only one of us to use it.

FLICKERS OF LIGHT and shadow attack my face complimented by sounds of whirling thunder working in tandem. Drawing me from my drug-induced slumber, I open my eyes. Daddy closes the blinds as the helicopter lifts from the helipad.

"Sorry Princess, I didn't mean for it to wake you."

"It's okay," I say, "I wanted to get up." The remnants of the morphine shot continue to drift throughout my body making my body warm and sluggish.

"How are you feeling Allie?" Tremors in Daddy's voice produce an upwelling of anxiety inside me.

"Better. What's the diagnosis?"

"I don't know. The doctor is on her morning rounds. She'll stop by in a little while."

Something outside the window directs his attention from our conversation. I sense Daddy knows more than he's letting on, still I don't press him. We wait in an unfamiliar silence until the doctor's arrival.

Sharp clumps strike at the floor as the doctor's footsteps approach. I can tell she's wearing pumps. A few seconds later she peeks her head through the curtain with a slight smile. After wishing me a good morning, reading my chart, and a physical examination she asks Daddy to join her in the hall.

"I'll be right back Princess."

He's gone for a long time. Nurses pop in and out of my room making sure I'm okay. They're nice and I spend most of the time talking to them about my nursing interests. I hope they don't think I'm being too demanding as I ask question after question.

Daddy walks back into my room. Something in his demeanor is skewed. It's not as recognizable as the transformation between Dr. Jekyll and Mr. Hyde. Still, he's different.

"Come on Allie we're getting out of here," he states with an unsteady voice. A nurse enters the room and helps me out of my gown and back into the clothes I wore yesterday. Daddy grabs my hand and walks a brisk pace to the elevator. Once downstairs, we exit the hospital and wait for the valet to bring our car.

"Is everything okay?" I ask wondering at his strange behavior.

"Allie, there's something I've been meaning to show you."

We drive for a half hour and arrive at the state forest, my first time here. We pay a fee upon entering and follow the path down a winding hill that ends at the most beautiful body of water I have ever seen.

"I've been meaning to bring you here for a long time," he says before exiting the car. Daddy holds onto me acting very protective.

"Daddy, what's the matter?"

He ignores me and continues walking towards the lake holding my waist with a tight grip. When we arrive at the edge of the lake, the mesmerizing effects of the lake stall my breathing. Trees are void of leaves leaving an interminable stark beauty to the landscape. I imagine I'm in one of Ian's paintings as I border the unpolluted lake.

For November, the afternoon air is mild. I have my winter coat, hat, and gloves in the car in case Mother Nature has plans to make alterations. From the other end of the lake where I'm standing, a large hill rises to join the mountain behind it. Large patches of brown grass sit where I imagine green grass grew months before autumn settled. Oak and fir trees cover the mountainside resembling camouflaged soldiers on a battlefield.

An indigo sky completes the backdrop. I wonder if Daddy and I have stumbled upon 'heaven on earth.' With the lake's mirrored image, I'm blessed to view two opposing landscapes at the same time.

At the edge of the lake is a manmade beach complete with fine-grained white sand. We walk towards it holding hands. Daddy and I are alone. He sits me up atop the table as if placing me in a highchair and seeks to make sure I'm comfortable. When he's convinced, he kneels on the sand with his back towards me. I watch him draw long parallel lines in the sand ten feet apart.

"Allie, do you see the two lines I've drawn?" He asks.

I nod.

Next, he plops on the table next to me.

"Good because I want to ask you an important question. This is the most serious thing I've ever asked. I need you to think long and hard before answering."

"Okay," I reply in earnest, curious to hear his question.

"Imagine a frog stands at the line on your right facing the other line. If you ask the frog to jump half the distance, and with each subsequent jump you ask the frog to jump half the distance, will the frog ever reach the other line?"

"Yes," I reply. Daddy's question is too easy. His swift silence disturbs me. Transfixed by the lake he stares off into the distance. His silence gets me to thinking that perhaps my answer's incorrect. I inspect the lines again and envision the frog jumping half the distance each time. The forward progress of each jump propels the frog towards the line. For ten minutes, I ponder his question until I'm forced to recant my earlier answer.

"It'll get close," I say, "but the frog will never reach the line."

"That's right Allie," he says excited as if I discovered the answers to the world's fathomless mysteries.

"You brought me to the state park to ask me about a frog?" Daddy ignores me again. He extends his hand. I place mine in his and walk with him towards the lake. Our feet are only inches from the edges of the chilly water.

"You see, this body of water in front of you?" I nod. "How long would it take you to swim across it?"

The lake is large and I'm not that good a swimmer. I don't factor that last part into the equation.

"Three or four hours," I reply. "I'd drown before getting there."

He smiles.

"I'd save you." His voice curdles. Animated movement from his hands reminds me of a charismatic choral director. "How long for a squirrel?"

"A squirrel? Daddy, what's going on?"

"Stay with me Princess."

For the life of me, I can't follow his train of thought. Frogs, squirrels, swimming... "Three days?" I answer him.

"An ant?" He moves along the shoreline. I follow him.

"I don't know a week I guess," I say raising my voice. With each question, I experience fresh frustration.

"Allie, can you think of something smaller than an ant?"

"A lot of things," I want to yell out hoping to bring an end to this bizarre line of questioning. My mind reverts to middle-school science where I learned about atoms and the parts that make up the atom that were impossible to see without a microscope. "Electrons, protons and neutrons."

"Using your best guess Allie, how long would it take a proton to get from here to the other side?"

"A year?" He turns and grabs me by the shoulders.

"Each of those will reach their goals even if you can do it in three hours and it takes the proton a year."

"Daddy, I don't understand what you're getting at."

"Allie, I know you must think I've gone crazy by asking you these off-the-wall questions. I want you to see something." He turns me around and we meander back to the table. "The space between the lines, on the sand or from side to side of the lake or even the distance from earth to the stars above, is an infinite sum of space and time. The frog will jump forever and never get to the other side. Do you understand what I'm trying to say?"

I shake my head.

"Listen Allie. You should never allow anyone or anything to steal that time from you because you always have as much of it as you need. The time God gives us to accomplish our tasks on this earth is always enough."

Daddy and I often enjoy discussing deep spiritual matters. I sense something significant taking place in this conversation. I'm drawn to his words as a magnet to metal. Back at the car, his large hand cradles mine. Dense murky-looking clouds infiltrate the sky shading us from the noon sun. Individual drops of water spot parts of my face. I blink away heaven's cold tears. Daddy opens the door for me. I'm uneasy as I take my seat. He turns the engine on and lets the car warm as we stare out over the lake one final time.

A Trumpeter Swan soars from the sky and flies less than a foot above the water. I watch as it races to the other side. I lose sight of it.

"Allie," Daddy says to me. The croaking in his voice makes me wonder if he isn't coming down with something.

"Daddy are you okay?" I ask.

"No Princess," he says. His heavy breathing eclipses the noise of the rumbling engine. Sighs from his chest graft new boundaries to cradle his broken spirit. The final rays of the sun illuminate Daddy's face. When I see the sparkle of tears stream from his eyes I know something is dreadfully wrong.

"What is it Daddy? Please tell me. I can handle it I promise you."

He turns to look at me. Wetness covers his face. I now reach over and hold his hand with both of mine.

"Is it about my headaches?" I ask thinking the worst. He nods. "Then please tell me the truth Daddy."

"Allie, the results from you blood work came back, you have…"

I can't say I've ever seen my dad breakdown. Sure, I've seen him sad, but nothing this startling or devastating. He cries unashamed next to me. I put my arm around his shoulder. As much as I want to comfort him I need to know what's wrong with me.

"Just tell me," I say squeezing his hand tight.

"Allie, you have leukemia."

These aren't words I ever expected to hear following my name. My role is to be the savior for the hurting and dying, not to be the one who needs the saving. Instantly, my hands recoil into my lap. Patches of fog appear on the window as I lean my head against it. Daddy reverses the car, puts the gearshift into drive, and we journey back up the hill towards home. Neither of us says a word during the return trip.

With each mile marker we pass, a small piece of me strips away attaching itself to the post, a piece I'll never salvage. My dreams, hopes, and desires disintegrate much the same as sand castles underneath a rising tide. By the time we arrive home, I'm empty, emotionless, and exhausted. My heart's response? Become stone.

Chapter Twenty-Three

I wonder if in every person's life a challenging issue hunts you down and tests you with such earnestness it becomes *that* moment which defines the type of person you are going to be for the rest of your life. This is mine. In the twinkle of an eye, my life has reversed into an unavoidable pothole. Suddenly, I understand the futility of life. Living a life filled with hopes and dreams is nothing more than trying to hold the wind with clasped hands.

My decade-long wish of changing the world has sizzled resembling an overcooked piece of bacon.

I sit in silence, detached as Daddy registers me at hospital admissions. When they've completed check-in, a nurse appears at my side with a wheelchair. She smiles. I've lost my sense of joy and can only elicit a frozen scowl. I sit in the chair without prompting.

We travel through a maze of hallways and elevators till we arrive at the children's cancer ward; my abode for the next several weeks—longer—until I die. Who knows? The children I encounter have something in common with each other. They're hairless or soon will be.

This stark realization hits me more powerfully than a kick in the abdomen. I double over in my seat. It won't be long till I look as pitiful.

I'm not them.

In a daze, I touch my hair. Fear grips me refusing to let go. Energetic children run the halls. Others walk with determination while several sit on hospital beds or huddled in groups spending time with family members or in consult with physicians. Still, I see a few laughing. Hope radiates from their eyes. Why? Don't they understand the truth? This is what separates me from them, what makes me different. I'm willing to accept the truth. I'm dying.

The same nurse from admitting pushes me into a semi-private room vivid with color. It takes a few seconds for my eyes to grow accustomed to the flamboyant decoration. Bright orange curtains highlighted from behind by the sun are shut keeping the intense light at bay. The floor is a mural made of tiny colored vinyl tiles. I'm too close to make out the image.

A mural on the wall to my right depicts children at a park. They're jumping, hopping, skipping, and throwing balls. The grass is thick. Children are barefoot and skip through the lush green carpet.

The opposite wall is a solid dodger blue color. A two-inch black line divides the wall into two equal sections. Multiple cans of paint sit on a cloth tarp and a bucket of upside down brushes is nearby. I wonder their purpose.

Two desert tan loveseats which double as hideaway beds for family members who choose to stay overnight sit against opposite walls. Two beds, one purple and the other apple green complete the rainbow of colors. Weighted cotton screens create semi-privacy. One is plum purple; the other apple green.

The nurse sets the brakes on the wheelchair and bends to flip up the metal plates where my feet have been resting. She extends her hand to help me.

I ignore her pity.

"Since you're the only one in the room, you can choose either bed," she says.

After standing on my own, I walk to the green bed. Daddy says nothing about my precipitous choice.

I pull the curtain around me and change into the robe placed on the bed. The thin garment opens in the back and is difficult to tie. I feel exposed.

I'm glad the other bed is empty. The last thing I need is a stranger staring at me wanting to make conversation. I shudder at the pointlessness of it and close my eyes to shut out the world.

Throughout the day nurses and doctors tread in and out of my room. My front row seat allows me to critique their movements. It's during this exercise my reason for wanting to become a nurse eludes me. What in the world was I thinking?

My refusal to communicate is not an adolescent knee-jerk reaction to having leukemia, but *my* right to declare to myself and others I still have control of at least one thing in my life.

Multiple tests have been scheduled for me. At least two of them hint to be painful procedures. A minor operation to insert a catheter into my chest to undergo chemotherapy, I fear the most. Yet, no matter how many needles they stick in me or how many procedures they administer I refuse to flinch. I realize I have control over this as well.

A thin man with a tangled black moustache wearing dark blue scrubs enters the room with my meal tray and places it on the table next to me. I push it away. He doesn't care, after all, it's not his responsibility to see to it that I eat. Unhappy nurses frown at my defiant posture explaining the importance of a strict diet during my stay in the hospital. I see through their tactics. Here is one more thing I realize I can control.

Daddy's refrained from addressing my atypical behavior. It's obvious he's troubled by it. He keeps apologizing to the staff on my behalf. I wish he wouldn't.

SLEEP ELUDES ME. The intermittent cries and shouts I hear coming from outside my room are not what keep me awake. My own fears drown their voices. I turn the television on hoping to concentrate on something else—anything else.

Around three o'clock in the morning a nurse walks into my room. She flips on the bright overhead luminescent light blinding me. She grabs the device that controls the TV and serves as a communication link to the nurse's station and pushes the off button. I'm desperate to break my oath of silence and give her a piece of my mind.

"Give me your arm Allie," she says her voice abrupt, "I need to draw blood."

Any nurse this brash deserves firing. I am deliberate and take my time to follow her demand. I swallow and a large gulp of air gets trapped in my throat when I realize Karla is standing over me with a large syringe in her hands.

Chapter Twenty-Four

I turn over onto my stomach refusing to obey Karla. When she reaches over to grab me I swing my arm missing her face by less than an inch. She's ready for my hand and deflects it. The collision of our wrists sends a sharp pain up my arm to my shoulder.

From the intercom in my room, she calls for added help. One male nurse, that's it, saunters into the room. My shape is small up against his stout frame. My body's tired I don't have the strength to fight him even if I wanted to. Tight grips circle my wrists and ankles, then with a single movement he flips me over flapjack style.

My arm slips through a tourniquet above the elbow. Karla secures it too tight. It puts a great amount of pressure on the brachial artery. With her fingers, she smacks my arm waiting for a vein to rise. It sounds as if I'm getting beaten by whips.

She snaps her latex gloves before putting them over her hands. I flinch from the sound. The purposeful act is confirmed by her smile. After ripping open a small square packet, the strong aroma of alcohol permeates the room. She cleans a spot on my arm and feels again for the vein.

Rather than fight, I go back to my original plan and tough it out. The male nurse tightens his grip while Karla tapes the intravenous tube to my arm. She hooks a drip up to the Travenol and measures the volume of saline going into my bloodstream. I know once they've both left I'm going to yank out the needle. Karla is prepared for this ploy.

Leather arm and leg restraints deliberate in their position sit next to the bed. Karla secures my left arm to the metal bedframe. The male nurse only needs to look at me and I concede. Now that I'm unable to cause any harm to myself or others the male nurse leaves me alone with Karla.

This is the first time I've seen her since I got her kicked out of the house. Being this near her makes me nauseous. If I do throw up, I want to wait till she's right next to me and then let it spew on her.

I'm extremely uncomfortable in this position. Sharp pains in my chest make me wonder if I'm having a myocardial infarction. I lift my body to relax my shoulders. None of the positions brings relief.

"What are you doing here?" I blurt. My voice is tight and my words scratchy from my sworn silence.

"I work here in the hospital."

I ask surprised, "Since when?"

"For two weeks now." I watch her face, her body—I scrutinize every movement to gauge whether she's lying.

I don't believe her.

"Yeah right," I laugh. "With your tawdry past, and what you've done to make this city hate you, no one in Brescade is going to give you a job."

"I still have friends here."

Karla's words stump me. What friends? She's alienated an entire community.

"It's possible you didn't notice Allie. I can see you're blinded by hate, suffocated by bitterness, and overcome by vengeance. If you took the time to look, you'd see I'm dressed in a nurse's outfit. Oh and look, I'm wearing the proper credentials. If that's not enough proof for you, I could always show you again how good I am at inserting needles." She pulls a 7-gauge needle from her pocket.

My eyes blink at the thick nail she holds in her hand.

"And you want me to believe you're working here in the cancer ward is nothing more than a coincidence?"

"I'll have you know I work in Emergency downstairs."

I remember Daddy telling me years ago Memorial Hospital believed Karla was one of their finest nurses.

"Why drag your warm and fuzzy personality up here?" I say mockingly.

"Word around the hospital is that you've been a royal pain in the butt. What possessed you to act with such impertinence to a medical staff whose only job is to help you get better? This is unusual behavior even for you."

"Don't talk as if you know me Karla." My voice is warming up and is no longer irritating my throat.

"Anyway," she continues, "I got the necessary clearance and permission to work in both areas. Now you'll see first-hand how *warm and fuzzy* I can be."

Her sickly smile brings the bile to the bottom of my throat.

"What, did you think showing up here might make me compliant?"

"You're talking, aren't you? That's a start."

I don't have a comeback to Karla's question and her smug sneer tells me as much.

"Answer this question; why are you here?" Her breathing slows and a half smile appears on her face. If I didn't know better, I'd say she's almost friendly looking.

"Why do you think?" she asks. I shrug my shoulders and give her an expressionless look. "To aid you through your recovery of course."

"My recovery?" I laugh till my abdomen aches from frenetic cramping.

Three women stand in front of me claiming the same body. One is the drugged-out party girl Mag Steel who I'm sure killed a ton of brain cells during the last ten years. The second is the concerned woman impersonating a nurse. And the last is the female imposter claiming to be my mother. I have an even loathing for each one.

I say, "Didn't you get the memo. I've got cancer."

"And your point?" Karla finishes cleaning up her mess and folds her arms across her chest.

"My point is I'm dying," I say as if this truth is all that matters.

"Even when you were a baby, you gravitated toward the theatrics."

How dare she bring up a past she knows nothing about?

"Have you even bothered to read the stats on cancer? One of three Americans is affected by cancer during their lifetime."

"Cancer doesn't have to mean a death sentence Allie. The strides they're making to eradicate this horrid disease are remarkable."

From the way she says my name, I almost believe she cares. The sensation passes.

"If it's my time, I'm ready to die." I'm disappointed when Karla doesn't respond. "I'm ready to die," I repeat.

Karla moves toward me holding the thumb and index finger together. She begins sliding them back and forth. I know she's playing the world's smallest violin. Her scornful temperament triggers the vomit up to my mouth. I turn towards her and puke.

Half of the vomit lands on me and the bed. Tickled with satisfaction, I smile and lift my index finger, bend it, and straighten it again. Karla knows the sign.

One for me.

She surprises me by not retaliating and leaves the room returning moments later with a new uniform, mop and bucket, cleaning supplies, fresh sheets and pillow cases, and a new gown. I watch as Karla wipes off the bed railings, and the side of the bed where the vomit landed. She dutifully mops the floor unfazed by her job. It isn't beneath her. Characteristics of a real nurse.

Without undoing my restraints, she pulls off the sheets then lays a towel underneath me. A pink plastic tub sits on the counter next to the windowsill. Seconds later, filled with water, she wets the cloth with hospital antibacterial soap, and wipes it against my body. I'm not prepared for the icy sponge bath. My body shivers and my teeth chatter as I wait for a towel.

She mimics my earlier movement.

One for me.

She dries me off, dresses me with the new robe, and re-sheets the bed without having to undo any of the restraints.

"I want another nurse," I say. Karla's callous smile leaves me sick and with nothing left inside to vomit on her, I resign myself to quiet. I watch as she walks out of the room.

"As long as you're here Allie Adonia Anderson you are stuck with me." She flips off the light.

"Wait. Please. I'm begging you."

After fifteen seconds, Karla steps back into the room.

"What is it Allie?"

"What if I need to go the bathroom?" I say tugging at my restraints. My hope is that by having one released, I can land a punch.

Karla approaches the bed and leaving the sheet in place reaches underneath pulling my gown up above my waist.

"You've got a pad underneath you. Don't be embarrassed to use it."

She repeats the motion with her index and middle finger. *Two for me.*

I'm left alone without access to the lights or television.

HOURS LATER, I lie in the bed still bemoaning my misfortune. The delicate morning light filters through the windows brightening my room. I stay cheerless. For the exception of my leukemia, everything else that's gone wrong in my life is Karla's fault, including the hatred of an entire city, the loss of Cass's friendship, and the job I had working with the football team. I don't understand her reason for returning.

Before shift change, Karla enters the room. I close my eyes feigning sleep. She replaces the bag of Saline with a fresh bag. As she leans close checking the needle site, my nose picks up a citrus scent. And another smell is missing: the absence of cigarette smoke.

Once she checks the machine and makes notations in my chart, she pulls away. I assume she's left the room. I open my eyes and Karla's standing next to the bed staring at me committing my face to memory.

"I forgot what a beautiful girl you are Allie."

I don't know what to say—I don't want to say anything—I should say something.

"Thanks."

For the first time, I discern a look of truthfulness. Our history doesn't allow me to suffer her charm.

"Karla, my bladder is about to explode." She hesitates. "Please, I'm busting," I say with piety.

"Are you going to give me any more trouble?" I shake my head. "And the nursing staff?"

"I promise I won't give them any trouble."

"And the doctors?"

"Karla, I swear I'll be the epitome of gentility and kindness."

Karla's smiles and I catch myself smiling.

"Well, since you swore."

Before loosening my restraints, she slips on a pair of gloves and pulls out the intravenous needle from my arm. Once the blood has coagulated at the site, she undoes the restraint on my right hand and then my left. When she unleashes both of my feet, I jump off the bed and race to the bathroom.

Inside, I discover a fresh towel, a washcloth, a new bar of soap, and two bottles: one of shampoo and the other of conditioner sitting on the sink. While I'm in there, I decide to take a shower. Twenty minutes later I leave the bathroom. I'm alone. Karla and the restraints are gone. A tray with breakfast sits on the table next to my bed. There is a set of new purple pajamas lying on the fresh sheets. I wonder if they are meant to go with the empty bed since I chose the green one.

A nurse I haven't seen before enters reading my chart. She is broad-shouldered and matter of fact when she speaks.

"What are these?"

"They're your new pajamas. You don't have to wear the gown anymore."

"Where did they come from?" I ask holding up the PJs.

"Your mom."

Grrrrrr. I frown.

Chapter Twenty-Five

I rationalize that wearing the pajamas Karla bought me doesn't make me a hypocrite. I wear them because they're soft and silky and keep me warmer than the gown does. Once I'm dressed, I sit on the side of my bed and remove the stainless-steel lid. Underneath is a breakfast of sausage, eggs, toast, oatmeal, orange juice and hot tea. I hoe into the food imagining it to be my last meal. When I'm done my tray is completely empty. The only things I didn't touch were the salt and pepper packets.

Exhausted from lack of sleep the night before, I venture into a morning nap that lasts till noon. Daddy arrives at twelve thirty. I'm eating lunch when he enters the room carrying a paper bag that he sets on the floor next to the loveseat.

"And how are you today Princess?" he asks kissing me on the forehead.

"It didn't go well last night."

"I suppose not," he says.

"How do you know?" I say.

"Your arms and legs. You're not wearing the restraints anymore."

"Karla told you?"

"I'm the one who called her." My disbelief shifts to instant disappointment.

"You devised the idea of having me tied up?"

"I won't go that far. But after the way you treated everyone yesterday, and your first day here no less, you deserved it."

Rejecting his words is unproductive because they're true. I reflect on the events of yesterday. Feeling doubly uncooperative in particular after

Karla and my altercation last night, I understand that if I'm going to survive in this place with Daddy, Karla, and the medical staff ganging up on me, I need to play the game.

I decide to change the subject.

"You knew Karla worked in the hospital?"

"Yes."

"And you didn't think that was information I needed to know?"

"Hold on a minute little girl. In case you've forgotten, I'm the father in this family, which means I don't have to inform you of every decision I make."

Stung by his words, my spirit plummets. Is he oblivious to the hurt he's inflicted upon me? When he reaches into the bag, I sit up straight and wait for the gift he's getting ready to pull out. Remorseful for how brutal he came across; this is his way of apologizing. I await the present or meal he's made. When he retrieves a copy of today's newspaper I can't keep the displeasure from showing on my face. I turn back to my tray and push the table away.

For the rest of the day, Daddy reads or goes for walks throughout the hospital. He even watches football, something he never does.

My earlier feelings of disgust have rocketed to anger. By seven o'clock, my chest is weighted down—I'm smothered with rage. It doesn't stop there: my eyes have sunken in, my ears are heated, my core temperature has increased, and my spirit is that of a ferocious caged lion. Spiteful visions circle my mind. Can this be described as hate? This sensation is new to me. As I glance at Daddy, my fascination for him has diminished. I want nothing to do with him.

At nine o'clock Daddy informs me he's leaving. I let out a sigh of relief as if I've been holding my breath for hours. He says his goodbyes and leans over to kiss me. I can't bear to have his lips touch my skin. My face turns away in disgust When I turn back our eyes connect and in that one single instant I understand the meaning of disappointment. I see it imprinted in his eyes. On the other hand, he captures, in my gaze, an utter loathing for him. He pulls back, our eyes still frozen in each other's stare.

Another defining moment transpires in that instant. A person with leukemia, acquires a deeper understanding of life than someone with supreme health. How could Daddy possibly understand my situation? He doesn't I realize.

Daddy picks up his bag and exits the room.

The door bangs against the wall as Karla barges into my room seconds later. On her face is a wide-eyed expression of dismay.

"What did you say to him?" she asks her voice breathless and loud.

"Nothing," I reply.

"You must have said something. Your father walked out of this hospital with a broken heart."

"Well, he broke mine."

"Impossible," Karla states. "You don't have one."

She stomps out of the room. I don't see her for the rest of the night. Karla is the last person to lecture me on the breaking of hearts.

SOMETIME DURING THE night an older man accompanied by a similar aged woman pushes a wheelchair holding a young girl of my age into my room. A gaunt face, thin limbs, and no hair suggests she's been sick for a long time. I watch while trying not to watch as she attempts to unseat herself. Weakness besieges her body. Both parents long to reach towards her and help. They make a conscious choice to keep their hands to their sides and respect the girl's right to independence. At the end, the father helps her into bed. She closes her eyes the moment the sheets cover her gowned body.

Her mom says, "Goodnight Teresa," and leans in to give her a kiss.

Her father utters, "Goodnight my sweet princess," and he too plants a kiss on her forehead. "We'll see you tomorrow."

Weary parents smile feebly at me as they leave the room. Tired, I close my eyes hoping to make a quick drift back to sleep.

Teresa's moans pluck me away from my brief snooze. From the hazy light in the hallway seeping through the crack in the doorway, I can see her writhing in bed with no one around to help her.

"Ugghhhh," The chilling noise comes from the bed across from me. "Mom," she cries out.

Either she can't find her control to call the nurse or she's dropped it. I reach around looking for mine to summon help. *Dang it.* I can't find it. Teresa's groans boost me to my feet.

I walk over to her bed. From the grimace on her face, she is in excruciating pain. I promise her I'll be right back with help. I'm not sure if she understood me over her cries or even knows I'm there.

The clock on the hallway wall reads twelve midnight. Lethargy sets in and my feet can only trudge slowly along the corridor. A night nurse exits another patient's room. Her arms drop to her sides the second she sees me.

"What are you doing out of bed?" she asks her voice raised. I recognize her as one of the nurses I rudely ignored yesterday.

"Teresa, the girl in my room, is in an awful lot of pain."

"She's crying out?"

I say, "She's screaming."

The nurse rushes to a drawer on the wall which she unlocks using a numeric code. She brings out a syringe and a small vial and carries it to the room. I don't move as fast as she does. By the time I get back to my room she has given Teresa pain medication through her intravenous port.

"Thank you for finding me Allie," says the nurse on her way out as I'm entering. She's kinder now than she appeared a moment earlier. "You're a good friend."

Friend?

I slip into my bed. If Teresa awakens again, I know I'll never get back to sleep. The moment my feet slip across the sheets to the bottom of my bed the rustling begins for a second time. Without squeaking the bed or rustling the sheets, I peek over. Teresa is trying to sit up on her own. Once again, I'm forced to leave my bed.

"Can I help?" I ask.

"Raise bed please."

Not much of a talker. Who can blame her?

After a long search for the lengthy tan chord that comes out from the wall at the head of the bed, I place my fingers on the control. Teresa's nimble fingers reach for a chord she can't clasp.

"Mind?" she asks.

"Sure." I push the button that lifts the head of her bed. "When?"

She releases a sigh of relief. "Thanks."

"It's okay."

"Teresa, me," she uses every ounce of breath in her diaphragm to tell me her name.

"Hi, I'm Allie. It's nice to meet you." What an awkward introduction.

Chapter Twenty-Six

I've reached the line between consciousness and unconsciousness—
that moment when my mind and body float off together to a place above
my bed, the ceiling, and into infinity and beyond.

Red and blue pulsating lights outside my window accompanied with
blaring sirens and even more ear-splitting horns jolt me from limbo.

What now?

I flap both of my feet up and down, and kick the covers onto the floor.
Now I'll be awake for the rest of the night.

Outside the window, squads of cars have entered the hospital lot while
other police vehicles set up a perimeter around the hospital. They shut
down traffic on the main thoroughfare and police with fluorescent green
vests and orange colored flashlights direct traffic away from the hospital
entrance.

I glance over at my new roommate's bed, and she is in a dead sleep. I
used to be able to sleep the way she does. Now I'm lucky to get a few
uninterrupted hours of shuteye.

At 3:00 o'clock a male phlebotomist enters the room to draw blood.
How do they expect patients to get well in a hospital if they keep
disturbing them at these ungodly hours? The point is moot since I'm
already awake.

He joins me at the window and is quick to share the news. Apparently,
thieves broke into the hospital pharmacy and got away with hallucinogens,
painkillers, depressants, and opioids. I walk back to the bed where he
checks my identification bracelet and with the deftness of a top
phlebotomist, pierces my vein and draws blood.

His narration of what happened continues.

A group of individuals affiliated with FADE dressed in black hooded garments broke into the pharmacy. They locked the doctors and nurses in a room, not before confiscating their phones and pagers. They hurt no one thank God. Talk is it may have been an inside job because no one saw a thing until the thieves got away.

I'm forced to hold in my surprise because I knew the details of this robbery days ago. My mind travels back to the library when I overheard Deke and Koreil discussing it. I didn't expect to be a patient in the hospital when the huge theft took place.

Karla's absence last night is more than suspicious. I'm more certain now than ever of her role in FADE. She's K.

I can even understand Cass's restraint in telling me. "And by the way your mother is the ruthless bloodsucking leader of FADE."

At last I close my eyes. My sleep is a fruitless race to locate the sandman.

"SO, WHAT ARE you in for kid?"

The voice disturbs me and comes from my new roommate Teresa.

"What?" I say looking over—still drowsy–in an irritable mood.

"You've got cancer, right?"

"Yeah, so?"

"What kind?" she asks as if the 'C' word isn't one of the most feared words in Western Civilization.

"AML," I eject for the first time.

There I said it. I still don't feel any better.

"Me too. Welcome to the club." Her jovial disposition irritates me.

"This isn't a joke," I reply.

"Chill Allie," she says without any regards for my feelings. "You're going to blow a gasket and then the leukemia is going to be the least of your worries."

In less than thirty seconds Teresa's gotten on my last nerve. Leaning over the edge of the bed, and after several attempts, nearly falling off once, my hand grasps the green apple curtain. I'm able to jerk it around until it surrounds my bed.

Teresa's laugh fills the room.

"You know they're not soundproof, right?" she says.

I get out of bed and rip the curtain open. The chains running through the rail on the ceiling make an ear-piercing jangle.

"What's your problem?" I say.

"You're spun kind of tight aren't you kid?"

"You think this cancer thing's a joke?" I shoot daggers at her with my eyes.

"Don't talk to me about jokes. I've been dealing with *this cancer thing,*" she holds the index and middle fingers of both hands up and curls them several times to symbolize quotation marks, "off and on for three years now. I've been in remission out of remission. How long have you been dealing with it?"

I'm embarrassed to say. "Two days."

"Wow, two whole days. You must be pulling your hair out. No, wait a second, you have all your hair." Her words are cruel.

"Forget you."

"That's the best comeback you have roomy?"

"Leave me alone."

"Oh, you want to commiserate on your own and have a pity party for Allie."

"I didn't ask them to put you in here."

"You're right, I did. This was my room long before you came here. Get with the program."

I'm ready to throw something at her. I swear I will if she doesn't stop.

"You need to let up."

"Not for a second kiddo. There's too much of life to live out there to be sitting around in here complaining, 'I've got cancer,'" she says in a whining child's voice. I want to make a comment. Instead, I swallow it. "Holding it in is worse than letting it blow. Say what's on your mind."

"I used to think…"

"… the same way. I know, until you got bitten by the leukemia bug."

"Why do you have to be so in your face?"

"Because leukemia doesn't have to be a death sentence Allie."

I laugh to myself. "Now you sound like Karla."

"Who's Karla?"

"One of the nurses. I suppose you'll meet her."

"I applaud a nurse who's down with the program. It's impossible you know," Teresa continues, "to be positive a hundred percent of the time. The alternative is a billion times worse. How old are you kid?"

"The name's Allie Adonia Alexander and I'm sixteen and two months."

"Nice. I'm a month older. Think of me as your big sister while you're here. Kay?"

Big sister. Who are you kidding?

"It'll be a miracle if I make it to seventeen. If I do," Teresa says, "I am going to have one heck of a party."

"You're dying." I'm not sure if I should voice it as a question or not.

"Everyone of us is dying kid. It's only a matter of time till your number's up. When the man upstairs calls you, salute and say, 'yes Sir.'"

"I guess," I tremble, "you're here because you're not in remission anymore?"

"Bingo. You win the grand prize. If you want, you can choose what's behind door number one, door number two or the envelope I'm holding in my hand."

"Stop joking. It isn't funny."

Her *avant garde* approach to her sickness disgusts me. Doesn't she understand that she and I will never go to the prom, graduate from high school, marry the man of our dreams, have children, or even pursue a career? I can't think of a worse death sentence.

Teresa grabs the remote and raises her bed till it's perpendicular to the floor. I can hear her fighting back the groans this position is causing her. She stares me in the face as I wait for her to say something witty.

"This thing has you bummed way out." A smile curls at the corner of her lips. She's not making fun.

"You could say that."

"You know AAA there's worse news in this world."

"What did you call me?

"Triple A. it's the nickname I've given you."

"Why?"

"Because I give all the kids here in the cancer ward nicknames."

"Why?" I reply for a second time.

"Because they have enough on their minds to keep them worried. If for a single second I can take their mind off the cancer and make them smile, then I'm filling their HM."

Teresa knows I'm going to have to ask. She's doing this on purpose. "What's HM?"

"It took you long enough to ask. HM stands for Hope Meter." I shake my head. "You see every time I say something positive or I give a word of encouragement or even make someone else smile, I'm filling their Hope Meter. I didn't make this stuff up. The Hope Meter's been around since the start of time. I happen to be the one who gave it the coolest name."

I decide to play along for a moment and not a second longer.

"And what does this Hope Meter do?"

I should never have asked the question. Teresa lowers her bed and swivels her legs off the side. With help from the metal trolley holding her medicine, she hobbles toward my bed. She stands at the side staring at me until I lower it all the way and move over. Next, she sidles in the bed next to me as if we're having a slumber party.

"Ever had a sick friend?"

"Sure."

"If you do something nice for them, say buy them flowers or send them an E-card, you're filling their HM. It's like a bank account AAA."

Teresa's animated hands and enthusiastic voice unearth her intent. I realize she believes every word coming out of her mouth.

She continues. "It's money. You deposit it into an account and then one day when you need it, it's there. The HM works the same way. Say your friend's not doing well. When she walks by the table and sees the flowers, they brighten up her day. Even if it's only for a second. She might think of those flowers several times that day. That's when the HM kicks into full effect."

Now she has me intrigued.

"How does it work for the children out there," I say pointing towards the hallway.

"Well you can imagine contracting cancer is a little more devastating than having the flu. A couple of them know they're dying." Her voice goes soft. "You must constantly fill their HM. Because the HM can dwindle to nothing in a second." She snaps her fingers. "Nicknames are a fun way to keep them happy and their mind off their circumstances. Sometimes, the parents need the HM more than the kids do."

As Teresa talks I can clearly see the war her body has gone through to fight AML. She has hematomas on her neck, her arms and legs that will be permanent. Her skin is so pale her blue veins are easy to pick out. Even her facial features are difficult to distinguish. The normal rosy color in the cheeks and lips is absent. Her eyes, once a vibrant blue I imagine, have been dulled by the heartache of her disease, the same disease in possession of me.

"Meds," says the nurse entering the room. She throws a full smile our way. "I see you ladies have become quite chummy."

Teresa raises and lowers her eyebrows several times.

"You're impossible," I whisper.

"And you love me."

Our relationship is roughly ten hours old, and she's right, I do love her. She's the most real person I've ever met.

She slips off my bed and walks, each step purposeful, back to hers. The nurse watches and is careful not to intervene. When Teresa makes it back to the bed, the nurse pulls the curtain around the bed and administers the medication.

"She's asleep," says the nurse coming out from behind the curtain. "I don't know where she gets the energy. Getting in and out of bed saps the strength right out of her."

At that second Daddy shows up to the room. He doesn't appear mad at me today and leans over and gives me a kiss on the cheek. It isn't mechanical. I don't pull back. A whiff of citrus from his neck lingers in my nose. Maybe he had oranges for breakfast and they touched his face. Neither of us says a word about last night.

A lady enters the room after knocking. She introduces herself and informs me that this she is going to escort me to the radiology department where I'll have my first treatment of chemo. In truth, my body's reaction to this procedure worries me more than I care to admit. Pride keeps me from uttering it out loud.

On the way, Karla joins us. What is she doing here? Her shift doesn't start for another six hours. From my position on the bed, I can see the warm smile Daddy gives her. She responds with a sheepish grin. The kind that says a ton without having to say a word.

When I get to the room, they wait outside for me.

"If you want, I can go inside with you." I try to hold a brave front and shake my head telling Karla I don't need her there. Yet, I don't even believe myself. How could someone else? "I'll come in and make sure you're settled okay?" I nod, glad I don't have to answer, and glad I won't be alone.

THE LIGHTS ON the ceiling fuzz in appearance as they wheel me back from chemo. I'm glad the treatment is over. Karla stayed with me the entire time. The other nurses did everything they could to make me comfortable. I hesitate to face it again.

Upon my return, I notice balloons and more balloons circling my bed. Daddy decorated it and brought cool lava lamps with purple colors. Against the apple green backdrop, the new décor works.

The nurse helps me from the temporary bed onto my own bed. I am glad she is there because I'm very weak.

"Are you okay Allie," asks Karla.

"My stomach hurts."

"I have an antiemetic I can give her," interjects the nurse.

"It will help control the nausea," Karla says. I watch as the nurse leaves to go get it.

"You survived," Teresa says from behind the curtain. "Was it as bad as you thought?"

I say, "Worse."

"You newbies are always so melodramatic."

Chapter Twenty-Seven

My simple plan for today includes sleeping in late and recuperating from yesterday's treatment. Teresa has other ideas. She stands at the bed tapping on it until the monotonous movement wakens me from a needed sleep. The cane that is in her hands contributes to her erectness. I turn over not ready to face the day.

"There'll be plenty of time to chill when you get to heaven," Teresa's says. "Come on, we've got work to do."

"What work," I say turning over uninterested.

"There are patients, family members, and nurses here who are HM deficient."

"So?" I pull up the sheet bunched around my feet until it's snug underneath my chin.

Teresa reaches for the sheet and with one hand rips it off. I sit up exasperated.

"Let's go kid. I have a treatment at one."

I slip out of bed and lift the lid on my breakfast tray to see what I missed. The only thing worth eating today is a blueberry muffin. I grab it and follow Teresa. She hobbles in pain, to the end of the hall. The nurses smile and nod their heads unconcerned by Teresa's behavior. Odd, since Teresa is barely able to function herself.

Standing behind her I watch as she peeks her head into the first room. She steps back to allow a doctor and nurse to exit. They both acknowledge her with wide grins.

Inside the room sits a young boy paler than a winter snowfall. He lies on the bed his eyes closed. Hematomas on his arms show where needles have punctured his skin in recent weeks, I suppose, to give him nutrient through a saline drip because he's too weak to feed himself. The name on the wall above him states his name is Vinnie. His head is bald and he couldn't be much older than six.

A quick look around the room reveals tons of toys including a large set of action figures on the table positioned to face him. Warriors, fighters, and soldiers stand, combat ready, protecting Vinnie.

Teresa moves with determination towards the bed. Her frail hand reaches out and touches his feeble hand. Eyes flutter at the tenderness of her touch. When they open he looks at the two strangers lingering at his bedside. I expect sadness. He surprises me by revealing a most wonderful smile.

"My name is Teresa. This is my friend Allie. I call her AAA. What's your name?" Why ask a question she knows the answer to? His voice is high and very raspy; his words are weak and nearly unintelligible.

"Vinnie."

"That's a very nice name."

"Thanks," he says.

"I bet you didn't know," she says struggling to sit on the bed next to him, "Vinnie means Conqueror in Latin." He shakes his head. I wonder how she knows this information.

"That means no matter what battle you come up against in life you have the ability to conquer it." He smiles.

"How old are you Vinnie?"

Without lifting his arms, he holds up three fingers with one hand and four with the other.

"Seven?" she asks surprise in her voice.

"I thought at least nine maybe ten." His smile widens. "So, what do you want to be when you grow up MC?" Vinnie and I both shoot strange looks at her. "Oh," Teresa says, "you're wondering why I called you MC?" His eyes answer her question. "Well when I saw your toys especially the ones of these tough fighters and that your name means conqueror I nicknamed you MC which stands for Mighty Conqueror."

If Vinnie could jump out of bed and march around the room, I believe he would. In less than a minute, she has brought life to a weakened boy. She continues to ask questions and by the time our visit is over I understand why she converses in a hurried speed despite the fact it takes ample energy out of her. It's the only way to break MC from his shell and open up.

"I promise to stop by later. If not, tomorrow for sure ok?" His parched and anemic lips create an infectious smile I can't help feeling better as I leave the room.

After MC's room, we cross the hall to a room where a girl, the age of ten, sits on her bed drawing on a pad of paper with over thirty colored markers in a neat semi-circle around her.

"Hi Hailey," Teresa says. I notice her putting more weight on the cane to support her balance.

"How'd you know my name," she asks looking our direction.

"It says it right above your bed."

"Oh, I keep forgetting it's there," she laughs.

"Are you guys part of the library?" she asks. "I don't see the book cart."

"Nah, that's on Thursdays. I'm Teresa and this is my friend Allie. Everyone calls her AAA."

Hailey has been a patient for six months. She has close to a hundred cards on a wall. Unless you knew she carried a deadly disease in her body, you might think her health to be perfect. Her positive demeanor suggests a young girl joyful and full of life.

"Can I take a picture of you?" she asks us both.

"Of course." I follow Teresa's lead and we stand together while Hailey pulls out an old-fashioned Kodak that prints the picture in an instant. She shows us the developed picture then slides off the bed and sticks it onto the wall. There are hundreds of pictures creating an amazing purposed display that's been designed to resemble a mural of a young girl's face. The more I look at it the more it resembles Hailey and the more amazed I am at the gift this young girl has.

"How long have you been working on this creation?" Teresa asks.

"It's taken me over four months to make it. The pictures piled up in the drawer and I knew I needed do something with them."

"You're the photographer for these pictures?" I ask intrigued.

"Un huh. Every time someone visits me I take a picture to capture the moment. As you can see," she says pointing to the wall, "a few of the faces are sad, and some of the others are in between sad and happy. Most of them, I'm glad to say, are happy ones."

"How cool that you've divided them by mood," I say.

"Yeah, the sad pictures create the head and forehead while the happy ones make up most of my eyes and face. The in-between pictures make up the ears and neck. I figure I need another fifty to a hundred pictures to complete my masterpiece."

"Your mosaic is a true work of art," I say.

"Thanks AAA." This is the first time I've heard anyone else call me that besides Teresa. It's growing on me.

"Helena of Egypt," Teresa utters out of the blue. "She lived four centuries before Christ and is famous for painting a scene of Alexander the Great defeating Darius III. They called it The Battle of Issus. Later, an archeologist discovered a mosaic of the same painting in Pompeii. Your mosaic is equally breathtaking."

Hailey's cheeks redden with pride as she hears the comparison Teresa is making with her and a famous ancient female artist.

"Helena of Egypt." Hailey says. "She's going to be my new hero."

"And that's why I'm going to nickname you Helena of Egypt."

Hailey's face couldn't become any fuller or it might pop. "You are?"

"I sure am. You are a great artist. And if it's okay with you, I want to come and visit you tomorrow."

"Okay, Teresa. Will you bring AAA?"

Teresa glances my direction.

"I'll be here," I reply surprised I'm looking forward to tomorrow's post breakfast visit.

For the exception of Teresa and myself, there are fifteen patients in our ward under the age of eleven, and we meet and talk to each one. With each person we meet, Teresa gives a nickname. More than that, she makes large deposits into their HM. I find it uncanny that Teresa knows the meaning of each of the children's names. This isn't information someone stores in their memory banks.

The last person we visit is a girl of eight whose parents have exhausted every resource and treatment choice available. They are taking her home where Hospice will aid the family with her final days of care. It saddens me to tears I'm forced to blink back.

"Hi, I'm Teresa and this young striking lady is my best friend AAA."

Her words don't escape me. Two days and I'm her best friend. How is that possible? My own explanation, and I'm not sure of its accuracy, is that because cancer patients walk close to death they don't have time for the superficial relationships. There isn't the normal period to cultivate a relationship. Friendship can begin in a snap and mature in an instant.

When Teresa introduces herself and me the eyes of this young girl light into sparkling Roman candles. Even in her hopeless medical condition, she can afford to fill our Hope Meters. My eyes tear again. We spend a half hour with Sophia. For such a young girl, she is very bright and articulate.

"You have wisdom beyond your years," Teresa says making a definitive statement. "And in case you didn't know, that's what your name means— wisdom—wise."

When her parents return after meeting with the doctor we excuse ourselves.

"See you later T and AAA."

"Bye," says Teresa, "I love you."

"I love you too," replies Sophia.

I hold Teresa as we turn the corner to our room. Her exhausted body needs rest.

"How do you do it?" I ask her.

"Do what?" she almost doesn't get out.

"Every single one of those children experienced a dose of happiness because they spent time with you." She remains silent. "To top it off, how is it possible that you knew the meaning of every single name?" Teresa smiles and pulls out a sheet of paper with the name of each child on it including their age, meaning of their name and parent's name. I notice that my name is on it as well. "Where did you get this?" I ask amazed.

"From the nurses. They prepare it for me when I'm here."

Teresa's concern is not for her pain. She's keen to breathe light and life into others putting me to shame. She's making an impact in the lives of others—changing the world with a few choice words.

"I love you T," I say using the nickname Sophia gave her.

"That's the first nickname anyone has ever given me." We sit in her bed crying and holding one another.

Chapter Twenty-Eight

Four days later, during the late afternoon, before the sun disappears beyond the horizon, and an hour till the evening meal, I walk the hospital for exercise. My goal is at least threes time a day—morning, noon, and night. The doctors don't need to tell me what will happen to my body if I sit in bed all day. So, to keep my muscles from atrophy, I've taken up walking. It's either this or have a nurse escort me to rehab and workout under the eye of a body killer. I know how tough physical therapists can be.

A few days ago, I resigned myself to lie in bed and wait for death to come for me. Teresa's shown me how to peer at the world in a different way.

Sometimes when T's body has the strength, she'll walk part of the way with me. Tonight, her parents are visiting late; she stays back at the room.

By the time I reach the downstairs lobby my entire body cries out from exhaustion. I scout the room and locate an empty leather sofa situated behind a group of massive imitation conifers. My plan is to sit behind the trees for a minute till I can catch my breath. Then, I'll reverse my course and flop into bed. The pliable leather couch conforms to features of my body. I might need to ask the staff to move this up to my room and exchange it for my bed.

Doctors, nurses, and other hospital staff who have worked a day-shift leave in droves. It's easy to identify them. The doctors are the ones with the white jackets. The nurses are wearing bright colored uniforms or blue scrubs while maintenance workers wear dowdy work clothes. Locating the administration staff is not difficult either. They're the ones wearing the severe business attire.

Visitors swarm the lobby. Most have finished work and rush in to see relatives and loved ones. I observe flower carriers, card and gift carriers, food carriers, and those carrying purses or backpacks.

At a young age, Daddy and I used to play a game that I called the waiting game. I named it this because when we played it we were always somewhere waiting: an airport, in line at the store or even in the car sitting in traffic. The point of the game? To guess the occupation of the people we watched and create a story to accompany the description.

I observe a man in an expensive dark business suit carrying a briefcase enter the hospital. I imagine he's a lawyer coming to finalize a will for his client before he dies. A young woman pushing the child in the stroller is a nanny. She takes care of the young girl whose mother is recovering from a serious car accident. The couple holding hands are newlyweds. She found out she's pregnant, and they are rushing to tell her mom who learned less than a week ago she has Alzheimer's.

It's been years since Daddy and I've played that game. Of course, there's no way to know if any of our scenarios hit the mark. I've often been tempted to ask.

The buzzer for the elevator sounds and another crowd of people exit. Sighs erupt from my lips as I stand. The walk back is always the worst, and I prepare myself for the grueling ordeal. Among the exodus, Deke and Koreil meander their way along with the crowd. Right away, I know their reason for being in the hospital.

I offer a quick prayer for Estrada and hope it's not too late.

I amble to the information desk and ask the older volunteer lady sitting behind the counter if Ray Estrada is still a patient here. She confirms my suspicions and tells me his room number. Estrada's on the second floor in the south wing. There must have been some complications with the surgery or he'd have been sent home the same day.

Deke and Koreil's visit can only mean one of two things: they've strong armed Estrada into complying with K's directions or… I hesitate to dwell on it.

I ride the elevator up a floor and locate Estrada's wing. As I turn the corner Karla walks out of Estrada's room. Her pace is quick as if she's trying to get away without being seen. She's carrying something in her hands. I'm too far away to see what it is. Now I'm worried. Is she covering up what Deke and Koreil did? My heart skips a beat thinking of Estrada lying on the bed dead.

Karla stops in mid-stride and does a one-eighty. I duck into the nearest room. Inside is an elderly man with incredibly wrinkled skin sitting on the hospital bed. From the crimson blotches on his weathered flesh, he's suffering from skin cancer. The patch underneath his eye suggests a recently removed melanoma.

He looks up when I enter and smiles. I bet he's wondering to himself who this young chick is and why she's in his room. I'm obliged to smile back. After the longest minute of my life I peek my head out. I catch a glimpse of the back of Karla's outfit as she turns the corner. I turn and wave at the man before leaving.

Estrada's door is open. I take a deep breath and look through the opening. Estrada's alive. He doesn't notice me right away. He's concentrating on an eight and a half by eleven sheet of paper he clutches with both hands. The smile overtakes his entire face and I hear him chuckling to himself. I'm not sure what to make of it. I assumed Deke and Koreil's visit occurred to put pressure on Estrada. Both arms are intact, no facial bruising, cuts, stab wounds or abrasions to the body. It doesn't appear as if he is under undue duress. In fact, he looks at ease. Estrada folds the paper and places it under his sheet. That's when he notices me standing there watching him.

Talk about contrasts. His face freezes, and with it the smile and calm he exhibited only moments ago. Replacing his peace is fear. Muscles in his face tighten resembling a person with too many Botox injections.

"What are you doing here?" he asks, less than happy to see me.

"Passing by," I reply.

The pajamas I'm wearing should give away the fact I'm a patient here. Estrada's wearing a gown. Maybe in this ward they don't do the color thing. My mind mulls over a thousand questions: What were you and Karla discussing? What's written on the paper you hid under the sheet that thrilled you? Why the sudden change of emotions when I entered the room?

A similar conversation takes place in Estrada's mind, only I'm betting his questions are different.

I ask, "How's the leg?" to break the awkwardness.

"I heard you had cancer," he replies.

I detect his calculated move to change the subject. He has no concern for my wellbeing. I ask him again about the status of his leg.

"Surgery didn't go as expected. A few more days I'll be caged in this place. I—, I've been better." His words don't flow and his answer breaks off in bite size pieces. It's like the day he tried to ask me to be his girlfriend. This fumbling has nothing to do with nervousness. He's afraid of me and I don't understand why?

"Leukemia, huh?"

"That's what the tests show," I reply playing down the cancer for the first time since my diagnosis.

"And you're not scared?" I can't tell if the question is an accusation or a compliment. Either way, he knows why I'm in the hospital. My suspicion is Karla told him.

"I'd settle for a trimalleolar fracture," I say too cheerful.

He responds with a forced smile of his own.

"I heard you saved my life on the football field."

"You had a fractured ankle, that's not life and death. I prepared you for the paramedics who brought you here to the hospital where the doctors fixed you, and the nurses, who are the real heroes, are taking care of you."

"Yeah, well, the doctors screwed up the surgery, didn't they? And now I'll need a second surgery to fix my ankle and the mistake they made." His words are genuine, so is the emotion that accompanies it. "I'm not sure if I'll be able to play football ever again."

"Your fracture is severe, but it isn't a career ending injury necessarily."

"Meaning what?"

"More than likely you'll be able to play down the road."

"Do you know of anyone who's come back from an injury like this?"

"On the internet, you can read of many documented cases where athletes with trimalleolar fractures are back on the field in seven to eight months. I know the doctors have told you, you have a year of rehab ahead. It doesn't need to take that long if you're willing to work hard."

"I didn't know that. Thanks," he says.

Weird vibes ricochet back and forth banging into walls as the conversation comes to an abrupt halt. Our stares mirror one another and for twenty seconds nothing is said. Estrada breaks the silence. His ten-word sentence sends me into cardiac arrest.

"Allie, what is it you want to know about FADE?"

Daddy has never given me a credit card, taken me shopping, and told me get whatever I want and charge it to the card. That's how I interpret Estrada's question. I have a thousand I want to ask. For the next ten minutes, I badger him with inquiries and he fills me in on things I didn't know: the money, and the new initiation rites to become a member. He even shares details of the numbers of members and explicit details on the next heist. I process better when I'm writing my thoughts on paper. I ingest as much information as I can.

To my dismay the gong in the intercom sounds declaring visiting hours over for the evening. I need to return to my room. There are still more questions I need to ask. Estrada can see me itching to pump him for more information including the question I'm fearful of asking, *"Is Karla the leader of FADE?"* The answer is obvious. Why do I need confirmation?

A nurse walks in as I open my mouth. The first words out of her mouth are, "Miss, I'm going to have to ask you to leave. Mr. Estrada's going to surgery."

I wasn't aware surgeries other than elongated surgeries and emergency related surgeries were performed at night.

"You're Karla's daughter, the nurse who works in the ER?"

I know when I've overstayed my welcome. A quick nod at Estrada and I make my way towards the door.

"It's Allie, isn't it?"

I leave without responding. I'm not a nervous person, however, on the walk back, I take repeated looks over my shoulder for fear of being recognized. The last thing I want is knowledge of my visit to Estrada getting back to Karla.

The nurses' station on my wing is busy with half a dozen nurses congregating around the computer mulling over charts and other stuff. They don't acknowledge my presence as I pass. Karla isn't in the group. I wonder where she is. I enter the room and bump into her as she's coming out.

Our eyes widen in a strange expression. Both at a loss for words, I recover first and walk into the room and notice Teresa's bed is empty.

"Where's T I ask?"

"She's in the lounge downstairs with her parents. They didn't come in till late. I invited them to enjoy the main lounge over these cramped quarters. Where have you been? I looked everywhere for you and even had you paged."

I bet.

"Your father wanted to say goodbye. He had to leave early to review another restaurant."

"The two of you are getting very cozy, aren't you?"

Faceless expression, eyes that refuse to blink, no unnecessary non-verbal movement, classic symptoms of someone who's working too hard at trying to hold onto a secret.

"It's going to take more than citrus perfume to sway him back into your arms Karla. He's not that gullible." She becomes busy with things around the room.

"You really do hate me." If her remark is rhetorical, I opt to respond.

"I don't hate you Karla; I feel sorry for you." She turns. I see her eyes widen. Daddy made a correct assumption. She hates others' pity.

Chapter Twenty-Nine

I fight grogginess as I make unsuccessful attempts to open my eyes. The task is tedious, my body tires, and I drift off again for how long I can't say. Sometime much later I awaken. It's easier this time. Teresa sits on the edge of her bed her legs folded into a lotus position playing with the necklace around her neck.

"You were out for the count."

What time is it?

My mouth is tacky and I can't move my lips. A Styrofoam cup of ice water sits on the table. Crushed ice crests the top of the cup filled by a nurse minutes before, I'm guessing. I reach to clasp it and pull my shaking hands back. Terror grips me as I entertain the thought of being struck with a second illness. After a few seconds, I rub my hands together before trying again. They're steadier this time and I'm able to grab the cup. Water spills onto the table. More trickles on me jolting me awake. With both hands gripping the cup, I lift it to my open my mouth enough to push the straw in between my gummed lips.

I suck in a mouthful swishing the liquid around before swallowing. My putrid breath adds a nauseating flavor to the water.

"What time is it?"

"Somewhere after eleven," T says smiling in full view. "You okay?"

"Tired," I reply. "My mouth was dry." I get the feeling Teresa needs to talk. She rubs the necklace incessantly as if summoning a genie.

"Where did you get that?" I ask.

"It's a gift my mom gave me the day we found out I had cancer. I never take it off." She stops talking and reflects on the memory. "How are you coping AAA?"

I shrug my shoulders. "Not as good as you," I sigh. "How do you manage it T?"

"I either cope or die. There aren't a lot of choices. If I beat this cancer, great. If I don't, I can't let it steal everything else away from me on this journey."

I nod with minimal understanding.

"I watch you. You are always so positive. I can't fill those shoes."

"Whoa sister, don't put me on that pedestal. I don't belong up there, trust me. You don't see the negative because I'm good at hiding those terrible days." She pauses as if something of importance occurred to her. "Each morning when I open my eyes to a new day, I want to live.

I nod at her again.

We sit comfortable in the silence that follows staring across the room reassured by the sight of one another. This camaraderie I want to last me my whole life.

"I've only ever had one close friend."

"Ian?" she asks. I smile. "I'd love to meet him," says Teresa.

"You will. What I meant to say is he's the closest friend I've ever had until I met you. I imagine if I had a sister, she'd be like you. Our kinship is closer than people who share the same bloodline."

"You're right. It's as if we've known each other our whole lives."

"On top of that, we care about each other. Weird, huh?"

"It's not crazy AAA. I'd love to think the world is supposed to behave this way if it wasn't so crappy. What's twisted is that it takes cancer or a deadly illness for some people to truly experience life."

"You make a lot of sense," I say.

I get up from my bed and join her.

"You didn't a few days ago."

"Yeah, well I hadn't met you yet."

"And now we're best of friends."

"I love you Teresa," I say without expecting the emotion that follows.

"I love you too Allie." We hug one another as the tears caress our faces cascading onto the sheet beneath us.

I'm running along a path with a girl keeping step with me. We hear the dogs moving closer unable to distinguish who's chasing us. Arriving at the edge of the cliff together, I look at the girl for the first time and realize it's Teresa.

I stare at the rope. There isn't a sign to tell us only one person can use it at a time. We just know.

"What do we do T?" I ask. Inhaling is a struggle; I'm out of breath.

"You go first AAA and toss the rope back to me."

I argue with her. She screams at me to grab the rope. I follow her instructions. After swinging over the chasm to safety, I push the rope back to Teresa. The dogs round the corner as her fingers touch the fibers. Their barks sound vicious. Teresa turns to face them. They leap upon her and she and the dogs fall into the water and rocks below.

I awaken with my body trembling and covered in sweat unsure why this feeling of terror exists in inside me.

Chapter Thirty

After consulting with doctors from oncology and following a brief meeting with Daddy and me, my doctor has chosen to take a more forceful approach to eradicating my cancer. For the next week, I'm scheduled to have several chemo sessions.

Dr. Seville tells me there's a good chance the cancer will go into remission by taking an aggressive stance. I'm in agreement with the change despite how my body falls apart after treatments. It's going to be a very long week.

TODAY DADDY SURPRISES T and me by catering breakfast. Dressed in his black tuxedo, he looks fabulous. He made lemon ricotta pancakes and cranberry compote my favorite all-time breakfast meal. Thick slices of kielbasa creates an aroma that causes my mouth to water more than Niagara Falls.

Added carbs include; fried potato patties dusted with Himalayan salt and Tellicherry Peppers, and he's made Almond-Cranberry Bread with White Chocolate Glaze with his personal recipe of blended butter.

He wheels in a table that he's borrowed from the nurses' floor. Next, he carries in two straight back padded chairs. He flaps out a white tablecloth that floats onto the table reminding me of swans coming in for a landing. He sets the table and escorts T and me to our seats. I watch her place her arm in his. She walks with the air of a princess. He returns for me.

Small firecracker pops fill my ears as he snaps the napkins open then places them in our laps. Two crystal goblets sit above the knife. One is filled with spring water; the other contains fresh blood orange juice.

Daddy opens the aluminum containers carrying the prepared food and fills our plates. The aroma hovers around us. Our excitement to eat something other than hospital food exposes itself through the constant giggling and uncontainable excitement. T tells me she's never eaten a meal this fancy in her life.

Daddy says two prayers before we eat: One for the food, and the second for Teresa and me. He asks God to bring us through our sickness to where we can live healthy and dynamic lives. He disappears allowing us to devour the feast together.

While we're eating T and I talk about everything. We giggle away, two adolescent teenagers lost in a magical wonderland. Sometimes sickness makes you act older, and other times much younger. When we've consumed our fill, Daddy surprises us again.

Ian walks into the room dressed in cream-colored painter's pants and a white long-sleeved shirt. I'm so excited to see him and introduce him to T I can't remember either of their names.

T ignores my senior moment.

"I'm Teresa. My friends call me T."

"I'm her only friend," I chide. T and I start giggling. It's not a joke, but T and I can't stop from laughing which only intensifies our merriment.

"It's a pleasure to meet you T. I'm Ian."

"You weren't lying when you said he's cute," T says this to embarrass Ian and me on purpose. Ian's face reddens. I don't think it's because he's flustered, rather, he's flattered by her comment.

"What are you doing here?" I ask.

"Besides coming to see you? Your dad told me this bland wall needed an artist's touch. That's what I'm going to do, cover it with art."

"You're going to paint it?" I ask with genuine excitement. "I wondered why the paint cans were stacked in the corner."

"They do this in the children's cancer ward to perk the kids up. Sometimes the kids paint the walls themselves," T says.

"That's a cool idea. How come you haven't had your section of the wall painted?" I ask.

"To be honest, I didn't think I'd last that long." The moment turns melancholy in a split second. Ian steps in salvaging the gaiety of the previous minutes.

"If you'll allow me, I can paint your side of the wall as well."

This brings T back to life.

"What are you going to paint?"

"You'll have to wait," Ian says with a smile that makes me experience lightheadedness and a squishy sensation in my stomach. I remember our last moment together.

I hear T giggling next to me.

"Alright, Picasso," shouts Teresa, "Dazzle us."

Ian bends and sifts through the different cans of paint.

"Even from this angle he still looks amazing." T says, and we enter another round of giggling.

Ian pulls the cans away from the wall and grabs the bucket of brushes inspecting each one individually. He mumbles under his breath disapproving of the poor care taken to preserve the bristles. For a second, he steps outside the room and returns with brushes he brought with him and several more cans of paint. We watch fascinated as Ian, I guess I can call him my boyfriend, begins to transform the plain wall into a grand masterpiece.

MR. BLUE SCRUBS knocks on the door and enters at the most inopportune time. He is my chauffeur to my first chemotherapy treatment this week. Karla shows up the same time as Daddy. It's better with her by my side. Still, it bothers me how she can keep such a cool temperament while she lives a despicable double life. I'll have to confront her once I finish these treatments.

I give T a huge hug before leaving. It's something we started doing the other day. When one of us leaves the room to go for a treatment or a procedure or even for a walk, we clasp our arms around each other.

"I love you T," I say.

"I love you more AAA," she says.

Our embrace is long and meaningful.

My hair is almost gone now. Several long straggling pieces and a few tangled clusters continue to hang on. I'm surviving because T is. Having Teresa around has made me a better person. She and I would've been friends even without the cancer. I'm sure of it.

After today's treatment, the effects settle in at full force. Overwhelmed by nausea, I vomit until my insides are empty. The antiemetic they've administered since my very first session takes longer to work now. After a while, the nausea subsides.

Ian isn't in the room when I return. My glimpse of the mural is brief as I cannot keep my eyes open.

I awaken to the hushed tones of Daddy and Karla conversing. I listen in unable to decipher what they're saying. When I stir, their conversation pauses.

"How are you feeling Princess?" Daddy asks. I detect a quiver in his voice.

"Better. That's the worst it's ever been."

I sit up and take in the mural. Ian has laid the groundwork for an incredible masterpiece. Teresa and I are on a hike. We stand atop a mountain overlooking immeasurable lands before us.

"Isn't it amazing," I ask struggling to get the words out. "Hey T, have you seen this? What did I tell you? Ian, isn't he awesome?" I glance over; the plum curtain is open. Teresa isn't in the bed. "Where's T?" I ask

Daddy and Karla who have inched closer to my bed. Daddy's contorted face reminds me of the days when I'd done something wrong. He sits on the bed and places his arm around me. My insides churn. "Daddy, you're scaring me."

"I don't mean to Princess," he says.

"Is it bad news?" He nods. "Then tell me now, please."

"Teresa's gone."

"What do you mean she's gone?" My voice raises to a high-level pitch. "They moved her to a different hospital?" I ask.

He fumbles for the words. "No princess. She's not here."

"She's always stepping out to talk to one of the other children on the ward." I slide my legs off the bed and amble to the door to peer out. A minute of waiting and my nerves refuse to settle. The storm inside me brews into a squall. Fighting the gale, I shrug my shoulders and lean against the door jamb. "She'll be back."

Shadowed images on the floor converge upon the archway. I turn to see a nurse enter. It's not Teresa; My disappointment shows. From the swelling of her eyes, I can tell she's been crying? Another despondent nurse enters. The two of them dodder to T's bed and strip off the sheets. When they start to fold T's belongings, I let them have it.

"What are you doing?" I scream, forced to accept what I knew to be the truth the moment I saw Daddy's face.

From the door to T's bed, I stumble and snatch her belongings from their hands taking them to the corner of the room. My body slides until my knees are underneath my chin. I bury my face into her clothes and breath in as deep as I can. Teresa's scent fills my nostrils.

"Don't touch me! Don't touch me!"

When the nurse ignores my hysterics, and reaches for me, I kick and scream. My loud voice draws more nurses and orderlies into the room. Everybody's come to watch the Looney Tune girl.

"She's not dead. She's not dead." I yell over and over until I exhaust myself—until I can't scream or fight anymore—until I am ready to throw the towel in and die myself.

God, how could you betray me like this?

Jabbed in the arm by a needle, I fall into a heavy sleep.

Chapter Thirty-One

Streaks of light radiate through the window burnishing silhouetted images of clouds, trees, cars, and even the occasional bird onto the contours of my face. I sit as I have for an entire month now—frozen in time—staring outside—lamenting the loss of my best friend.

In my short association with Teresa, she and I got deeper than knowing one another well, we understood each other. We shared the same dream of changing the world. She wanted to become a pilot; not one of the commercial kind that makes a bunch of money, but a small aircraft pilot. She dreamed of flying into hard to get to places around the world and delivering medicine and food to the needy and underprivileged.

A single drop of water lands on the window in front of me where I'm sitting. For the exception of a few scattered clouds the sky is blue. I watch as the bead hangs motionless against the pane clinging on for dear life until it slides and evaporates into nothingness. It reminds me of my loss. Everything does these days.

I'm not sure I've loved a person that completely in my life. I'd have given up my life so Teresa could have lived. The fact she felt the same makes the loss that more unbearable.

The noise at the door doesn't distract me. I am surprised when Daddy and Dr. Seville appear at my side with smiles on their faces. I can't imagine what has made them this cheerful.

When I hear the news that I've gone into remission I expect to feel something—anything. Vacuumed emotions leave me expressionless

Three days I'm told, and I'll be able to leave, go home, and return to school and my old life.

Hooray.

Why reintegrate into a place where I'm not accepted? I've been keeping up with school assignments to keep from falling behind the other students. I work better on my own anyway. Will Daddy see it the same way? I wonder if he'll consider homeschooling as an alternative.

Breakfast, lunch, and dinner have come and gone; trays of cold food stacked up on the shelf. Thus, the intravenous needle remains in my arm. Since I started chemo, not only have I lost my hair, I've dropped twenty pounds. Clothes that used to fit no longer enhance my appearance. They make me appear wayfaring and frumpy.

Daddy visits me every day. I don't have much to say to him anymore. Everything that made me who I am ceased being the day T died. He sits quietly in the chair until visiting hours come to a close. Karla and he are extremely close and spend time together downstairs in the cafeteria on her meal break and other times I suppose.

He shouldn't trust her and needs to hear the truth.

Soon as I regain more energy, I *will* confront her.

I'm tired and walk from the chair to the bed. Daddy asks me if he can do anything for me. I shake my head because there's nothing he can do unless he can bring T back from the dead and only one person I know can do that.

As far as God goes, my faith, once solid and sure, wavers in the wind of adversity that's come my way. I'm not sure I even believe in Him anymore. Of the people I blame for my loss, I blame God for taking T from me. I'm not sure He and I will ever connect again.

My nap lasts an hour. I awaken to Ian sitting in the chair next to my bed. As usual, he's sketching something on his pad. I can't make out the drawing. As much physical exertion as it caused him to create the mural, it triggers an unfavorable emotional response and I can't bear to be around it. I haven't told Ian that.

He smiles as I raise the bed.

"Congratulations Allie."

"For what?" I reply. Ian ignores the surliness of my response.

"Your dad told me the cancer's gone. I'm happy for you."

I can tell by the unforced inflections the genuineness of his words. I don't share his enthusiasm or his optimism.

"Remission doesn't mean the cancer's gone or that it won't return. The average life span from diagnosis to death is five years. At most I'll be dead by nineteen not much cause for celebration."

Ian's not sure how to respond. "Your dad tells me you're going home in few days. That's good news, isn't it? You'll be back at school—."

"What's great about it? The students hated me before I contracted the cancer. It'll only be worse now."

"Allie, what's wrong with you? Did something happen?"

"Why do you keep calling me Allie? My name is AAA. If you were a real friend of mine..."

"Allie, I'm sorry, I mean AAA. And we are friends. I realize you've gone," he pauses, "you're going through something no person ever should. Things are tough right now, I get it."

Provoked by Ian's attempt at empathy, my words go on the offensive readying for battle. "What would you know about a tough time Ian?" I snap. The words leave my mouth and I can't retract them. It's me that's talking and at the same time it's not. "Your biggest issue in life is whether to follow the path of least resistance and become a doctor or take an alternate more difficult path to get you to your dreams. I bet you didn't even show your parents the check you got for the paintings I sold for you."

He moves uncomfortably in his seat.

"I've been waiting for the right time to ask. Why did you lie to me about the paintings? I gave them to you because you told me your dad wanted them for his restaurant. I couldn't wait for him to have them."

"I had to do something to get you to pull your head out of your butt Ian. You needed someone to jumpstart your career. I lit the match that ignited the fire underneath you."

"I wish you hadn't done that Allie." He stands as if he's preparing to leave.

"Somebody needed to move you to action."

"I showed my parents the check. They weren't excited. The entire thing made them irate. Their response was to confiscate my art supplies. I'm not allowed to paint anymore."

I ignore the hurt on his face.

"You have the perfect opportunity to stand up to them."

"You don't get it do you Allie?"

"AAA Ian. It's AAA."

"AAA," he says through clenched teeth. Foam seeps through the crevices of his ivories. "Not only am I banned from painting, they've made it clear that you and I are no longer allowed to hang out."

"That's life." I shrug.

"That's your response for making my home life a nightmare?"

Ian is furious. Veins push vigorously against his skin making disfigured lines of blue green, hisses spray from his mouth more corrosive than acid. For the first time, I see a different Ian transformed before me.

"Now that's what I'm talking about. Where was that anger when you were talking to them?"

"I don't believe this, you're making this out to be my fault?"

"Your unwillingness to decide about a career is on you Ian. At some point you've got to decide. You can't hesitate because you're afraid of hurting your parent's feelings. They need to hear the truth. Are going to be a doctor or an artist? Make a stand. Which one is it?"

Ian walks over to the wall where a few cans of paint sit. He opens the lids, and one by one he tosses the paint onto the wall splotching over the work of art destroying it completely.

"I guess you have your answer." He leaves without another word.

Karla barges into the room with arms folded across her chest.

"Break another heart, did you?"

I face the opposite direction and hear her gasp when she observes the mural.

"If you weren't sixteen, I'd take you over my knee and wallop your butt."

"You lost that right years ago when you walked out of my life," I say without moving. Karla walks around the bed to face me.

"You're hurting everyone around you. Of course you can't see that can you? No, because your life ended when Teresa died. You want to hear something Allie? While you sat around these weeks bemoaning your loss, three other patients on this hospital floor died. You remember Vinnie, don't you? He went by MC; a nickname Teresa gave him. He wanted to be a Marine like his dad. Is his life or the lives of Lisa Bear or Olympic Champ, less significant than Teresa's?"

Not MC.

I remember the day I met him how he came to life when Teresa gave him the nickname Mighty Conqueror. It pleased him he'd grow up be a conqueror. Now he's dead. No one leaves this place. Everyone dies. I see Teresa's face in my mind and my anger for Karla grows from a small pimple into a full-fledged boil filled with putrid puss ready to burst.

"Don't lecture me on loss. You rejected staying in Brescade to take care of your own daughter when you had the chance. Now you're going to stand here and make me feel what? Bad? Teresa was my best friend, and when I lost her, I lost everything. I don't expect you to understand that."

"Maybe I didn't have the same relationship with Teresa you did. I imagine if she saw you now, she'd pick you up by the collar with one hand, slap you across the face with the other, and tell you to get off your butt and to do something with your life."

"Don't you even." My eyes are sharp knives that I throw her way. "You might have everyone else fooled Karla. I'm not buying your nurse cover. I know what you're up to and don't think I won't turn you into the police." Karla's hurt and confused expression doesn't dissuade me from my bloodthirsty attack. "I have the scoop on the break-ins, the drugs, and even the hit you put out on Estrada."

Daddy walks into the room.

"That's not true Allie. I don't have a clue where you're getting this stuff."

"You know Karla, lying suits you. You know who you remind me of? Satan."

"Allie," Daddy interrupts. "That's enough."

"You," I say to him, "stay out of this." shooting him identical daggers. "*I'll* say when it's enough. I've held my tongue long enough. Not anymore. I'm tired of everything that's going on around this godforsaken city." I focus on Karla. "People blame Daddy and me for everything that's gone wrong." I focus on Daddy. "And you're so blinded by puppy love you can't see the truth. Karla can do no wrong. Well I'm here to tell you that's not the case. Karla is the leader of FADE and always has been. Go ahead and ask her. She won't deny it."

Karla's eyes pop open in vagueness. she appears clueless. Then I remember.

"Want to settle this once and for all?" I don't wait for an answer. "Turn around and lift up your shirt." Another befuddled look comes from Karla and an added one from Daddy. "She's got the tattoo on her back. Every member of FADE does."

Karla can't restrain her fear from showing.

"Scary, isn't it, that I have this much information on you? I've got to hand it to you, you are a pro when it comes to deception. You see Daddy, the tattoo is part of the buy-in into the gang. Lift up your shirt Karla and prove me wrong." My voice is loud and demanding. "Show him!"

Karla surprises me by caving. Sure enough, her back shows the FADE tattoo underneath her shoulder blades. From Daddy's stunned look, his eyes have never seen it, which means she didn't have it when they were married.

I continue. "Ten years ago, the robberies stopped when she left us and moved to Asia. They started up again when she returned. Estrada, in his naivety revived FADE. To make an example of him, Karla had his ankle broken."

Daddy opens his mouth to protest. His heavy tongue won't form the words.

"Jack, listen please. Yes, I have the tattoo. I promise you there's a simple explanation for all of this."

I don't give Daddy time to process or ask questions.

"And she's responsible for Cass's injuries." My words rush forward—a gushing waterfall ready to unleash fury. "FADE's planned a robbery for next month at a warehouse outside Tacoma," I say. "I can name more than a dozen members. The moment I get out of this hospital I'm going to do what I should have done a long time ago, call the police and blog so the entire city of Brescade knows the kind of person you are." I squint my eyes sending more daggers her way.

If Daddy hasn't connected the dots for himself, I've linked them. His baffled expression I count as a victory.

Two for me.

"It must have been difficult for you Karla when they admitted me into the hospital. You knew I had to be getting close. What you didn't realize is how quickly I fit the pieces together. The night Cass visited, you told me in no uncertain terms to stay out of this. Your physical intimidation didn't keep me off your rotten scent."

Widened eyes, crinkling lines in the forehead, perplexed look, and crimson cheeks are evidence of the storm brewing inside Daddy.

"See, I understand everything now. I learned the truth from Cass, even Deke and Koreil had tons to say not realizing I overheard their conversation. You needn't worry about your precious Estrada. He didn't implicate you. After all, you hold his life in the balance. What I don't understand is the charade. Why come back to Brescade? Even a stupid criminal couldn't escape being a prime suspect of crimes and robberies committed by FADE past and present. Why get Daddy to fall back in love with you? Did you think him a patsy you could use up and throw away a second time? Did you think you could run from the past? Wasn't it enough you left mayhem everywhere your feet touched ground? Did we really have to come face to face with your immorality in our home?"

"Allie——."

I cut her off quick. "Don't you speak to me you whore."

I don't see the slap that hits me. It stings and I can tell without looking it'll leave a large welt on my cheek. I will wear it proudly knowing I've exposed the miserable truth about her.

That's game, set, and match.

I wear my victorious smile with pride.

I turn to Daddy. "Do you need more proof now Daddy? Can you finally see Karla's not the woman for you?" He remains silent.

Karla walks away her head bowed.

Chapter Thirty-Two

Brescade receives its fair share of snowfall over the course of the year. Tonight, white snowflakes drift from the heavens covering everything in its path with a thin frosty blanket. It's doubtful any of it will stick beyond tonight. A breathtaking event to witness. After being cooped up in a hospital for two months, even a cyclone warning would be a welcome change.

Christmas lights and decorations brighten the entire city. During this time of year, Brescade goes berserk. It's a visual wonderland. Every lamppost on Main Street and on many of the smaller feed-in roads have forest green vines circling them with red bows at the top of the posts.

On our way home from the hospital, Daddy stops at a favorite restaurant to pick up our meal. Since my major *tête-à-tête* with Ian and Karla several days ago, I can't be bothered communicating with him or anyone else. I shake my head declining his invitation to go with him into the restaurant to pick out my meal. He leaves the car to make choices for us both.

Before leaving the hospital, I overheard a couple of the nurses talking in the hall. Karla left the children's ward and is back in Emergency full-time. Since I'm in remission, I guess she doesn't need to stay. More likely, she's running away.

It bothers me. Even with the truth right before him Daddy hasn't acted on the information. As far as I know he hasn't spoken to Karla and I know he hasn't called the police. This infatuation he has with her is muddying his thinking. I get that they're still married, but it's in name only. Same as her relationship with me.

A family of three captures my attention as they walk, without rush, on the sidewalk towards our car. The young girl has her mouth open and is trying to catch snowflakes with her tongue. She laughs with gusto each time she's successful. The parents allow her to frolic to her hearts content and feast on the artic treats.

It's the perfect picture Christmas card moment. I wish I could immortalize it.

I reach for the heart pendant around my neck and rub it. T's parents gave it to me today, only a few hours ago when they heard I entered remission and stopped by the hospital to pass on their good wishes and tell me how much they appreciated the joy I brought to Teresa's life during her last days. I told them she did more for me than I could ever have done in return. They presented me with the necklace. I wanted to tell them to keep it that I lacked the worthiness to wear it. They insisted. "I'll treasure it always and never take it off—not ever," I told them.

The snow starts to fall heavier now. The little girl is bustling with excitement and pulls from her parent's grip to chase after more snowflakes. As she runs off, her father slips while reaching for her. He knocks into the mother and they both land on their backsides. Another picture-card moment.

A vehicle roars around the corner its occupants thinking its tires are invulnerable to the slick substance. I'm out of the car barreling towards the girl. The speeding car slides sideways certain to careen into the sidewalk where she stands staring at the flakes as they light up when passing through the illumination displayed from the lighted posts.

Time lags and everything occurs in slow motion. I race to the girl and reach out grabbing her into my arms. The car will collide with me in seconds. I can't escape the impact. The important thing is to get the girl to safety.

I toss her towards a bush that is cattycorner to me. Her body rises in the air several inches until it reaches the apex of the curve and then drops hard landing on the rough and pointy bristles of a castle holly. I kneel to the ground and cover my head with both arms and wait for the impact.

I'm ready to die.

Seconds later I hear the car speed off its occupants laughing.

My body's shaking from an adrenaline surge. I race to the sobbing girl and grab her into my arms. The parents are not far behind me. I'm in tears as I ponder what could have been a disastrous Christmas for them.

Daddy races to the scene dropping the containers of food. He puts his arms around me and asks me if I'm okay. My body rises and falls uncontrollably. The sobbing keeps me from answering. With gentle prying, he pulls the girl from my arms. I can see the ground where my release of tears has made dotted indentations.

"I'm sorry," says Daddy handing the little girl back, "a few weeks ago she lost her best friend to cancer, and the emotion is still very raw."

"Is this your daughter?" the woman asks.

"Yes, her name is Allie." The lady hands her daughter to her husband. He pulls the little girl to his face as if never having laid eyes upon her before. The lady stoops and puts her arm around me.

"Allie, thank you for protecting our daughter," she says between sobs. "Her name is Teresa, we call her Tessa for short. She has cancer too. The likelihood is we won't get to spend many more days with her as precious as this. When the car skidded towards her, our lives stopped…" Tears freeze as they leave her eyes. "Thank you, thank you, thank you, for saving Tessa's life." Warmer tears fall upon my face as she grips me with her arms. "It takes a person of great courage and strength to risk her life for someone she's never met."

Through my stream of tears, I notice the father tug at Teresa's woolen cap. I can see she is completely bald. Her pale head glows like a glorious halo underneath the Christmas haze. As I continue to sob I realize I'm crying for my Teresa.

When the tears stop. I'm faced with *thee* defining moment of my life.

We exchange numbers and multiple hugs promising to keep in contact with one another. Daddy puts his arm around me and we walk back to the car. He says nothing, yet his demeanor towards me for the first time in many weeks has softened. On the way home, countless notions fill my mind needing immediate attention.

THE DECORATIONS ON our street rivals the best that Brescade has to offer. Our house is the solo undecorated home on the block.

WELCOME HOME ALLIE.

A larger-than-life banner stretches the width of the house. Painted on large treated white butcher paper, the inclement weather won't destroy it. Daddy tells me Ian made the sign the day before we had our altercation. Ian hasn't contacted me since our fight in the hospital.

The garage door opens. Anxiety overwhelms me.

Inside, I stare at the house where I grew up, the only house I've ever known. Everything looks different and it's not because the house has changed.

Upstairs in my room I stand in the doorway and switch on the light. I remember the headaches I suffered in this room months ago. Now the headaches have stopped along with the growth of my hair. I smile at my mind's image of Tessa and how absolutely striking she looked with a bare scalp.

I stand in front of the mirror and stare into it. It's something I've been avoiding since my hair started coming off in clumps and because I knew I didn't want to meet the person on the other side of the glass—the monster I'd become. I don't recognize the girl in the mirror. She looks malnourished. More than that she looks exasperated.

I turn the faucet on letting the bath fill with luxurious hot water. When the steam starts to rise, I add a little cold water. I pour in Epsom salts and slip into the bath. The water jets in the tub buffet my body like a gentle masseuse kneads skin. The water woos me to sleep.

A strong steady knock on the door jolts me from my snooze.

"Are you okay Allie?" Daddy asks.

"I'm fine, I'm fine," I repeat a second time. "I must have fallen asleep."

"Well I'm going to bed now. If you need anything, yell out. I'll leave my door open."

"Goodnight Daddy," I say, waiting eagerly for his response.

"Goodnight Princess."

After the bath, I dress in my purple full length footed pajamas. My tablet sits on my desk where I left it, only it's plugged in and charged. For the next four hours, I make the longest entry into my diary, to date, detailing the events of the seventy-six days of my absence.

Chapter Thirty-Three

I awaken in my own bed. My body is more energetic than it's been in weeks. Now that I'm off the chemo I want to do something useful. The smell of breakfast wafting up the stairs makes the first choice for me.

Downstairs, Daddy is in the kitchen. I walk up to him and place my hand in his. He squeezes back gently. For the first time in ages, I set the table, surprised I remember where everything is.

After pulling two square patterned plates from the shelf above me and two forks, two knives, and two spoons from the drawer, I make two place settings opposite one another rather than one at the head where Daddy sits. I need to have a heart-to-heart conversation with him today.

Using a spatula, he scoops up the thick pieces of French toast stuffed with papaya and places them next to the poached eggs and Moroccan lamb sausage patties. I forgot how great a cook Daddy is and sit back enjoying my moment of heaven. Though my appetite's returned, I can't eat everything on my plate.

"Daddy, you've never cooked a better breakfast." I say kissing him on the cheek and clearing the dishes.

"You were hungry." He starts to stand.

"I've got this."

In two minutes, I've placed the dirty dishes, into the dishwasher that doesn't appear to have been used for months.

"You've been eating out a lot, haven't you?" It's not an accusation.

I turn the cycle onto the normal setting. The rush of water enters the machine.

"I prefer to dine out than eat alone at home, if that's your question."

At the table, I recline in my chair

"Daddy, I need to talk to you. It's important."

He starts to rise.

"No, no, no, I'm fine. I'm talking about a different important."

I've seen him every day since I found out I had leukemia. He looks older now. His sideburns and eyebrows are grayer. A small wrinkle line sits at the corner of his right temple. I noticed earlier as he walked around in the kitchen, in contrast to his usual deft swagger his steps called for more energy.

Did I do this to him?

Even with an older face he still sports the same smile—the one that tells me everything is right with the world. I don't detect any anger residue. He's forgiven me for everything.

"I've been a butt these last months," I say out loud. He isn't shocked by my words and sits in silence. "You could protest a little louder."

This brings a smile to his lips.

"I've been confused about a lot of things Daddy: you, FADE, school, this city, me, and mainly what I'm supposed to do with my life."

"Those are heavy burdens for a young woman to be holding." He leans forward his hands clasped giving me his full attention.

"I'm not sure how to express these new feelings I have regarding T's death. I know she'd want me to move on with my life…" The words stick in my throat.

"And now you're ready to make steps towards that end?"

I nod.

"I'm desperate to."

"Why the change?" he asks.

I fumble for the words hoping I can say them before I lose the courage.

"When Teresa, little Tessa," I say qualifying who, "almost got hit last night, I saw an end to a young life that never really got started. I got joy watching her catch snowflakes with her tongue. I couldn't bear to see that taken away from her. She had to be saved.

"As I held her moments before you came over and took her, I realized that I needed to go on as well. I could mourn T's death every day for the rest of my life and turn apathetic towards life. If I wasted mine in the interim, I'm misusing my grief? It's wrong, I think, to want to die when someone you love passes away. I'm sure the person who's died doesn't want or expect that sort of reaction."

Daddy reaches out for my hand and the heat from his palm warms it.

"Will the pain ever stop Daddy?"

"The simple answer is yes. Most of your healing," his tone turns soft, "as it relates to the releasing of your pain, is contingent upon what you do with your emotions, your fear, your anger…" His voice trails off.

I understand anger too well. This one-sided relationship has made us close companions of late. The more I cling to anger the worse I become, and the more I alienate myself from those around me. When I alienate myself from those around me, the angrier I become. This vicious merry-go-round refuses to stop, and anger is the person at the controls.

"In time, you'll learn to live with it and it won't always be unbearable," he says.

"Daddy, there's no fairness in what happened to T."

"I agree Princess. Teresa was an extraordinary girl with a zest for life few people have."

"Why does God take the good ones before their time?"

"I really don't know Princess. I'd like to think maybe it's because they're too good for this world. One day I'm going to ask him that very question." He gets up from his seat and sits in the chair next to me. "Who knows, maybe then the answer won't matter." He pauses. "I guess that's why it's important to use the time God has given us and not to waste it."

"What if you don't have much time? What do you do then?"

"You're referring to the leukemia?" I nod.

"Today I'm not sick. I can't bank on that being the case tomorrow."

"Do you remember the question I posed to you at the lake?"

After a moment of reflection, I say, "The frog question?"

He chuckles. "Yes, the frog question. Remember what I said, 'it doesn't matter how little space exists between the lines because eternity lies within them.'"

I seriously consider his words recalling the image of the lines he drew in the sand.

"First, I have to learn to control my anger? Until the leukemia came along, I never knew I had a problem."

"Allie, think of anger as fire. It can be used for good or destructive purposes. You've seen the pictures of fires burning up thousands of acres this summer including people's homes and many lives were lost." I nod. "This is terrible and of no lasting benefit to anyone. Controlled fires, those set on purpose, on the other hand, allow farmers and ranchers to clear large areas to rid themselves of growth that makes them prime candidates for brush fires. Fire can spawn new growth to spawn and you can witness the creation of a new ECO system. Once again, the responsibility falls on you. You get to decide how that anger inside you gets used."

I have a bunch of thinking to do, and some bridge building to undertake. I'm glad I didn't shy away from the talk.

Chapter Thirty-Four

My first order of business to make amends is to see Ian. I'm not sure I've ever been this nervous about seeing him. I stand outside the estate gazing at the immensity of his parent's house. I've only seen it once before this close, and only from the outside, the same day I took the paintings that started the downhill slide in our relationship. My pulse rate quickens, my breathing is off-pace, and I stumble every few steps. I hear the opening of a car door from behind. It doesn't surprise me. I turn and wave to Daddy that I'm okay. Reluctantly he gets back in the car. I must do this on my own no matter the cost.

The sky is void of clouds. Last night's snow has melted. Many of the roads and driveways still glisten from the quick thaw.

It's possible that Ian isn't home and I'll have to walk back home without seeing him. Speaking with a friend I wounded, especially over the phone, defeats the purpose. That's why my pulse rate is off-the-chart.

Things did not end well between us the last time we were together.

A panel the size of my cellphone sits affixed to the side of the solid gate of iron. Cameras point in multiple directions around the property. If someone's watching, they know I'm here. I prepare to place my fingers on the panel when the gates slide apart. The hum of them retracting comforts me. I turn and wave to Daddy. I watch him drive off before walking up the long stone-paved driveway.

Three minutes later I rest my back against the tall white columns to catch my breath. The front door opens and Ian stands in front of me. He's wearing a licorice suit with a white shirt and teal tie. I must confess he looks more delicious than I've ever seen him.

"AAA."

His acknowledgement terrifies me. What's worse is what he doesn't say, *"Hi Allie,"* or *"Come in Allie,"* not even, *"How are you Allie?"* just, *"AAA."*

"Hi Ian," I reply trying to be bubbly. "I'm sorry to show up without calling first. I needed to talk to you and phones aren't my thing."

He motions me in with his hand. Not, *"Come in Allie,"* or *"This way Allie,"* or *"Would you like to come in Allie?"* just a brisk wave of his hand.

Unrecognizable is the boy I used to know. Ian is a stranger.

As I enter Ian's house I feel as if I'm walking into a museum. A surplus of art work and antique furniture borders me from both sides. His parents are extremely wealthy yet he never discussed any details. I fear I'm the proverbial bull in the china shop as I walk through the treasury of artifacts. I fear tripping or bumping into one of these dated pieces.

I follow Ian down a long hallway; we pass by a large formal room with Queen Anne seating and other odd-looking furniture. He leads me to a less informal lounge room that still looks ostentatious compared to ours— by far the most stunning room I've ever encountered.

Three vanilla leather pieces make up three sides of a square. They have low backs which makes for uncomfortable sitting in my opinion. The rest of the décor is fabulous. The wall behind the couch is somewhere between a lime and a java green. One of Ian's abstract paintings captivates the wall. I can tell it's his by the signature.

A glass table with a single magazine and an old-fashioned scale is in front of the couch. It sits on an Oriental rug. The room is large. The expensive tile on the floor is similar in color to the couches. Oversized vases, two and-a-half feet tall, hold large brown dried leaves and match the colors of Ian's painting. I find it ironic the other walls are covered with paintings by Ian as well—a passion his parents choose to call a waste.

I sit on the couch that faces the open room. Ian's hands are in his pockets. He traipses to the leather seat opposite me and sits. The glass coffee table that separates us creates a second chasm.

Ian is paler than I last remember and replacing the smile he used to carry is a look of dreariness. He's focused on a painting next to the windows. I turn and see an oil painting of me on a field of grass somewhere surrounded by a diverse group of children. It's clear I'm telling them a story. My animated hands and infectious smile is testimony enough. Each child's focus is on me as they hang onto my words.

"What am I saying to the children?" Ian removes his hands and crosses his arms over his chest. He places his feet on the table and crosses his legs, uncrosses them, re-crosses them, and eventually places them back on the floor. His arms unfold and he struggles to slip his hands back into his pants pockets. "I imagine it's a wonderful story."

"Why are you here AAA?" From his monotone voice, I struggle to judge his temperament. In his suit, I find him more menacing. I detest the way he says my name.

"At the hospital, I said some terrible things. I'm here to apologize."

He adjusts himself till his back is straight. He looks as uncomfortable as me. "It's too late for that, don't you think?"

I want to react to his words. Prudence says to stay silent. Ian stands and walks towards the window. He seems farther away than my house across the lake.

"What you and I had, was something special."

His inflection of the word 'was' bothers me. Identical to a branch on the verge of shattering, a twinge in my heart confirms the same.

It's my fault. I've ruined us. In my zeal to help and change Ian, I destroyed him. I knew his heart when it came to painting. I wanted to get behind him and support him. Nothing more. I violated the prime directive.

Ian stands as if our conversation has concluded giving me no opportunity to apologize. His face is blank. Eyes once filled with longing for me, are cold and unfeeling. He walks towards the door and stops short.

"From the first time I saw you, I fell in love with you. Third grade I think. No way I could tell you because…well… it was third grade."

His eyes light up for a moment then return to their dull look eliminating any hope I might have had.

"The day I kissed you made me the happiest guy in the world. I saw it as the fulfillment of a lifelong dream which you destroyed that day in the hospital, and everything else we had."

"Ian…," I can't think straight enough to get the words out.

"By the way," he says standing outside the doorway, "you're telling them the story of how you and I fell in love."

"What?" I ask, still processing his response to my previous question.

"The painting." He points towards it. "You're telling them…," he stumbles, "our story."

A hiccup of emotion. Please God, don't let it be over between us.

"After today I can't see you again. My parents have allowed this onetime meeting."

"Ian, I'll do anything to take it back. Don't shut me out."

"As you announced to me in the hospital Allie, 'that's life.'"

My unresolved feelings and unrest create a sound inside me that is both dissonant and unnerving. I stare at the painting again and see it exactly as he described it.

"I love it. Ian," I say.

Back through the artifact-filled hallway I follow a young man who used to be my best friend to the front door. He opens it for me.

"Goodbye AAA."

Not, *"Merry Christmas Allie,"* or *"Happy New Year Allie,"* or *"It's been nice knowing you,"* just goodbye AAA.

My heart snaps.

Chapter Thirty-Five

December 24, 2016

Dear Diary,

On a vacation that I took with Daddy during the summer when I was ten, we hiked from Roanoke, Virginia to Knoxville, Tennessee a small portion of the Appalachian Trail. My hike back from Ian's place today took a lifetime. Half-a-dozen times I found myself standing still or leaning against a sign or lamppost entrenched in contemplation.

In my mind, I relived the evolution of Ian's and my relationship, from the moment I fell in love with him, to the day he reached out and pulled me close, to that horrible moment in the hospital when I weakened him by attacking his manhood, to our conversation today when the relationship disintegrated. Surreal is only word I know to describe it.

Not in the mood for celebration, Daddy and I attended the Christmas Eve service anyway. I fail to remember singing the Christmas Carols, listening to the message or watching the live nativity. Emptied from my mind were any prospects of substance, leaving me to ponder how barren and lonely my life had become during the last few months since being diagnosed with leukemia.

December 25, 2016

Dear Diary,

Today I awakened early not anticipating the day before me. I didn't do any shopping this season and as far as Daddy goes I don't think he did any either. I know it's not about the gifts under the tree, ironically, we don't have a tree, or the feasting I've become accustomed to. Daddy and I are going out to eat for dinner, it does have everything to do with the reason for the season.

As I stare at the ceiling in my room I'm reminded of my sixth Christmas archived as my favorite of all-time.

I wake up around five in the morning two hours before my usual getting up time. Cold weather made me shiver last night until Daddy put an extra blanket on my bed. It takes me several seconds before I can kick off the heavy comforter. Once I'm free, I make my grand escape. My slippys which Daddy calls jammies are the ones that cover my feet. They have become slick after months of sliding on the wooden floor. I race from the end of my bedroom where I can get a good grip on the carpet and build up my speed. When my feet hit the oak floor I lower my body and slide across the room with my arms out copying a seasoned surfer on a slithery wave.

Only once since Daddy bought the slippys, have I ever made it near the top of the staircase. This time I slide past the top step. My awkward body bends forward preparing to carry out my first impromptu forward somersault. My heart lifts into my mouth as I prepare for the impact when I see him. Not Santa, Daddy.

"Ho, ho, ho, Merry Christmas Allie."

"Daddy," I yell at the top of my lungs plunging to my death.

"I've got you Princess," he says catching me in mid-flight. My arms close tight around his neck as he carries me to safety. My breathing returns to normal.

The purple lights on the tree coupled with the silver tinsel are my favorite and have even more sparkles today.

"Ahh," I scream as he lets me down. "Where did those presents come from?" A massive pile of gifts circles the real winter pine we bought after Thanksgiving.

"Santa brought them of course."

"No way," I say unable to contain my excitement.

"Yes way."

"Santa was in our house?"

"Yes Allie, how else do you explain these gifts?"

I agree with Daddy and race to the tree and grab the present closest to me. A square box wrapped with shiny red paper picks up the oscillating lights. My eyes widen when I see my name written on the tag. I twirl around and around unable to keep from smiling.

"This one is for me daddy." I say taking the box to my dad.

"They're all for you."

 "Can I open this one Daddy?"

"Yes Princess."

Daddy and I spend the next hour opening presents. With each gift I open, his face is as excited as mine.

"Daddy," I say after opening the last gift, "is mommy coming back home today?"

He reaches over and scoops me up into his arms.

"Your mommy is still on a trip overseas."

I nod my head in acknowledgment saddened by his comments. Mommy left three months ago and we haven't heard from her.

"Don't despair my little princess. She sent you a huu-gge gift."

"This big?" I ask stretching both of my arms far as I can.

"Bigger."

"Really? Bigger than this?" I say standing on my tippy toes.

"Follow me," he says, "and I'll show you."

I follow him into the next room. The gift is in the room where mommy used to practice her guitar and write her music. Daddy doesn't go in there anymore. Sometimes I sit on the hallway floor outsider her room, when he's upstairs, and work hard to remember her, afraid I might forget one day.

Right where I sit, is a rectangular box as tall as me. I tear into the paper excited to see the box's contents and fall backwards on my bottom.

We open the box together and I step back in awe as he lifts a car out. It's purple. I jump up and down squealing with delight. He carries the car out to the hallway and places it on the floor. I want to make the car go varoom…room. Before Daddy allows me to get in, he pulls out another gift from inside the big box.

This one is much smaller. Inside the wrapping paper, I discover a small wallet. It too is purple. Inside the wallet, is a picture of Allie Adonia Alexander, me. Daddy tells me this picture is very special because it's my first driver's license.

"Anywhere you go in this car you must promise to keep this license with you always."

"I promise Daddy. Can I drive it now, can I?"

He lifts me up into the seat and gives me a quick lesson on how to make it go forward, backward, and how to turn it. I put my seatbelt on and push the lever forward. I take off bearing a resemblance to a jet plane leaving a destroyer.

Daddy chases me around the house.

Later after Christmas lunch, that Daddy cooked himself, he says it's okay to go outside and drive. I'm a big girl and can put on my boots and jacket by myself. I only need Daddy to zip me up, put my gloves on, and tie the scarf around my head and neck.

I take off again. Daddy jogs by my side. When we get to where the sidewalk ends and the street begins we stop. Not once during the millions of miles I drive does Daddy complain about the cold, running after me or having to change and recharge batteries.

I smile as the memory fades. My nose catches the captivating aroma of baked caramel-pecan French toast. It's time for me to get up and celebrate Christmas with Daddy.

Chapter Thirty-Six

Christmas passes. I'm fortunate with the thirteen days of vacation to have a reprieve before attending school. I begged in earnest for homeschooling, Daddy ignored my pleadings saying isolating myself from others served no useful purpose. He said if I wanted to make a change *in* my world, then I needed to be *in* the world.

Daddy has been seeing Karla on a regular basis. He doesn't tell me where he's going when he leaves the house and I don't ask. It's easier that way for both of us I guess. Whatever spell she's cast him under he's unable or unwilling to fight his way free. He's very happy right now. To divulge what I know to the police means messing up Daddy's life. I'm not sure his forgiveness stretches that far.

TODAY IS DAY fourteen since I spoke to Karla in the hospital. Daddy informed me that we will be dining at Legends tonight for New Year's Eve and that he's invited Karla. I don't argue with him and smile telling him it will be good for us to get out of the house and celebrate.

I wear my best dress; a Maison Jules Striped Midi Dress. Daddy dresses in a bespoke suit with a non-conservative tie. We arrive at the restaurant. Karla will be coming on her own. In the hallway, as we're being escorted to Legend's best table, I notice Ian's paintings adorning the walls. My heart leaps with joy and jumps off a cliff when I see them.

Fifteen minutes after our arrival Karla enters. Daddy stands as the *maître d'* escorts her to our table. I have never seen a woman that I know look quite this beautiful. She's wearing a Ralph Lauren Crossover Bodice Gown, the perfect dress for her body showing every curve and accent.

199

Her makeup is perfectly applied. Daddy pulls out her chair. She sits with such grace it's as if this is a customary outing for her. Every eye in the restaurant is on her. And for good reason; she's stunning.

I force myself to momentarily choke back the truth of Karla being K, the leader of FADE.

"Hi Allie," she says with a genuine smile.

My response is a simple "hi."

"You're looking well." I can tell she's having trouble making conversation with me.

"Now that I'm off chemo my body's going back to normal I suppose."

"You look amazing in that dress."

"And you look stunning." I'm shocked to hear the words leave my mouth as are the two-other people at the table.

"Thank you."

This is my second time at Legends and the food is more amazing than my first visit. Everything is going great. The conversation is light hearted and the mood at the table amongst the three of us for the first time in my life is what it's supposed to be, familial.

Sometime after ordering dessert Karla's phone buzzes. She opens the small leather clutch that matches her dress and pulls out the phone. She excuses herself from the table to take the call. A few seconds later I excuse myself on the pretense of visiting the ladies' restroom. Careful to keep quiet, I push open the door. The room is empty except for a voice coming from the last stall. I identify the voice as Karla's and position myself with an empty stall between us. My ears stand up on end as I eavesdrop.

"I told you I'd take care of it...............No, you listen to me. I warned you this might happen if you tried to get out ....Running only delays the inevitable and I couldn't help you at that point...............You don't want to end up dead like Desmond...............My advice is don't go...............I'm at dinner with my family...............Fine, I'll be there as soon as I can."

Who's Desmond?

Karla sighs and exits the stall. Fear's burly grip tightens, and I can't breathe. My feet lift as Karla's shadow passes and she's exited the ladies room. I don't want her knowing I've been snooping. I take an opposite path to hers back to the table. She makes it before I do. Karla and I make eye contact as I approach.

"Wow. Have you noticed all the lovely paintings?" I ask.

"Totally amazing," she replies. Her face is no longer as composed and I can tell the conversation in the bathroom unsettled her.

"Is everything okay?" Daddy asks.

"Ray, there's an emergency and I have to go." She makes it sound hospital related. "I'm sorry, I've enjoyed our lovely evening."

"You work in a business that doesn't adhere to normal business hours," says Daddy standing at attention. "We can do this again anytime."

"Allie, it was good to see you."

"You too Karla," I say plainly. There is an awkward pause as we both try to determine whether physical contact is appropriate for our goodbye. We decide to leave it at the verbal farewell.

"Happy New Year."

"Happy New Year, Allie."

"I'll walk you to your car." Daddy and Karla leave me alone at the table. While I'm waiting for dessert and for Daddy to return, I rack my brain. Who is Desmond and how did he meet his death?

At Karla's hands. I'd swear to it.

My eyes drift towards the paintings on the walls. There are several paintings that weren't there on my first visit. This isn't unusual I suppose since he's making his place a showroom for local artists. I am taken back by two familiar paintings. I leave the table to get a better look. Before I get halfway there, the joints in my legs stiffen. My breath chokes in my throat and my eyes water. They're Ian's paintings. The very ones that used to be in the living room in his parent's house. And that includes the one where I'm telling the story of how we fell in love.

Ron walks by and sees me gawking.

"That's you in the painting, isn't it?" Ron asks. I nod self-consciously intrigued to know how Ron got hold of them. "It's lovely don't you agree?"

"You've been in touch with Ian?"

"Are you kidding? Since I placed those two paintings in the hallway, I have had more comments on this artist. 'Where did you get this? Who is Ian McPhetridge? How can I buy his work?' When I found out where he lived I called to make an appointment. Each time the caller responded that Ian wasn't interested. Then on Christmas Eve I get this call from guess who?"

More tears fill my eyes and I'm forced to turn away from Ron.

I can't believe he parted with this one. My hand touches the frame.

"He told me he stopped painting and gave me these and a few others. I even have a few in my home. Of course, I told him to keep painting and presented him a check for his work. Can you believe he refused to take it? I deposited the funds in an account that will gain interest and if he ever changes his mind the money will be there." A waiter a few tables away motions to Ron. "Excuse me Allie, I'm needed in the kitchen."

"Why did he do this?" I ask Daddy who now stands next to me. "I'm responsible for this. If I hadn't pushed. If I hadn't been overtly mean to him. How I wish I'd listened to you."

I turn back from the painting and place my wet face in his chest. He circles his arms around me and holds me for a long time.

Chapter Thirty-Seven

Back to school.

Yeah—not.

Today is Tuesday, January 3, 2017. I've dreaded going back since my admittance into the hospital and can longer put off the inevitable.

Before getting dressed, I borrow Daddy's razor and shaving gel and while I'm in the shower I shave my head. I'm not interested in wearing a wig or hat or scarf to cover up my bareness. This is who I am now. People who have a problem will have to get over themselves.

After arriving tardy for breakfast, Daddy drives me to school getting me there on time. Having missed two months, I've no hope Mr. Reynolds will happen by.

School starts with an assembly. The staring and not staring occurs the instant I enter the gym. The crowd grows awkward in its silence. My own breathing throttles my ears as I walk up the bleachers. My fear, I hope can't be heard. I take my seat and stare back at the gawkers. One by one they turn away until the focus of the crowd is on the Principal.

It seems in my absence several drug related arrests have been made with several Brescade High students being taken away in handcuffs while fellow students watched. When a description of the types of drugs confiscated is given, I understand why the quiet stares came my way. They blame Karla for Brescade's drug problem and for good reason.

The rest of the assembly is on the harmful effects of drugs. I watch as students tune out the Principal's spiel. They've sat through this speech that many times they've become inoculated.

When the assembly is over the students file out. The Principal and Vice Principal cast a snide glare my direction. We don't speak. I can't imagine having to endure this treatment my remaining years of high school.

In my hurry to get to class, I turn the corner and accidentally bump into another student. I turn back without focusing and utter a quick apology over my shoulder and continue to class.

"Hey, you baldheaded freak."

Knocked back by the hot-bloodedness of his words, I stop dead in my tracks.

"What did you say?" I turn and walk towards the offender. The astonishment on our faces begins when I realize Estrada is the person I careened. He shuffles towards me with the help of a varnished wooden cane. His eyes widen as I get closer.

"Allie, I swear I didn't mean it." Fear breaches his voice like the fluctuating tones of a prepubescent boy.

"Okay, Estrada ease up. I won't deck you." I stare at him as he leans against the wall. "No one would blame me for retaliating."

"Okay, I said I'm sorry."

"No, you said you didn't mean it. That's a long way from saying I'm sorry." I notice Estrada is traveling alone without his FADE posse. "Where's Cass and the rest of the gang?"

"She's gone."

"Who's gone?"

"Cass's gone."

"Gone where?" I ask.

"Taken."

"Taken where? By whom?" My voice is a screaming whisper.

"Quiet, they'll hear you."

"Estrada, what in the world is going on?" I ask lowering my voice, "And where is Cass?" He hobbles into an alcove and I follow him with stealth checking over my shoulder to make sure we're not being followed.

"There's a meeting tomorrow night for FADE members. I have a suspicion K is going to make Cass the fall girl for the heat surrounding the gang."

"How will K make that happen?"

"Probably plant incriminating evidence on her or something."

"Why Cass? Why not Erin or you or somebody else? Cass has no clue how to pull off these pharmaceutical raids. The police won't buy it. Plus, the moment the police get hold of Cass what's preventing her from telling the truth, and giving up its members including K?"

"I'm the point," says Estrada pointing to himself. "Over here," he says opening the door to the janitor closet with a key. I don't ask him where he got the key and light the room with the flashlight on my phone when the door is closed. "I've got a knife," Estrada says and pulls a black leather sheath from inside his pants. The gleam from the six-inch blade mirrors into my face blinding me.

"Why are you carrying a knife?" I ask suddenly fearful of being in a small room with a desperate boy.

"K promised to kill me if Cass talks."

"What, and the knife is for protection?"

"Yeah." His matter-of-fact attitude unnerves me.

"And if they come for you?"

"Then I'll do whatever I need to protect myself Allie, even if that means killing, Deke, Koreil or K."

"You'll be a wanted man, a fugitive on the run. The police won't let up till they find you."

"It's me or...."

We halt our conversation and hold collective breaths when a body moves past the room. Deafening silence fills the closet and chokes me.

"The only choice I have is to go after K and end this then maybe everyone else will fall in line and things can go back to the way they were."

My loyalty is not to Karla. However, knowing Estrada's contemplating killing my mom puts a whole different spin on my position. I need to act now before Karla, Estrada or the others get hurt or killed.

"I don't want to use it Allie," he says. The trembling in his voice, the shakiness of his hands as the blade adds weight, and the fear in his eyes define the length he'll go to when it comes to protecting Cass.

"When is this meeting supposed to take place?" I ask hoping for details.

If I can get to Karla first, it's possible I can talk her into stopping this. If accepting her back into the family is the only way for her to call off the meeting, then I'll become the good little daughter. I can't stomach the idea of seeing Cass or Estrada killed. One death in my life is one death too many.

"It's tomorrow night Allie. And don't bother asking me where because I'm not going to tell you. Did you know K's already responsible for one murder? There's no reason to think it'll stop at one."

The killing he's referring to has to be Desmond, the guy I overheard Karla talking about at Legends.

Brilliant ideas don't often strike me in the moment. The magnitude of this thought almost pushes me over. There may be a way to save Cass, protect Estrada, and get rid of Karla once and for all.

"K needs to be stopped," I say.

Estrada's eyes gleam at the words. Good, the bait's working.

"I just wish I knew how to end K for good Allie."

This side-stepping of shortening Karla's name has far exceeded its use-by date. Estrada's got to know I'm privy to the identity of K. He's inducing me as much as I am him.

"I might have an idea."

"What?"

"Nothing I can share. But first, I will need you to do me a favor."

"Anything for you Allie."

"I've got major issues with my mom, and I need some…unique supplies, I can't get myself so I can settle those differences."

"Name it," he says. I verbalize the list of items I need. Never once does he flinch at the bizarre request.

The fire alarm sounds which means one of the students forgot to complete their over-the-holiday assignment.

"I've got to go," says Estrada. I watch as he ambles away to put distance between us before the hall crowds.

Because of the holiday on Sunday, Monday was the final day of Christmas vacation. Today during lunch time, DREY sings songs from their new album. As much as I'd like to be there, I need to visit the library.

The banks of computers are visible to anyone as I enter. There are obvious reasons for this. I pick the one at the end. It has no less visibility than the others but makes me feel not as obvious. Once I'm online, I search for this Desmond guy. I remember a conversation I had with Daddy months ago when he told me of a man who died the day Karla left to go to Asia. A search for Brescade deaths ten years ago should be a good place to start. Desmond's name doesn't pop up. Search after search reveals nothing.

Near the end of lunch period an idea surfaces. I search through the newspapers concentrating on the obituary section for the year in question. I don't remember the exact month Karla left. Starting in January seems plain enough. I've worked my way through till September when I locate an article about a man gunned down with a single shot to the chest.

His name was Alvin Reynolds aka Desmond. I discover as I read further through the obituary the persons surviving Desmond include his wife and three children, his parents, and one brother named, Jarrod K. Reynolds, my bus driver, who happens to be married to Kamren Jorgenson, my principal.

Chapter Thirty-Eight

A critique at a new Brazilian Churrascaria in Tacoma keeps Daddy away for the night. He'll return sometime tomorrow evening. Reynold's refusal to wait for me after school means having to walk home. On the way, I call the hospital and ask to speak with Karla. I'm told her shift doesn't start till six o'clock. I leave a message for her to contact Allie as soon as she arrives at work.

At 6:18 the doorbell rings.

"It's open," I yell out through the kitchen into the hallway. I hear Karla barge through and the door slam seconds later.

"Allie? Allie?"

"In the kitchen," I reply.

Dressed in her nurse's scrubs and looking panicked, Karla enters the kitchen breathless.

"What's wrong Allie?" she asks afraid of what she might find. "I called your phone that many times. You never answered. I got worried."

"I need to speak with you Karla. Hungry?"

On the table, sit two plates; dinner for Karla and me. Swedish meatballs, rice, and lingonberry sauce attack the air tempting her. I made cranberry tea to drink on the side. It's the easiest meal I could put together in a short period.

Karla glances at the table then at me. "I assumed because of the message you gave the head nurse you were in trouble. They called someone in to cover my shift and I rushed right over."

"Daddy says, a meal is better when two can share it. It's true don't you think? Since you're here, why don't you join me?" I motion for her to sit at the place setting across from me. She doesn't move right away and eyes me and the meal with suspicion.

"What's this about Allie?"

I motion for her to take a seat and wait for her to sit before joining her. Eloquent it isn't, yet I offer a blessing for the meal and pray for Daddy's safety.

Careful to touch only a fork and knife, Karla picks up the utensils and slices off a small piece of the meatball swishing it with a light touch in the cream sauce before lifting it to her mouth. It's reminiscent of a wine connoisseur sniffing the bouquet to determine the caliber and authenticity of the wine.

"You made this yourself?" she asks.

She closes her eyes before sticking the fork into her mouth. Tiny drops of sauce touch her tongue exciting her expression and turning it into delight. Explosions of minced onion, melted butter, brown sugar, and ground pork and beef, rejoice in perfect union as her teeth close over the tiny morsel. Moans of culinary pleasure slip from her lips and she takes more care with the second bite inspecting it for faults. Her verdict of my meal is especially important as laced in the sauce is a drug to cause fatigue. I wait in anticipation for her verdict of my meal and to lose the feeling in her legs.

"I'm surprised you cook this well."

"For a sixteen-year-old you mean?"

"Jack never told me you'd expressed an interest in food. I have to ask where you got fresh lingonberries this time of year?"

"Trade secret," I reply.

"It's an excellent blend of onion and," she pauses, "raw sugar," she pauses again, "no, brown sugar. Allie, you have a gift."

"Inevitable I suppose, considering my genes and upbringing."

"Your cleverly worded message had me racing over here to make sure you were okay."

"You're not upset, are you?" My tone is syrupy.

"Not at all Allie. It's a tactic I might use." Her eyes pierce mine with a shrewd squint. "Like mother, like daughter." Karla adds a smile. "I'd enjoy the meatballs more if you had——."

"Pickled cucumbers?" Unsteady fingers push a small ceramic container towards her. Her cunning remark related to our genes inwardly has me reeling. I fight not to show it. "Here, I had Daddy make it before he left."

"Wow," says Karla with a maniacal laugh. "Aren't you the quintessential chef?"

She slips more of the meal into her mouth and chews for enjoyment's sake.

"Like you Karla, I have hidden talents."

The tone of my remark jostles her. She stops in mid-bite and places her fork onto her plate. From her lap, she lifts the cloth napkin, and with an undetectable touch dabs at her mouth before folding it up and placing it next to her plate.

"Finished so soon? From the way you've praised my meal, I assumed you were enjoying dinner."

Now her tone changes. "I gather this isn't a social get-together."

"You tell me Karla, are you feeling social?"

Steam from the hot cranberry tea targets her nostrils. Karla reaches for the cup, and after several lingering blows through tightened lips, she takes a deep sip. The cup rattles and hits the table prematurely. I'm careful to hide the smile wanting to cradle my lips.

"Am I missing something here? Is this about Jack and me? Because…" She pauses to decide if she should continue.

"I've gathered the two of you are together. I might not approve or even understand it. At the end of the day you are still husband and wife. This dinner has nothing to do with you and Daddy enjoying a nostalgic trip to the past."

"Then what?"

"Not what Karla, who? And you are the who."

"Me?"

"Little ole you," I smile wide.

"I'm flattered," Karla says. "After all these months, my daughter wants to have a heart to heart with her mother." The feigned sincerity of her words eclipses the deceitfulness of mine.

"You should be."

"What do you want from me Allie? I don't have time for this," Karla says. Her legs lose traction as she stands. She topples over onto the floor.

"Karla," I exclaim, "what's wrong?"

I move to her side and help her to her feet. Her wobbling legs make it difficult to stand. With my arm tight around her waist, I tug her to my side. The nearest room is her room downstairs. Inside is a queen-sized bed, a dresser with mirror and pictures of Karla before she left for Bangkok. A small hard backed chair and a wooden desk sanded down to the natural color of the wood are positioned next to a bookshelf laden with books and papers. A heavy curtain covers the window making the room pitch black during the day.

Dazed, she sits on the bed massaging her temples. When the feeling doesn't pass she falls back and her mind loses momentary focus. On the bed, attached to the bedposts, are four leather restraints delivered earlier by one of Estrada's companions in addition to the potion I've used to incapacitate her. Karla lies still as I secure her arms and legs without difficulty.

My eyes cannot pull away from the woman I refuse to call "Mother." I want to argue in court that we're nothing alike, yet her eyes have the same fire within, her nose curves at the end in the same way mine does, and her skin sinks beneath the cheekbones. We're nothing alike, yet it's impossible to argue against our similarities.

Karla's eyes stare back at me. I avoid her gaze knowing tonight I've crossed a line.

211

"You must really hate me."

Encouraged by the growing anger inside me, I turn to eyeball her. "Karla, you have no idea."

"Jack will be home tomorrow," her voice rises as the transient potion wears off. "You can't keep me prisoner here forever."

"I'm not interested in forever, only twenty-four hours. After that, Daddy can ground me for life if he wants. Tonight, you'll stay here. Tomorrow I'll skip school. You'll be my guest until then."

"Guest? Allie." Muscles ripple and veins pop in a sudden burst as Karla's body lifts from the bed.

"Karla," I say refocusing her attention, "I know about the meeting tomorrow night. You've set Cass up and are going to make her take the fall for FADE. I won't let that happen. When you don't appear, they'll assume something happened to you. I'll place a call to the police. When they arrive, I'll explain the facts. You can tell them about the drugs you stole and Alvin Reynolds or should I call him Desmond, the man you killed ten years ago. Then Daddy and I can go back to the lives we had before you returned."

"Allie, you can't do this."

Arms and legs twist in blurred motion as she fights against the restraints. Her muscles are strong. Her body lifts as effortless as a sheet when the wind blows underneath it.

"I need to go to the bathroom."

"I expected as much Karla, don't you worry. Underneath you, I've placed a pad for this very purpose." Behaving very businesslike, I pull the blanket over her body, reach underneath, and pull her clothing to her ankles. "Don't be embarrassed to use it."

"Please, Allie! I'm begging you, untie me."

Declared the best thing next to sliced bread, my fingers search for the edge of the roll. When I have enough for the job, a roaring rip echoes from my fingers as I tear off eight inches of Duct tape and place it over her mouth. All is calm.

Chapter Thirty-Nine

My sleep lasts well beyond eight o'clock.

After I shower and dress, I walk downstairs to check on Karla. Soft snores indicate she's sleeping. Sometime during the night, in a failed attempt to escape, no doubt, the blanket worked its way off her body. I pull it up to her neck and tuck it underneath her chin. Her face warms. For a moment as I gaze at her and inspect her face, I can't believe I'm looking in the mirror. I always believed that I resembled Daddy. There is no doubt about it. I am my mother's daughter.

Karla awakens sometime later. My heart shifts to fear as I read the terror on her face. I swallow my feelings. What I'm doing is for a higher purpose—to stop her from ruining other people's lives or killing Cass, Estrada or any of the members of FADE.

I leave her for several hours because I can't bear to examine my handiwork. When I return, I must change the pad. She's embarrassed. I make no fuss and clean her up replacing the old pad while keeping the blanket over her.

In my front pocket, I reach my hand in and pull out a knife. Her eyes widen at the sight of the blade. I can only imagine what she's thinking. It's only a tiny pocket knife, yet, any sudden movements could damage, leave scars, and cause pain.

"I suggest you keep very still." These are the only words I've spoken to her since last night.

Her eyes are extremely telling. She's scared I'm going to do something to pay her back for the years of neglect. I point the knife at her. Her eyes widen. To get the best angle I decide to kneel with my legs on either side of her chest. As I move the knife closer to her face she quivers.

"I said keep still!"

Her eyes begin to water as the blade comes within inches of her face. I hear the muffled screams from underneath the tape. Without meaning too, I memorize the sounds. They become the very sounds in my throat. I fight to keep silent not wanting Karla to hear.

Once I'm positioned, I cut a small hole in the tape. Frozen, Karla doesn't flinch, move a muscle or blink. When I'm done I get off her. She breathes again. My breath returns soon afterward. After tossing the knife on the chair, I give her a drink of water with the straw I've inserted through the hole.

She sighs in relief finishing the cup of water.

Hunger pains, by now, have set in, and as much as she needs sustenance, her voice can carry and I can't have passersby call the police because they heard screaming. She won't starve if I keep her this way for a dozen more hours. By then the meeting will be over and I'll call the police to come arrest her.

Redressing her will not be any more difficult than undressing her. I've planned in my mind the next steps. After threatening Karla that I'll let the police come and find her in her current state if she gives me trouble, she turns very compliant.

I undo the shackle on her left leg and take the left opening of her undergarment and scrub pants and pull them over her ankle. I secure the restraint and repeat the process with the right leg. Once the restraint is secure, I change her clothes. There's no need for embarrassment as the blanket covers her from neck to toes She lifts her body and I pull them up to her waist.

Maintaining her dignity on the upper part of her body is trickier. After releasing the restraint, I pull her left arm out of the robe and then place the robe back keeping her covered. There's no way on earth I can manage the bra without having to undo both arm restraints. Instead, I grab the scrub shirt and put her arms through the holes.

The shirt is snug and pulling it over her head is going to be difficult. I close my eyes and ask her to lift her head the best she can. It takes several attempts before I succeed.

Drops of sweat cover my face. Wet patches develop underneath my arm pits and around the collar of my shirt. Using my shirt, I dry off my hair, face, and neck. It leaves a wet stain.

Now I open my eyes.

Karla's face surprises me. I expect anger, disgust, scorn or even unbelief to baste me. In contrast, I gauge it as appreciation and dare to go as far as say gratefulness.

When I tell her I'm ready to call the police, she's no longer calm. Her body rises and the bed shakes with the legs lifting off the floor. I plead with her to control herself. When she eventually settles, the index finger of her left-hand points towards the book cabinet.

There's something important she wants me to see. Music books, texts books sit neatly stacked, nothing of significance captures my attention. On the next shelf below, I notice for the first time the journals. As I pull one from the shelf, I recognize the thick rubber band holding its cover and pages together. It's identical to the ones I use on my diaries upstairs.

The date on the one in my hands is from 2004, three years before she left. I place it on the bed and run my fingers across the leather bond journals till I locate the one farthest to the right.

Karla is still and quiet now. Unable to discern her reason for wanting me to find this. I flip through the pages until I get to the last entry.

I take a deep breath realizing what I have in my hands. Reverently, afraid of what I might find, I touch the pages again and flip back several days before Karla left.

September 10, 2007
Dear Diary

The pressure I'm feeling is worse than any I've experienced in my life and I'm getting it from every side. Jack knows something's wrong. For the past few weeks, I've been distant, a stranger. What he doesn't realize is that I've been given an ultimatum. Either I leave Jack and become one of Jarrod's possessions or he'll kill Jack and Allie in front of my eyes and swear to the police I did it. I'm not sure what to do.

Kamren's infatuation with Jarrod is spooky and she doesn't want to share him with me. She's told me if I leave town she'll make sure Jack and Allie stay safe. I must make a quick decision.

The Jarrod she's referring to must be Jarrod Reynolds, my bus driver. And Kamren is Principal Jorgenson.

September 11, 2007
Dear Diary

Dizzy called. He's been trying to get me to leave Jack and go with him overseas to start a band with a few of his friends. This is not the first time he's approached me and up till today I've said no. I have no interest in leaving Jack or Allie. This turn of events could be the answer that's eluded me thus far. Dizzy still wants me. I won't lie and say we didn't have a good thing going in high school, but he's a coke head and I've worked hard at being a better person.

Dear Diary
September 12, 2007

I've made my decision. I'm leaving with Dizzy. The fear of going away is overwhelming. Dizzy is the lesser of two evils. He wants to leave day after tomorrow. I told him I needed to pack and tie up a few loose ends. He asked me to grab money and a suitcase and forget everything else. I admit I'm shallow with little backbone. Even when I'm with Jack, I lean upon him too much he must think I don't have a will of my own.

I went to the bank and took twenty thousand dollars out of one of the accounts Jack and I have. He won't notice the money missing till I'm gone. And with the money he's making from his restaurant he and Allie will be fine.

The pace things are moving, I can't see straight. I purchased the tickets. Dizzy and I will be flying to Europe where we will catch up with one of his band friends and then we'll make our way to Bangkok. What we'll do when I get there I have no idea. I'm scared.

Dear Diary
September 13, 2007

Good news. Desmond is talking to Jarrod tonight. He fears his brother and the new direction of FADE. Up to this point stealing from pharmaceutical establishments has been enough. Jarrod has bigger ideas. He wants FADE to start robbing banks. He says the pharmaceutical robberies were a quick way to get income to buy the necessary equipment to bypass hi-tech cameras and alarm systems.

Desmond agrees with me that this change in direction is senseless and could land us in jail or worse. Most of us got into the gang to score cash and a few party drugs. None of us wants this.

September 14, 2007
Dear Diary

I called Desmond late last night to see how the talk with Jarrod went. He never answered. I'm worried. Of the two brothers, Desmond is the easy going one. Jarrod sees this as a weakness he can exploit. On top of that, Jarrod is mean, ruthless, and cares only for himself. He will do anything necessary to get what he wants.

Late tonight Kamren called me. Desmond's dead. She told me to leave town as Jarrod promised to pin the murder on me. My reputation in Brescade is pathetic and it won't take much of a leap for people to believe I did it.

Will Jack ever forgive me? Will I ever see him again? And then there's Allie. By making this decision I may lose her for good. How can I ever hope for her to understand what I'm doing? As much as it pains me I accept the fact that she'll hate me for the rest of her life. What saddens me most is that tomorrow is her birthday, and I wanted to be there to give her the purple car.

I flip through the remaining pages till I get to the end of the book. Blank sheets flicker through my fingers. No entry after September 14th. As Karla stirs, I realize keeping her here prisoner was never the right move. I have made the biggest mistake of my life.

Oh God, what have I done?

I walk over to her and one by one I undo the restraints. She sits up and massages her hands and feet. When she reaches towards me with her hand I recoil. I suspect her anger is at boiling point and will blow at any second. I'm ready for whatever recourse she dishes out. If she hits me, I deserve it. If she berates me, I'll take it. If she leaves, I'll be worse off without her.

Karla puts her arms around me and pulls me into an embrace and holds me. This I don't expect. My body molds to her shape and then melts into her. For the first time I can remember, we are mother and daughter—we are family—we are one. She is no longer Karla the woman whose choices affected my life—Mag Steel whose escapades made the tamest blush—K the ruthless leader of FADE—she's Mom, the lady who sacrificed herself for me.

Gentle fingers touch my scalp. I don't pull away. Shock waves of ecstasy travel through the sensory receptors in my neck and spine. At the base of my back a warmth shoots out heating my entire body.

A few words on a page, a few diary entries and everything I've heard, known, and felt about Karla changes. It's too much to take in—happening too fast—it's perfect.

Chapter Forty

Other than normal, emotional woman stuff, I'm not the crybaby type. I pride myself on being strong, confident, and unwavering. What's happening inside of me now I can't describe or comprehend. A wave of sorrow engulfs me and I drown in the emotion.

At first, tears trickle down my cheek at irregular intervals. I wipe them away with my sleeve leaving no sign of their presence hoping to be rid of them. Moments later, over-salted rivulets stream from both tear ducts bathing my face, my chin, and my neck and saturating Karla's wrinkled top.

"I'm sorry, I'm so sorry. I didn't know, I didn't know."

Karla tightens her hold on me. I'm warm and safe. If she wants to embrace me forever, I will let her.

"I love you Allie."

These are the first words she utters since I held her hostage. I'm too grief stricken—too filled with joy to respond. I can only swim along with the current of tears.

When my crying ceases I sit. My eyes drop when Karla's eyes connect with mine aware of my grievous transgressions. She puts her hand underneath my chin and lifts it till our eyes meet again.

"Can you forgive me?" she asks.

I move away and turn my back towards her. I want to run to the bottom of the mountain and scream for it to fall and crush me. Never in my wildest imagination did I ever think I could treat another human being with such cruelty. To look upon another person, one of God's creations with such disdain is an abomination. I'm the one who requires forgiveness.

"Will you forgive me?" I ask.

Karla's arms encircle me from behind, I lose all breath and fall to my knees. Karla falls with me. As her squeeze hardens, the feelings of hate, anger, revenge, the hopelessness, and ten years of loneliness evaporate through the pores of my body.

Neither of us needs to hear the other vocalize the words. From this point forward, she and I are no longer monsters of the present or captives of the past. Today we have been reborn.

"You need to get to the meeting," I say remembering the reason why I detained Karla. "Jarrod is holding Cass as leverage against Estrada. Estrada showed me the knife he planned to take to the meeting. I'm betting things will get out of hand."

Karla's arms release from around me. I'm no longer afraid.

"I didn't know about Cass's abduction. Allie, I need to find her, then stop Jarrod."

"Will he listen to you?"

"His reign of terror is over in Brescade. I've met with each of the FADE members and they're in agreement this gang needs disbanding. This was the reason we were meeting in the first place. Ten years ago, Jarrod murdered Desmond when Desmond visited him to discuss FADE's future. I never doubted Jarrod killed him; I couldn't prove it. When Jarrod threatened to hurt you and Jack. I considered staying and fighting. Fearful I couldn't win against Jarrod; I took the path of least resistance. I left town with Dizzy because he offered me a way out. Now, ten years later, I find myself back in the same fight. I can't, I won't let it destroy my family, not again."

Karla grabs her purse and walks towards the door. I follow her.

"Where do you think you're going?" she asks.

"I'm going with you," I demand. "I can't let you face Jarrod on your own."

She offers me a smile that softens my spirit.

"Allie, I need you to stay here." She glances at her watch. "When Jack gets back tell him to meet me at Simpson Avenue. Can you remember that?" I nod. "Next to the twin warehouses."

"Simpson Avenue," I repeat. "Twin warehouses. I've got it. Are you going to be okay?" I ask.

"I'll be fine Allie." She reaches towards me and I dart into her arms. "I love you Allie. I'll call the police on the way."

She opens the door and runs to the car. I watch as she backs out of the driveway and speeds into the night.

Sometime later, I recall my conversation with Estrada. He said nothing about FADE's disbandment, in fact, he intimated the gang would go back to the way things were once he dealt with K. I call Karla. The call goes straight to voicemail with a message stating the box is full. I cannot contain the fear inside me. If anything happens to Karla, I'll never forgive myself.

Half an hour later, illumination of the lights from Daddy's car spill through the window. I flee outside before he can pull into the driveway. After I enter the car, I spout the address Karla made me memorize. Our car careens towards the downtown district.

Thumps in my chest won't go away. Tachycardia is well pronounced. My heart beats well in excess of a hundred bpm and Daddy's the same. He wipes the sweat off his brow and taps his fingers onto the steering wheel in an inconsistent rhythm.

He races through the back streets moving closer to Brescade's downtown district. Every second of the chase the car comes close to losing control. I grip the handle above the window and push my feet hard against the floor to keep my body stationary.

Two abandoned warehouses sit off Bradley Street at the site of the meeting. Broken lamplights make it difficult to see. Sharp lines of light point out our path. As Daddy decreases his speed, I double check to make sure the doors are locked. I don't want to be surprised.

Having grown up in Brescade, Daddy knows the roads well enough that he doesn't need the GPS. When he reaches the end of Bradley and makes a left on Simpson that's where we see them. Bodies scatter across the roadway hoping to avoid detection. Deke, Koreil, and a couple of others hightail from view.

Slowed to a crawl, the car continues forward until I notice a pair of legs sticking out on the street. They don't appear to be moving. Sheets of eight and a half by eleven paper litter the ground. I yell for Daddy to stop and race out of the car. He exits the car and follows me with an LED flashlight. Erin is on the ground. I think the worst. A steady pulse beats from her neck; I breathe easier. I inspect her body for injuries; none exists.

I put my ear to her mouth to listen for breathing. Erin grabs me with both hands and flips me over on the ground. She raises her hand to strike when she realizes it's me.

"What are you doing here?" she asks.

"Where's Karla?" I ask. Erin's eyes dart back and forth. "Tell me where Karla is."

"She's not here," says Erin releasing me. "She went to Jarrod's home."

"Why?" Erin's answers are turtle slow. I grab her by the shoulders and shake. "What's going on at Reynolds's house?" I ask again. This time a fever pitch accompanies my voice.

"When Karla didn't show, Ray took it upon himself to question Jarrod about Cass's whereabouts."

"Jarrod was here?" Why would Jarrod show up to a meeting where the gang ostensibly planned to disband? "You're lying."

"I swear Allie. Someone must have tipped him off. Ray went ballistic when he saw Jarrod. You know how mean-spirited he can get. He took his cane and smashed the side of Jarrod's head. They scuffled, and that's when Ray pulled out his knife and stabbed Reynolds in the leg. Reynolds punched Ray and limped to his car and drove away. Karla got here seconds later and she and Ray left together to chase Reynolds. His place is on Juliette road, number twenty-five."

Erin's hesitation leads me to think she's left out part of the story.

"What is it you're not telling me?" She waffles. I grab her by the shirt collar and lift her until she stands on her tippy toes. "Tell me."

"Reynolds has a gun."

"How long ago did they leave?"

"I'm not sure Allie. When the gun fired I slipped and hit the ground. I came too when you found me."

"Are you okay to make it home?" I ask.

"Yes."

I grab Daddy's hand and we race back to the car.

"Where are you going?" Erin yells after me.

"To stop Jarrod."

Daddy turns the car around and we drive away. In the side mirror, I'm puzzled by the look of satisfaction I see on Erin's face.

Chapter Forty-One

Fifteen minutes from our present location is Juliette Road. I call Karla on my cell. No answer. Worse than my imagination is the lingering guilt I feel that much of what's going on is my fault. By releasing her, which needed to happen, I may have sent Karla to her death. My nervousness launches skyrocketing my sanity along with it.

Juliette Road has two lights to illuminate the winding mile-long street. They're stationed on same side of the street twenty yards apart. The cheap incandescent lights barely illuminate our path. Off the road, fifty yards away, I can make out a two-story older style home. Smoke drifts from the chimney at a ninety-degree angle. The vapor is heavy and crystallized frozen by the artic wind. A single flickering orange porch light burns out instantly darkening its surroundings. If other houses exist on the street, the dying light has extinguished them.

With only our headlights to guide us, we arrive at the end of the cul-de-sac. A gravel road lies before us. A dilapidated mailbox with the faded number 25 and a for sale sign that is equally pallid indicates we're at the right address.

A slivered moon peeks out from behind a cloud cluster exposing our path. Daddy reads my mind and douses his lights. We move forward in the dark. In our clandestine approach, stones crunch underneath the tires like fresh popped popcorn. The noise will give our position away. The entire state of Washington will know our location.

Heat blows on medium force from the face and foot vents. I stick my hands and shoes closer. Cold air whisks through the open windows. It is easier to view our surroundings with them lowered and will allow us to pick up distinct sounds whether screams or gunshots. Bundled in a jacket, gloves, and a woolen hat does nothing to lessen the chill.

Our senses are on high alert—our threat level severe.

Clumped clouds scurry across the path of the moon. Their malformations create eerie shadowing against the wooded façade. A half mile down the road lights flicker amongst the trees. From here it's impossible to tell if they are car lights, house lights or flashlights. It might be a campfire. Somehow, I doubt Reynolds is in the mood for cooking weenies, making S'mores, and discussing old times. We approach with continued stealth and caution.

The dark outline of the Reynolds's house takes shape until I can nearly make out its full design. The for-sale sign states a property of over a hundred acres. A house and barn make up the only manmade structures on the moderate acreage. I imagine Cass is being held in one of the two buildings.

We traverse the winding incline. One hundred yards in front of us fractured light makes it difficult to determine if they are the rear lights of Karla's car. Daddy pulls off the gravel road into the tall grass on the left. The blades bow before us. When we're five feet off the path Daddy stops the car. Long blades of grass rise behind the car concealing it from passersby. Daddy squeezes my hand and tells me I'll be safe here and to stay in the car.

Who is he kidding? Isn't that the line used in every horror movie ever made? "Stay here, I'll be right back." Despite his assurances, I don't feel safe.

Daddy's bravery never crossed my mind. I guess most kids grow up believing their fathers to be all-powerful. On the ride over, he seemed contemplative.

After majoring in business and getting a Master's Degree in Business Management, Daddy attended a culinary arts school. By the time of his arrival, his superb chef skills made him revered amongst the other students. He assumed a self-taught chef needed to verify the fundamentals of his craft in a classroom environment. Six months later, he realized his far superior skillset and left school to open his first restaurant. By my tenth birthday he had a total of three restaurants two featuring Spanish cuisine and the other Portuguese comestibles.

Two years ago, the Takoma newspaper approached him and asked him to contribute to the Food Section. This led to his renowned food critic role. He visits restaurants each week, writes reviews and blogs on occasion. His following on Twitter is descent somewhere over fifteen thousand.

Daddy's affection for food pales in comparison to his love for Karla. We haven't discussed what happened during the last twenty-four hours or the months preceding. Even with the knowledge of why Karla disappeared ten years ago, it doesn't erase the behaviors or activities she participated in overseas. Daddy's behavior towards Karla suggests complete forgiveness, acceptance and total reconciliation. Only a man of remarkable character, immense peace, and an unshakable faith in God could do that.

In seconds, the darkness sucks away his body.

With phone in hand, I sit in the quiet. I'm not afraid of the dark. Now that my eyes have adjusted I have better visibility. Three quick blasts from a gun destroys the ominous quiet making the night darker.

Breaths wanting to escape catch in my throat. I stiffen in my seat. Daddy doesn't own a gun and I'm partly sure Karla isn't a gun person. Reynolds must be the one doing the shooting. I pray he's not targeting Karla or Daddy. Two minutes have passed. I can no longer adhere to Daddy's command to stay in the car. What if someone's hurt? Karla's a nurse, she could take care of the injury. What if it's Karla's the one hurt? Who's going to help her?

I exit the car through the window careful not to trigger the beeping sound and the inside light. The choice between walking through the woods or traversing the gravel path is easy. I can't read a map and my poor sense of direction might make Girl Scouts blush.

I opt for the road. Twenty short steps later my feet kick gravel. I walk the pathway to the house making sure to stay on the grass as much as I can. I don't need popping rocks to give away my position.

Sharp cracks some distance away immobilize my feet. My eyes scan the darkness. Nothing. I walk taking deliberate steps. Tremors of fear move as quickly as the grass in the path across from me. I'm being shadowed. A stronger shudder travels through me. Goosebumps the size of goose eggs form on my arms and neck. I regret nixing the idea of traveling through the woods. It might have been wiser.

Sounds of the fleeing rabbit send my heart into spasms. It darts out of the grass and scurries across the path in front of me. I come close to letting out a scream and wetting my pants from fear. What is it about dark nights and unfamiliar surroundings? Oh yeah, I know, *stay away from them.* It takes several seconds to locate my heartbeat and even longer to find my courage.

Reddish flames appear seconds before I hear the gunshot blasts pierce the air again. More flames exit the mouth of the gun as Reynolds shoots. I pick up my pace.

Where are the police? Karla said she'd call them. Did she make the call? Are they downtown questioning the members of FADE? I pull the phone out of my back pocket and kneel in the grass. I touch the red emergency call button on my homepage.

"This is 911 what is your emergency." Her voice sounds as if she's screaming into a megaphone. I lower the in-call volume and whisper.

"My name is Allie Alexander and I'm calling from 25 Juliette Road. There are gun shots being fired."

"Are you hurt Allie?"

"No, but you need to come…" I turn the lighted side of the phone to the ground. I freeze. I'm sure someone is behind me. My face grabs grass. I taste dirt and something else—fertilizer?

Crunched gravel and swooshes through the grass move closer. If I move, I'm dead. I hold my breath and wait making nary a sound. Exploding nerves bounce against the inside of my arms and chest when the feel of a hand grabs my shoulder. The grip is strong and firm. When the other hand covers my mouth, I wait for the blade of a knife to slit my throat.

This time moisture seeps through my legs.

"Shh, Allie. It's me."

Chapter Forty-Two

Rubbery legs make it impossible to stand straight. My knees knock against each other. While bent over, I steady them with my hands. The onset of nausea has settled into my body. With deep breaths and willpower, the feeling subsides. When I'm sure I won't fall over, I turn and pull Cass into the grass protecting her from Reynolds.

"What are you doing here?" I ask. I'm surprised, happy, and angry at the same time. "How did you get away?"

"Get away from where?" she asks.

"Reynolds. Aren't you his prisoner?"

"Allie, have you gone crazy? I've been staying with my aunt while a construction crew remodeled the house."

In my mind, I categorize the bits and pieces of the drama-filled moments of recent days, weeks, months, and line them up vertically. The sum of them doesn't compute. I try a horizontal approach. Bad math is still bad math. I remember Estrada telling me that Cass was being held captive by Reynolds. Did I misunderstand?

"If you're not a prisoner of Reynold's, what are you doing here?"

"Ray's in trouble. A few of us came to help him."

That's the first thing that makes sense in this horror-filled mind-numbing day.

"Where are the others?"

"Around the property. We entered from different directions."

Something else that makes sense.

Goggles sway around her neck. What good are goggles at night unless they're equipped with night vision? Did Cass happen to have a set at home?

"Is that how you found me?" I ask.

"Oh, the goggles," she says tugging at them. "Yeah." Her herky-jerky changing of the subject bothers me. "How did you get here?" she asks.

I lie.

"Karla brought me."

Her eyes light up as the words leave my mouth. She is excited to the point of delirium. I can't explain my reticence to tell her the truth. If Cass discovered me while wearing the goggles, it's possible she saw Daddy's car enter the property. Even worse, Erin called and told her we were on our way. When she doesn't mention it, let's just say, I know when to keep my mouth shut.

"I'm sorry you had to find out this way."

"Find out what?" I ask.

"Your mother is K, the leader of FADE."

"Cass, you've got it wrong," I say. "Karla's not the leader."

A shiver travels from the bottom of my spine to the top of my head. I do my best to control the obvious trembling and new wave of nausea.

A barrage of gunshots jolts my focus for a second. I turn in the direction of the gunfire. When I turn back to confront Cass, my eyes stare into the barrel of a gun held by my moderate friend. The moonlight picks up the shininess of the blue-tinted metal giving it a menacing look. She backs up several paces measuring me with the gun. My body trembles before her.

"I bet you didn't see this coming."

She's right. Until a few seconds ago I understood nothing. Glutinous globs of mucus stuck in my throat prevent me from answering. I can't form a single word let alone put together a complete sentence. Obedient to her instructions, I walk the dark path as our feet kick and pop rocks. A girl who used to be a friend of mine now holds a gun on me.

The moment I said Karla wasn't the leader of FADE an adverse reaction triggered within Cass. She wanted me to believe in Karla's guilt. At the beginning I did. In my blind lust to see Karla come to justice, I became judge, jury, and executioner misreading the signs along the way.

At the hospital where Estrada, of his own accord, regurgitated what he knew about FADE, he danced a lure in front of me to keep me dogging for more information. At the school he made sure to dangle the carrot about the meeting while excluding time and location. He showed me the knife knowing my desire to stop Karla trumped all other desires. He had to know I wouldn't kill her or let her be killed even in my quest to stop her. His help in getting me drugs and restraints to constrain Karla fit into FADE's plans. They wanted…no more than that, they expected me to turn her into the police, once I found the courage to act.

When Erin saw me a few minutes ago her improvised recounting of Jarrod, Estrada, and Karla's movements, was enough to send Daddy and me over here.

Oh God, what have I done?

It's a trap for the three of us. This was always the contingency plane. And I'm betting evidence from Desmond's ten-year-old murder will magically turn up implicating Karla. But instead of going to jail, she'll die along with Daddy and me, and Jarrod and the members of FADE will have the freedom to create more havoc for the residents of Brescade.

"It looks as if she's finally figured it out." The female voice is directed to Cass.

Out of the darkness Principal Kamren Jorgenson appears.

I breathe hard. "Karla had you pegged the moment she saw you Kamren," I say. The loathing evident in my tone.

Cass and Principal Jorgenson share a smile.

"And we played her from the moment she arrived in town. And for that Allie, I want to thank you. You were our biggest contributor."

Memories flood forward. Karla offered Estrada a way out of FADE when she visited his room. Estrada didn't want her help. I see that now.

"Jarrod must pay you well to stay this loyal."

"Our intense love for one another," interjects Kamren, "is what binds us. That's why we've been married for ten years."

It's embarrassing and shameful to realize that Cass, Kamren and the rest of FADE could play Karla, me, the police, and the town as expertly as they did. The call Karla received at the restaurant on New Year's Eve? More superb playacting from Erin I learn. In her desire to help release FADE members from Jarrod's grip, Karla did nothing more than tighten the noose around her own neck.

"Karla's return to Brescade fit our plans with flawless perfection. With the anger of the community pitted against her, anything suspicious meant everyone suspected her. And by now, she's dead, your father's dead..."

Blades of remorse prick at my skin, hundreds of them force me to see the kind of person I've become.

"...And Jarrod will swear it was self-defense, and of course the rest of us will corroborate his story. When the police ask me what the other students are doing here, I'll tell them we were engaged in an impromptu astronomical field study when the three of you barged onto the property."

How could I have been so blind?

"What are you going to do with me?" I ask. Tears for my parent's death refuse to come. Why is that?

"Your death will be what they call collateral damage. Now move."

Chilled moisture coats my palms, the areas around my ears, neck, and underneath my armpits. More questions fill my mind as we approach the house. How does she know Karla is dead or Daddy for that matter? Less than five minutes ago he left. The barrage of shots I heard couldn't have been for him, and I hope not Karla. Maybe they got away. Or am I once again, trying to see something that isn't there.

My feet turn to lead. I stumble in my tracks and fall. My hands reach out to brace for the fall. I hit the ground hard. Several of the sharp rocks penetrate the palms and fingers of my hands. I scream out in pain. The sound of my heart drowns out the noise.

"Get up," Cass says. "Now."

Multiple cuts and abrasions on my hands keep me from supporting my body weight. Turning my body to the side, I scrunch my legs till my knees hit my chest. With my elbows and legs working in tandem, I maneuver my body into a kneeling position.

"Allie, get up." Kamren's voice is cold and harsh.

I glance at the woods to my left. Rush towards the grass and hide? If Daddy and Karla, are still alive it might buy them time.

"Did Estrada ever want to date me?" I ask.

"You've got to be kidding. Why settle for ground beef when filet mignon is on the menu?" Cass replies. "He tried to seduce you into becoming a member of FADE. I told him you were too religious and would never agree to dating him or getting a tattoo. I've got to admit Allie, you surprised me. I didn't realize someone with your faith and church background could act so disloyal and conniving. I guess you were right when you said, 'the apple doesn't fall far from the tree.'"

Her truth adds fresh wounds to an already scarred heart.

"Were you ever my friend?" I ask. It's hard to believe our entire relationship was a farce.

"I tolerated you Allie."

"So, the day you cried in my lounge room…"

"Reynolds's philosophy is simple, to make someone believe a lie, you plant a small seed and let others come along and water that seed until it sprouts and becomes a truthful reality. We enjoyed toying with you Allie. You believed everything we said."

"What about Karla? You couldn't have known of her return to Brescade."

"Manna from heaven fell when she showed up," says Kamren. "Jarrod couldn't believe his luck."

I continue to think.

"What about Estrada's ankle? I was there."

"Freak accident. It ended up working for our benefit. Even the incident at the library Allie. We wanted you to eavesdrop on Deke and Koreil's conversation. We played you from the beginning."

Her words are unnecessarily cruel.

"Cass…"

"No more talking. I've told you everything I'm going to, now walk," Cass says.

"When this is over Allie, Jarrod and I are going to own this town. Of course, you won't be around to see it," Kamren says.

Chapter Forty-Three

"I wouldn't take that to the bank if I were you."

A voice from the dark sounds from behind Cass and Kamren. I've heard it only once. I recognize the deep bass tones. I've never been happier to hear it. "And if I were you," the voice continues, "I'd keep very still. Right now, rifles are trained at your heads. This shindig of yours brought out our top snipers. If you think I'm kidding, look down, but do it real slow."

My eyes pickup on the red dots jittering from their hearts back to their heads.

"I'm surprised you didn't pick that up with your night vision goggles." I think he chuckles. "It would be a shame to mess up two such beautiful faces. Now, I want you both to listen. Make no mistake if you don't do exactly as I say you will be shot dead. Listening?" Both women nod. "Good. Take the guns and place them on the ground and allow me to memorize every move."

I watch as they follow the directions of Detective Wiles and bend over making sure to follow his orders to the letter. Once they've placed the guns down, he gives them orders to lie on the ground with their hands interlocked on top of their heads. Officer Dominguez emerges from the dark her gun drawn.

A hand underneath my elbow doesn't elicit fear this time. Officer Wiles, who is at my side, helps me to my feet. He asks me to hold out my hands and sprays disinfectant onto them. I prepare for the sting that doesn't come. He takes a roll of gauze he's procured from a pack on his side and wraps each hand.

Officer Dominguez and a slew of police officers surround Cass and Principal Jorgenson. Officer Wiles and I walk towards the lighted house. We're fifty yards away when his hand tightens around my arm. He's listening to what's going on inside the house with his earpiece. He stops as another barrage of gunfire takes place. It reminds me of hail raining down on a corrugated iron roof. In a few seconds, the storm is over.

Daddy. Karla.

It takes a year for us to make it to the front door. I've aged half a century by the time we arrive. Somewhere on the walk down the hill daylight illuminates 25 Juliette Road. Light beams from police cars, officers holding flashlights, blazing flares, and two hovering helicopters with spotlights aimed at the property create this phenomenon.

Dozens of police men and women mill the property marking off boundaries with yellow tape. Others with flashlights and dogs search the grounds. The dogs are fit and excited, not here to play. I surmise they're here to sniff for drugs. From behind us, gravel explodes underneath the tires of an approaching ambulance.

Officer Wiles leads me to the house and then let's go of my elbow when we get to the threshold. There are more police officers inside the house. Tentatively I step inside. Right away I smell the blood. For the odor to be that pungent, someone lost the quantity they needed to stay alive.

Several officers stand in a group with their eyes focused downward. My eyes follow their gaze. On the ground, is the body of Jarrod Reynolds with Karla on top of him, her head on his chest. The rest of her body is on the ground her legs bent in the fetal position unmoving. Blood matts her hair. Her blood-soaked clothes and the scent of death reignite the wave of nausea. She is facing away from me. I can't find air. My heart stops beating. This is what it feels like to die. My legs lose their elasticity and my knees knock together again.

Two EMT's move towards Karla and Jarrod.

"How is he?" One of the paramedics asks. None of the officers answers him.

"I've tried everything. He doesn't have a pulse." Karla lifts her head from Reynolds's body. "He's dead. I need to check in there," she says tearing.

As she walks by me her hand brushes against my side. We should be celebrating her life. Someone else is down. Who? I'm afraid to find out. Still, I follow at my own pace. Then I see it. I take a deep breath to reaffirm my findings and enter.

The paramedics are doing their best to stabilize Estrada. He has a GSW to the chest. The doleful look between them states the obvious. I don't have time to find a bathroom. A potted plant nearby will do and I rush to it and vomit. Karla's hand circles my waist as I finish. She hands me a bottle of water and a wad of gauze. I rinse my mouth several times spitting the foul mixture into the pot. I wipe my mouth. If the plant dies, it won't be from lack of moisture.

Karla helps me to my feet. She unwraps the gauze from around my hands and inspects the wounds then re-wraps them. She tells me they will have to address my hands at the hospital. Gravel wounds can be especially painful as the only way to prevent infection is to scrub the wounds with a special disinfectant. I can't think about that now.

When she asks me if I'm alright, I nod. Daddy's entrance into the room uprights my imperfect world. My knees weaken. I manage to keep my feet. The three of us stand hugging one another with me in the middle. I fail to remember an experience this comforting.

"He's asking to speak to Allie," says the EMT interrupting our unit. "We've done everything we can for him. He's comfortable." The EMT shakes his head. "He'll be gone in a matter of minutes."

Why me?

Multiple eyes watch me as I make my way to the edge of the cot where Estrada's lying. With each step, I become warier of this decision. I don't want to face another death. Next to his feeble body is a folded piece of paper. On it are written the words:

If you want to get out of FADE, I can help you.

It's signed by Karla.

I whisper Estrada's name. It takes several moments before his eyes open. A syrupy glaze coats them. I can tell by the slight smile on his face he recognizes me.

He attempts to open his mouth.

"Don't speak Ray. Save your strength."

"Ray? That's a first. If you're using my first name, it must be serious."

"Stop talking and rest."

"I'm about to enter a long dirt nap Allie, let me say what I need to. This might be my only chance."

My head lowers to his mouth. "

"I'm sorry Allie. Please forgive me."

"It's okay Ray," I say.

"I restarted FADE to make a few bucks. My old man died in an accident last year. Mom had to take on another job. You know the story. After the first couple of robberies, it didn't take long for Jarrod to find me. He owned me after that."

"Ray."

"I lied to you, I hurt you, I treated you terrible Allie. I need you to forgive me." His eyes focus on mine and he waits unblinking for an answer from me.

How long does it take to forgive someone? A lifetime, a year, a month, a day, an hour, a second, less? The group of people standing around me wait along with Ray anticipating my answer.

"Yes, Ray, I forgive you. More importantly Jesus forgives you. Will you accept that forgiveness now?" I feel like a priest administering last rites as I wait for his answer.

"I want to," he says.

"Then do it now Ray." I urge him. "Ask Jesus to forgive you." His eyes are glass, the kind a taxidermist might use to stuff a deer or a bear. "Please Ray, do it now."

His eyes close and his head sags to the side. He's dead. Then Ray surprises me.

"Jesus, I deserve no favors from you. I won't lie; I'm scared. Forgive me for the things I've done. Don't forget me please." Tears of joy trickle down from my face. Ray surprises me again. "Allie, will you hold me?"

This guy tried to have Karla and me killed. How can I oblige him this request knowing it will be his last?

"Cass is somewhere outside. Let me ask the police to find her?"

"I never loved Cass." His words are sharp and direct. Does that mean he loved me? I'm torn about what to do and then I remember only seconds ago I told Ray I forgave him. I look to Karla who gives me the nod. An EMT assists me onto the couch and places Ray's head in my lap.

"Allie, I never told you this. I've always dreamed about becoming a park ranger in Montana." I want to laugh. I want to cry. I cry. "Have you ever been to Montana?" he asks me.

"Once on a vacation with Daddy," I say sniffing.

"Tell me 'bout it." His slur scares me. Yet, if this is his final moment on earth, I want him to experience part of his dream.

"You couldn't have picked a more beautiful state Ray. In the spring, Montana is picture-card beautiful and luscious green. When you come out of Yellowstone Canyon on the Montana side, the sight of gigantic mountain ranges steals your breath.

"They're in constant need of park rangers. I've no doubt you'll make a great one. You have the warm spirit that's needed for someone to watch over and care for God's beautiful creation."

A wide smile has covered his face.

"They have clear lakes that allow you to see down to the bottom and rushing rivers where fighting fish swim against the force of the water.

"Perhaps the best thing about Montana Ray is the space. You can travel for days in the wild and never come across another soul. If you appreciate the quiet and solitude, it's the perfect place. Imagine yourself on a horse. The two of you disappear with no destination in mind. How awesome is that? Who knows Ray, maybe one day you'll settle down, get married and build a home there on a hundred acres with a stream that runs through your property. Every morning you'll get up to the chorus of animals singing hello. I'd suggest you make a trip to Montana first to make sure you it suits you. It gets mighty cold in the winter and you don't strike me as the fair-weather type."

I stop talking.

For a moment in my mind's eye I'm standing on the porch of a log cabin home looking at the splendor of Montana. Ray is on a horse with his dog standing next to him. They take off into the wilderness for a long stay. Now it's over, the vision, the dream, gone forever.

I don't need the eyes of Mom or the EMT to tell me Ray has slipped into death. I felt his last breath as he exhaled onto my arm. With both hands, I place Ray's face onto the bed. His eyes are closed thank God. My breathing becomes rapid and I feel lightheaded. Karla sees my struggle and rushes over to help me. Once again, my grief is instant and uncontrollable. I fall face first to the ground. She covers me with her body refusing to let me go.

Chapter Forty-Four

We need showers. Once we leave the Reynolds's property and arrive home, I use the remainder of my energy to crawl upstairs. For thirty minutes, I allow the hot water to blast away at my body. Soap stings my wounded hands. In my mind's eye, I see Jarrod's dead body and what I believed to be Karla's dead body draped over him. The image ends with Ray cradled on my lap. Finished showering, I meet Daddy and Karla downstairs.

The three of us drive over to the police station and walk into an interview room where we give our statements. It's while listening to Karla's account of what happened the last pieces of the puzzle form the complete picture that's eluded me.

Karla ached to return to Brescade for years. She stayed in Asia under the impression she was protecting us. When during a sober moment the pain of being away overruled her heart, she made an important call and reached out to the Brescade Police Department informing them of her return. Her decision meant coming face to face with Daddy and me, and an entire community who hated her. Convinced this was the right decision, Karla prepared herself for the anger, hatred, and rejection she'd experience.

A return to Brescade meant having to face Reynolds and face her sordid past both in Brescade and Asia. She took it on willingly. Unbeknownst to Daddy or me, Karla worked with the police with hopes of bringing to light the person responsible for killing Alvin Reynolds ten years earlier.

Dizzy's attempt at smuggling drugs was legit. The publicity from the story and Karla's return served to bring Reynolds, and the others out of the shadows. He'd been operating in secret targeting different counties around the state though he ceased operations in Brescade. When FADE started robbing pharmacies around Brescade, suspicion was thrown back onto Karla.

Reynolds supposed Karla suspected him as Desmond's killer and became unnerved by it.

Interestingly, when the story broke, and I began to stick my nose into FADE's activities, Reynolds concocted the brilliant idea of letting me believe Karla led FADE. It didn't take much persuading since my loathing for Karla peaked even the tallest mountains. By pitting mother against daughter Reynolds gambled I'd never side with her. He hoped I hated her enough to turn her into the police or do his dirty work for him and kill her myself.

I shudder at the thought.

Reynolds's reacquired his position of leadership of FADE stealing it from Estrada and picking up where he left off ten years earlier. Everything pointed to Karla except the police knew the truth. They needed irrefutable evidence to prove Reynold's culpability in the death of his brother. No one could know Jarrod Reynolds was the subject of an ongoing investigation. And so, the police rousted Karla at our home the night she arrived, and arrested her on school property. These moves allowed FADE to continue their exploits, believing the police were focused on Karla.

The afternoon at the hospital when Karla saw me enter Ray's room she knew they were stringing me along. Sworn to silence for fear of breaking her cover and tipping Reynolds off, she weathered my attacks knowing how misplaced they were.

Karla spoke to every member of FADE asking them to denounce their affiliation. This, her obsession, became the one opportunity for them to come forward and meet with authorities.

The sad truth? None of the members took Karla up on her offer. They tricked her into believing they were quitting the gang and giving themselves up. She'd set up the meeting for that purpose. That's when Reynolds decided to have Karla killed

Since I opposed Karla at every turn, Reynolds thought of me as his ace in the hole. When I asked Ray for help and restrained Karla to keep her from showing up to the meeting, he knew a call to the police from me couldn't be far behind and planned to plant evidence for the police to discover.

The night of the meeting one of the members watched our house. When Karla left and Daddy and I followed soon after, Jarrod decided to kill three birds with one stone. Erin faked her injury and gave us a spiel about Jarrod rushing home and Ray and Karla chasing after him. This impromptu move to lure Daddy and me over to the Reynolds residence worked.

Soon after Karla left the house, she contacted the police. They scrambled a team who, using covert tactics, infiltrated and surrounded the one-hundred-acre property then waited to see who'd showed up.

The bullets I heard fired came from Reynold's gun as he shot at police and from return fire that led to his and Estrada's death. Lab tests confirmed it to be the same gun that killed Mike Reynolds ten years earlier.

The twenty remaining members of FADE including; Cass, Erin, Deke, Koreil, Principal Jorgenson, and the Assistant Principal, were arrested, arraigned, and taken to a Tacoma prison where they await trial.

No one will know of Karla's involvement in FADE's demise. We've been sworn to secrecy. They have, however, informed the residents of Brescade of Karla's innocence now and ten years earlier. Yesterday, one of those residents sent flowers. Instead of stomping on them and tossing them into the fire pit, I located a vase and set the flowers on the table in the kitchen.

January 9, 2017

Dear Diary

Two days have passed, and it's too difficult for me to put in words what's happened. Vacillating emotions, conspiratorial relationships, and the knowledge that Karla's not the monster I labeled her, makes me wonder if I can ever trust myself again. I doubt my ability to make sound judgments.

Don't get me wrong, I'm happy Daddy and Karla are together and that I have a real mother again. When in the middle of everything, untruth became truth, I supported those I should have opposed and disapproved of the one person whose trust I should've embraced.

What does this mean going forward?

A KNOCK AT the door alters my focus.

"Come in."

Karla walks in and sits at the foot of the bed. I move my feet to give her more room.

"Jack's going to Seattle tomorrow to review a new South African restaurant that's opening. He'll be out of town for a couple of days. Want to go to New York with me on a shopping trip?"

"If I agreed on the spot, you might think less of me." I say placing the tablet on the bed beside the table.

"Not on your life," says Karla pulling me into her side.

"There's the question of school?"

"And?"

"I'm supposed to go back tomorrow."

"Do you want to go tomorrow?"

"No."

"Then it's settled. I'll call and inform them you have a more pressing engagement to attend. They're bringing in a new Principal from the east; Boston or Bethesda? She's innovative and it won't be long before

245

Brescade High School is in the news for things other than football, drugs and murder."

Two days alone with Karla. It sounds too good to be true.

"And Daddy's okay with this?" I ask timidly because I've always cleared things with him first. I don't want Karla seeing this as an attempt to dodge her parental authority.

"I'm the one who suggested it," says Daddy entering. "What do you think, after the review and our trip to New York, we take a vacation?"

"Where to?" I ask excited and delighted I will be able to miss more school.

Daddy leaves the room and returns with a paper in his hands. Piece by piece he unfolds a map of the world.

"Where are we going Allie? The Caribbean and South America are nice. Please don't let my preferences influence you in making your decision."

I look at the map and with my hand I touch various countries and cities. Too many places from which to choose. I decide on one and seconds later another location captures my interest. It's impossible to choose. Sympathetic to my struggle; Karla makes a sensible suggestion.

"Allie, close your eyes. Take this coin I'm putting in your hands and toss it onto the map. We'll go wherever it lands providing the country is safe, and it's not an ocean or Iceland where it's freezing."

"Great idea Karla," says Daddy.

I agree the idea has merit. When my back is turned to the map, I flip the coin over my shoulder.

"Australia," Daddy says truly excited. "Let's plan to stay for six months."

Chapter Forty-Five

We returned from our trip around five p.m. last night and slept most of the day. Daddy and Mom left not too long ago to shop for food and other household items. Confinement in a long plane flight precipitates my need for exercise. I dream of stretching my legs and taking in the summer fragrances of Brescade.

As my fingers touch the knob of the front door, the doorbell rings. Fright, the kind that forces your heart into your mouth, and sends shock waves throughout your entire body, subdues me for a moment until the white-as-a-sheet feeling passes. When I'm able, I open the door.

"Hi Allie."

Life, time and again, targets us with moments we can't prepare for. Outside, with his hand clutching onto a leather case, Ian stands with a sheepish grin on his face. My involuntary action to glance at my phone he doesn't acknowledge as rude. The day is Saturday; the time is 4:00 p.m.

"Ian," I gasp, "what are you doing here?"

"Is this a bad time?"

"Yes," I reply still within the throes of the shock I suffered when touching the door knob. "I mean no, of course not, please come in Ian."

I hold the door open, Ian sets the case on the hallway floor careful to lean it against the wall and faces me. Dressed in dark pants and a long-sleeved business shirt open at the collar he's taller than I remember and more handsome.

Misplaced and confused heartbeats nail dynamic rhythms into the wall of my chest. Since I last set eyes upon Ian, eight months have passed—a lifetime. Conversation once simple to ease into is sticky with complexity.

A chasm of hurt exists between the man I fell in love with and the man who now stands in front of me. I assume a similar gulf exists for Ian.

While overseas, I considered the demise of our relationship now and then. Three-quarters of a year is a long time to stash away one's feelings. Right now, they appear to be equal in emotion as the day our estrangement occurred. Those opinionated expressions I hurled at Ian in anger led him to destroy a beautiful work of art and brought an end to our thriving relationship. How I wish the reconciliation between us could be as simple as, "oops, my bad," followed by a casual, "no worries."

God, if healing is possible…

On instinct, I walk upstairs to the lounge room. Ian follows, holding tight onto the case which he places against the wall. Conscious of sitting on the loveseat next to me, he chooses, instead, to pace.

"How was your trip to Australia?" he says breaking the silence.

"Awesome, indescribable, I learned so much about the Australian culture, and a lot regarding the person I am."

My statement falls on deaf ears. I wait for Ian to ask a reflective follow-up question which never comes.

Though I've seen the move a thousand times, it shouldn't surprise me when he strides to the window and stares out past the lake. Memories of that afternoon bombard my mind; feelings swell in my chest.

I remember.

"I've missed you Allie." His words leave a patch of fog on the glass.

Our hands touched and the earth opened beneath us. We kissed and our hearts became one changing us forever. And then…

"Do you think it's possible to go back?" He says. His body turns from the window. Light from behind creates a haze around him.

"Back…to, to…where?" I stumble.

"A time when you and I are still best friends?"

Powerless to think, my response is not to respond. Albatross wings flap amuck inside my chest pushing away the lingering remnants of my breath.

"What's in the case?" I ask.

Distinct as night is from day, my changing of the subject causes Ian's demeanor to slide. His lightning-fast recovery reminds me of the old Ian. He opens the case to retrieve a painting.

"The day you came to see me was the second worst day of my life. The first being the fight we had in your hospital room. My parents hated the fact you involved yourself into what they called, 'family business.' They gave me an ultimatum regarding my painting. What they held over my head is not important. The result being, you and I had to stop seeing each other. That hurt more than you know."

"Ian, I'm sorry."

"They appropriated my art supplies. Angered by their actions, I retaliated by removing every painting of mine from their walls and took them to the restaurant and gave them to Mr. O'Keeffe though I didn't have the guts to complete the action till after your visit."

I swallow hard as the saliva clumps its way through the canal of my throat.

"Ian?"

"It took a couple of months until I developed the courage to stand up against them. Believe it or not, I played the age card. I told them at eighteen I could make my own decisions without their involvement. My words weren't as in-your-face as that, but I told them my love for painting was a destiny I needed to fulfill."

"How'd they take that?" I ask. My eyes wander to the hill where Ian's house sits.

"We arrived at a compromise."

"Wow. And?"

"I will major in both medicine and art." Before I can respond, he continues. "No doubt existed in my heart as to what I wanted to do and yet I couldn't ignore their wishes. Inwardly, I realized, I had a deepening passion for medicine, something birthed by them and cultivated by you Allie."

Delight floods within me—an amicable tsunami unleashed.

"If you weren't so..."

"Pushy?"

"I was thinking pugnacious." A smile crosses his lips. "That day may never have happened."

From the leather case, Ian has removed a canvass. I shriek within myself when I realize it's facing away from me. Before I can vocalize my displeasure or extend a physical reaction, I soon recognize the painting of me sitting with a group of children reciting the story of how Ian and I fell in love. Tears surrender.

"Where did you get..." I remember seeing this painting on the wall of Legends.

Ian goes onto explain how he visited Ron and bought back the painting so he could give it to me.

"Ian, who told you we returned from Australia?"

His sheepish smile returns.

"I wasn't sure how long you'd be away. I've come by each Saturday since February hoping to see you."

No single prescription for healing exists. It comes in many forms. Despite my prayer, I didn't expect this. Within forty-five minutes of his arrival, I'm ready to throw my arms around him.

"Ian," I say, "I don't have another best friend."

Emboldened, Ian approaches me and places warms hands on my shoulders. When he pulls me close, heat from the earth's core cements us together for good this time. I don't remember the moment his lips touch mine nor when I respond. Even when the door downstairs opens announcing Daddy and Mom's return I'm trapped in a world of bliss that refuses to free me.

When we pull away, I hold onto him to keep from falling. Mom stands at the top of the steps turning to head back downstairs.

"Mrs. Alexander," Ian calls out.

Mom turns. She approaches Ian placing her arms around him.

"Ian, the last time you were here, I was extremely rude and unkind to you. I hope you can find it within yourself to forgive me." She pulls back from the embrace. "I'm Karla Alexander. It's a pleasure to meet you."

"Mrs. Alexander, Ma'am, you're mistaken. The pleasure is entirely mine," Ian responds with the refinement of a Count.

"I hope you'll stay and join us for dinner. Jack is making Saltimbocca. He told me it's your favorite."

"I'm humbled by your offer. Thank you."

Mom hurls an interrogative stare at Ian. "How is it that a guy with your amazing looks, ethereal talent, and extraordinary disposition has never dated another lady other than Allie?"

Instant pink flushes Ian's cheeks.

"Mrs. Alexander, Allie and I aren't dating."

"You're not?"

I shake my head.

"No Ma'am, we're not."

"Then Ian, it sounds to me you need to do something about that. Jack's downstairs in the kitchen."

Ian casts a curious glance my direction. Surprise and elation is how I'd describe his look.

Ian steals a look at me. "Answering your question Mrs. Alexander is simple, I can't help but love Allie."

When Ian leaves to speak with Daddy, like magnets, Mom and I cling together allowing the tears of joy to flow unashamed.

"Where did he come from?" Mom asks. "He's quite a find."

"I love him Mom."

Her grip tightens around me.

Chapter Forty-Six

In a blink, a year blurs by.

Mom, left her job at the hospital for two reasons—both delighted me: One, to homeschool me. After limited discussion with Daddy, she convinced him, for now, this was the right course of action. The second reason is as obvious as her protruding stomach. Excitement builds as her due date draws nearer.

Residents of Brescade, slow to act at first, have dropped by or sent cards to welcome us to the city. Mind you, I've lived in this same house all my life. In addition, apologies have been plentiful and Mom and Daddy have no shortage of relationships they hope will grow into strong and meaningful friendships.

On August 15th, mom throws a party. Neighbors and other Brescade residents are invited to the get together. During the meal, Officer Wiles and Officer Dominguez, and a slew of their police buddies stop by for a plate of food. Daddy cooked his world renown Shrimp with Cilantro Cream, Boliche, and Ropa Vieja.

Almost the entire town of Brescade shows up to our block party. When the last person leaves around midnight, I sit on the Lazy Boy with Daddy without saying much. Mom is in the kitchen. Her scream jolts us to a lucid reality. Daddy and I bolt from our seats and race to the kitchen. Doubled over and standing over a discolored puddle is Mom.

"Is it time?" asks Daddy rushing up and putting his arms on her.

She nods.

"Allie, get the bag in the downstairs closet and meet me in the garage," Daddy says.

"What are you doing?" asks mom.

"Taking you to the hospital."

"Not looking like this, you aren't. I need to clean up first."

Daddy throws me an inquiring look.

"Allie, take the bag to the car and I'll take Karla to the shower downstairs. Grab an outfit from her closet."

"The lilac cotton dress hanging on the hook behind the bedroom door and my essentials," adds Mom.

"Essentials?" I laugh.

"Grab my essentials and you," she says speaking to Daddy, "get me to the bathroom. This baby is early, and it's coming tonight."

I decline joining my parents at the hospital. This is something, I've decided the two of them need to do together. Plus, the party wiped me out and I need sleep. I wave goodbye on their way to the hospital.

AT NINE IN the morning my phone rings. My eyes fight to focus. I answer without looking at the display. I grunt a greeting.

"Allie?"

"It's me," I say grunting again.

"Did I wake you?"

"What? My greeting didn't give you a clue?"

"Sorry Princess."

"It's fine. I needed my sleep interrupted."

"Cute."

"How's Mom?" I ask more alert now.

"Karla's fine. I wanted to call you and let you know that you have a baby sister."

"You owe me twenty bucks."

"I could have sworn she delivered a boy at first. The doctor told me I was focusing on the umbilical cord. I moved my eyes down an inch and a half and voilà, you've got a baby sister."

"Twenty bucks," I repeat, "in twenties."

"I'll give it to you in pennies if you don't stop badgering me."

"Picked out a name?"

"That's the reason why I'm calling. Karla and I figured you'd might want to be part of the name choosing ceremony."

"Wow, a ceremony. This is a big deal."

"Huge."

"Should I dress up?"

"I'll be by to pick you up around noon. We're going to get a little rest?"

"Congratulations. That's great news Daddy. Tell mom I love her."

"Thanks Princess. See you soon."

Sleep interrupted, I rise and let the shower blast me. A new baby sister, and me, a big sister. She'd better watch out.

I stand underneath the hot water and allow the jet sprays to exfoliate my pores. I grab the large towel and wrap it around my body and another for my growing hair. My toothpaste tube is empty; I tiptoe to pull out a new tube from the cabinet. That's when a red-dotted blotch on my neck underneath my chin captures my attention stealing with it every ounce of joy. I fall to my knees in despair.

"Why God?" I ask repeatedly. "Why?"

Chapter Forty-Seven

What should be a day of celebration as new life enters the world, turns melancholy at the recurrence of my leukemia. I'm readmitted into the children's ward right away. A handful of the nurses I recognize. They do their best to welcome me understanding the all-too-taste-touch-hear-see-reality. No one wants to spend their days in a cancer ward? And that's the point: None of us wants to be here suffering from cancer.

Later during the day, I traverse the ward. Since the last time I was here, more children seem to have been stricken with the cancer. Each bed holds a precious soul undeserving of such a sentence. Family members are present in a few of the rooms. The majority of sick and dying children lie alone. I enter the room of a seven-year-old boy. He's surrounded by books, magazines, and toys. An Xbox sits on the bookstand next to his bed. I can tell he's bored out of his brain.

It occurs to me, after a second look, it's not boredom he's dealing with, it's his lack of understanding on how to cope with cancer. I figure I'll go in and talk to him or something and get his mind off things.

"Hi," I say entering his room. "My name is Allie what's yours?"

"I'm Jackie."

"That's my dad's name."

"No kidding?"

"Well he's a lot, lot older and they call him Jack not the cool Jackie they call you." I hop on his bed and sit cross-legged next to him. "Do you want to play a game?"

"No. I'm waiting for my mom."

"That's okay, I can go."

"Don't go," he says. I hear the pleading in his voice and see it in his eyes.

"Okay, I'll stay. You've got to know I can't sit here and do nothing."

"What do you want to do?"

"Do you want to hear a story while we wait for your mom to arrive?"

"Story?" I can tell he's intrigued. "What kind of story?"

"You tell me what kind you want to hear."

"I don't know," says Jackie shrugging his shoulders.

"You're not a love story guy, are you?" I ask.

"Love is for sissies."

"And you're not a sissy, are you? What about a story with adventure, action, and a little bit of sissy stuff?" I ask.

"Okay, but only if it's a real little bit." He squashes his thumb and index finger tight.

For the next fifteen minutes, Jackie is enthralled as I concoct a tale that includes giants, dragons, and of course the damsel in distress. Somewhere during the story, a young girl stops outside the room and peers in at Jackie and me. I motion for her to join us. As more stragglers appear, more invitations are given

Nurses walk by and cast marveling glances through the door. I continue the story until Jackie's mom walks into the room.

"What is going on here?" she asks surprised at the number of children packed into Jackie's room.

I fess up quickly. "I told Jackie a story while we waited for you. The group grew. Sorry."

Placing her arm on my shoulder, the mother whispers, "Thank you for making him feel important. He's been feeling low the last two days."

"I enjoyed it as much as he did."

I gather the extra children to walk them back to their respective rooms.

"Thanks Allie," says Jackie on my way out.

"No problem. Another story same time tomorrow."

"Promise?"

"You bet."

"Can we come?" ask the other children.

"Sure. Let's say after lunch."

"Can you tell one tonight after dinner?" asks a six-year-old girl with mangled patches of hair spotting her pale head.

"What's your name Princess?" I say lifting her to my chest.

"Kerry."

"Story time in Kerry's room after dinner. Spread the word."

Dinner is bland. My spirit is a mixture of jelly beans, a walk on the beach, and hot sauce. There's no satisfactory answer I can come up for it. Using the clock in my room to countdown, I give everyone twenty minutes to finish their meals. On my way to Kerry's room, I catch the eye of several nurses. I don't understand why until I enter Kerry's room. Eighteen children sit around Kerry's bed on chairs, bean bags, and lounge chairs from the playroom.

Before telling a story, I ask each of the children to introduce themselves. When I've learned the names, I launch into a story that includes every one of my listeners. Excitement erupts in their faces when their names are mentioned.

Thirty minutes later the nurse enters the room.

"Medicine time."

Medicine time, the most hated, dreaded, cursed activity in the hospital next to physical therapy, procedures, and operations. I know from experience. Before the children have a chance to scrunch their faces and utter a litany of boos, I jump from the bed and dance excitedly at the word medicine. Soon the kids are chanting along with me at the top of their lungs.

"Single file line," I say.

Stomps and shouts accompany the far-from-marching-band-technique. Askew behind me, their feet march to my cadence.

"Repeat after me.

Medicine is not our foe
Medicine is not our foe
This is why we have to go
This is why we have to go
If we're good and sleep the night
If we're good and sleep the night
Tomorrow's story will be outta sight
Tomorrow's story will be outta sight
Sound off
One, two
Sound off
Three, four

Nurses watch in amazement as the eighteen children, the oldest no older than eleven, march in unison to their respective rooms. When the last child is tucked in, I walk back to my room exhausted. Daddy is there with Mom and my new sister.

"Hey," I say running to see the baby. I gently pull the blanket from around her neck to see her face more clearly.

"She's beautiful Mom."

"She looks exactly the way you did when I gave birth to you," Mom says.

Suddenly Mom is overcome with emotion. Daddy reaches over and takes the baby from her hands. He motions to me with his head to take her for a walk. I stand behind her wheelchair and push till we reach a secluded place in the lounge. I wheel her up next to a chair where I can sit and face her.

"Mom what's wrong?" I ask.

It is hard to understand what she's saying between the sniffles.

"I want to apologize to you."

I'm baffled. "Mom, what for?"

"When, when, when, I, I…"

I've never seen her this distraught.

"Breathe mom." I take the deep breaths with her. We continue breathing together until she regains control. "Mom, talk to me. You've got me worried."

She turns her face from me as she speaks. "When I found out I was pregnant with you it turned out to be one of the saddest days of my life. I'd placed my career on the front burner and having a baby didn't fit into my plans. So, for six years I tabled my dream regretting every moment.

"From the second you were born, Jack's and my relationship changed. I began to blame him for every small thing that went wrong in our relationship. Ultimately, I left him making him shoulder the responsibility for the break. On top of that, I selfishly lumped him with the charge of raising you by himself."

Saying nothing, I wait for her to continue. Children with cancer are wise beyond their years. I understand if Karla doesn't exorcise her demons, the past will haunt her for the rest of her life.

"Allie, this morning when I gave birth to your sister an overwhelming sense of guilt came over me. I couldn't get out of my mind what I did to you. What mother treats her daughter that way? I don't deserve to be your mom or your sister's mom."

"Come on, that's crazy talk and you know it. You're a great mom. I'm a better person with you in my life Karla Alexander."

Her eyes latch onto mine at the mention of her name. Crocodile tears create two sparkly diamond lines on her face.

"Can you ever forgive me Allie?"

"I already have. The past is best left there. I won't bring it up. You shouldn't either."

She places her head in my lap and I stroke her hair.

"I love you," she says sitting.

"And I love you too Mom."

Boxes of tissues are always nearby in a cancer ward. I tug several from the snug sleeve and hand them to Mom. After she's wiped her face, blown her nose, and discarded the tissues, I stand and wheel her back to my room. On our return trip, I wave to the non-sleeping children.

"You've got quite a following."

"I told a few stories today. The kids needed a pick-me-up. Boredom can be as deadly as the cancer."

"The nurses told me you made the children very happy today."

I smile as Teresa's image surfs through my mind.

We arrive back at the room. Daddy is sitting on the couch holding my baby sister.

"So, are you two ready?" he asks.

"For what?" I ask.

"The naming ceremony. We can't call her, 'Hey You' the rest of her life."

Chapter Forty-Eight

Daddy and Mom returned from their meeting with the doctor. Confirmation that they've tried all possible treatment avenues leaves their hearts heavy with sadness and exhaustion. I can't fault them for wanting to keep me around a little longer. I'm prepared to die, then wonder if anyone can ever be ready.

I've seen five of my children die in my time here. It is the saddest thing to see these parents grieve the loss of their child. For a handful of parents, this child is their only offspring, the center of their universe. Walking through the grief with the parents is my way of helping them heal. I tell them wonderful stories about my/their children.

When these parents lament I'm reminded my parents will soon endure the same unforgiving, unreal, and unfair realization unless a miracle happens.

The look on their faces says everything. They do their best to hide the finality of my sickness. Daddy does a much better job at it than Mom. It's problematic for me that they are the ones trying to be strong because they don't want to add more pain to my life. I don't know where they derive the strength.

While sitting on the couch, I ask to hold Abbie, the name I gave her. It's biblical and means, *my father is joy*. She giggles every time our eyes connect. Maybe it's the funny face coupled with the buzzing sound I make with my lips that creates the joy. She knows we're connected—that we're sisters.

Unable to share with anyone what's going on inside of me, I often hold Abbie close. She senses the restlessness in my spirit. If I had time, I'd teach her everything I know in an instant, and show her what mistakes to avoid and what choices to make along the way.

A sudden wave of melancholy washes over me. I hand Abbie back to Mom. I can't hide my desperation from her.

"Are you okay Allie?" she asks.

"I need to rest."

"Do you want me to call the nurse?" asks Daddy.

I nod.

Olivia enters the rooms moments later and increases my pain medication. In a few minutes, I travel to a different world. My escape route from reality causes guilt to swallow me. I'm ashamed of my feelings and have kept this to myself: I'm afraid of dying.

I race through the valley at breakneck speed. The beast beneath me will not support this hurried pace for long. Still, I drive it as if I must reach my destination by a certain time or give up something in return if I'm delayed. The beast beneath me understands my urgency and makes it his. He increases speed.

I lean over onto the shoulder holding the long frowzy mane of the bistre-colored stallion. He emits an unfamiliar scent—the smell of an animal that lives free in the wild. I inhale his freedom into my body. Now, I have the same scent.

Steam from his nostrils creates a cloud of smoke—the strong powerful pounding in his heart is slow and purposeful at first then beats with an out-of-control tempo. My heartbeat merges with his until our pulse is one. Heat rises from his body warming me. I'm not sure how I know this ride is one of many we'll take together.

Landscapes, visually breathtaking, arrest my breathing. Before me are the infinite peaks of a vast mountain range. Immeasurable valleys are fertile and boast colors I have no words to describe.

The land, the horse, and I are free; at the same time, we submit and report to a higher authority. Today I ride through the ocean knowing I will be uninterrupted as I cry out to God; thanking Him, blaming Him, questioning Him, and arguing with Him, not necessarily in that order. My heart bursts with things to speak out loud. I want to discuss my past and my future, talk about Daddy, Mom, and Abbie, and Ian's and my relationship, things only He will understand.

I reach my destination and sit atop the stallion with my right leg folded underneath me in total awe of my surroundings. This place is perfect. I walk the horse into the undulating waves and let the water rush up to his knees, no further. I imagine the water is cold; my steed does not react to the change in temperature.

While sitting atop the horse I lean over and peer into the deep blue cobalt water. A young woman stares back. For a moment, I am perplexed. She is imprisoned. From what, I cannot tell. The image is real; I want to jump in and save her.

I choose not to describe her features. Because she is faceless? No. Because she represents women from every nation, tribe, and tongue. In the pool, she is a dazzling blend of black, white, yellow, red, and brown.

I lean forward still holding onto the mane and place my face against the face of my companion for the last hour. His breath is fast and rhythmic. His skin emits the moisture of perspiration. Sadness ineffectively trawls my spirit as I pull back. I do not want to leave him. For now, I must. Taking his cue from my mood, the horse walks deeper into the water. I slip off into a blue calm and the girl in the reflection and I become one.

Swallowed by the water, doubts and fears wane in their importance. I dive as far as I can then burst upward to the surface rising from the water. Regret and sadness evade me as I walk from the ocean.

Wet and energized, my body glistens in the light. It doesn't take long before I'm dry from the moisture and my spirit ready to do business with God. I will offer no bargains and refuse to plead for my life. I sit with my back against a cherry tree. The leaves provide no shade as the light around me does not emanate from the sun.

I keep my eyes open as I pray. All my life, I've spoken to God this way. Seconds before my lips open to implore him, the voluminous list of questions that once circled through my mind shortens leaving me with a mere two to ask.

"God, did you make a mistake by allowing me to contract cancer?" I wait a long time before reiterating my question. The ocean waves seek to draw my attention away from my purpose for being here. I won't be sidetracked and ask my second question. "If

I die this young, how can I accomplish the endlessness of dreams I still have in my heart?"

Within the foreboding silence I find comfort.

My horse wanders off, not far, to graze. My entire being becomes transfixed on the waves and sand. Small swells make a swooshing sound as they attempt to smooth out the glut of jarring mounds of bronzed granules. The sand, I realize, though I'm not sure how I know this, is my life, while the potholes and mounds and other blemishes are my inadequacies, my failures—those times when I acted on what was best for me failing to consider other's needs, and my propensity to rebel against what I knew was right holding tight onto what I understood to be wrong. The smattering of my defects covers the shore as far as my eyes can see.

Symbolism emanates from the waves. They are, I realize, God's method of grinding off the rough defects in my life. Gentle waves ease across them sometimes barely making a change, and upon closer observation, I realize many of the smaller imperfections cease to exist. Larger waves push towards the shore with tremendous force. They assault the larger mounds, sometimes, obliterating them altogether. Other mounds need countless attacks before diminishing. It takes the combination of gentle and commanding waves to free the sand of its blemishes.

One mound remains. Its refusal to lessen intrigues me. While I watch and pray, my focus turns to my illness. I come to the realization that this singular flaw, my sickness, will remain. With no time to consider this news, an even more compelling realization overcomes me: Wherever here is, cancer is impotent. It's powerless over me.

My fingers reach towards my face and curl around my lips that have formed into a smile. In my weakness, strength has its grandest opportunity to shine. In this place, my past neither haunts nor rules over me. Fear's tactics to coerce me into believing I failed to accomplish my life's goal fade into nothingness.

I stand to my feet invigorated.

"This is your home, my daughter."

I reflect on the significance of His words for a long while. When I'm ready, I stand and walk towards the horse. He lowers his body allowing me to climb onto his back easily.

Chapter Forty-Nine

September 15, 2017

Dear Diary

I turned seventeen today. The nurses and the children in the cancer ward celebrated with me. The cake Daddy baked fed almost the entire hospital. We sat in the lounge room on the floor in campground fashion. One by one they went around the circle with each person saying something they appreciated about me. Talk about blowing my mind.

Ten weeks in the children's cancer ward and I know every child's name, birthdate, and I've even given each one a nickname. Two more children have died since my re-admittance into the cancer ward. Breakage happens in my heart for the parents and loved ones. Though having no child of my own, I have a tiny inkling of the anguish their souls suffer.

Miracle of all miracles happened today. Tessa, the little girl I met last winter is a patient here. The doctors came back to her parents this morning and informed them that Tessa's leukemia is in remission. We were so happy to hear the news we marched back and forth through the halls yelling and celebrating. They'll keep her here for another week and then release her. These kinds of stories make living through the nightmares worthwhile.

After the party, I returned to my temporary space. A leek in the ceiling meant I had to take a different room until repairs could be made. The estimated time of completion is this afternoon.

I awoke after a short nap. A girl my age is being admitted. She discovered a few days ago she had AML. I can empathize with the torture her mind is going through; the lack of control she feels she doesn't have anymore. She is going to need someone to talk to and a person to build up her HM. I asked the head nurse to make us roomies.

The highlight of my day occurred when following my nap, they ushered me back to my old room. A weird vibe radiated from Daddy, Mom and the other nurses I couldn't explain until I entered the room and discovered a mural painted on the wall.

Teresa and I stand on a hill together, arm in arm, overlooking the open plains. The sun is high in the sky and we're dressed in hiking gear. We're contemplating which track we'll take to navigate through the hills and across the vast space. What makes the mural special and causes me to tear up is Ian is in the picture. He stands next to me, his arm around my waist and an infectious smile on his face. The mural leaves me breathless.

AN HOUR LATER a girl named Samantha walks into the room accompanied by her parents and Candice, one of the nurses. Samantha is wearing pajamas with various types of felines on them. Once she's settled, and the room is empty except for the two of us, she lets out a deep sigh. I can tell she's trying to come to terms with the cancer. She stands at the bed and glances over at me. Our eyes connect.

"So, what are you in for kid?"

"What?" she says looking over at me her mood turning irritable.

"You've got cancer or they'd put you downstairs."

"Yeah, so?"

"What kind?" I ask.

"AML. What's it to you?" she asks getting into bed.

"Welcome to the club. I've got it too I say grinning."

"It's not a joke."

"You need to chill Kit Kat," I say. "You're going to blow a gasket and then the leukemia is going to be the least of your worries."

"What did you call me?"

"Kit Kat. That's my nickname for you."

"My name is Samantha."

"My name is Allie. You can call me AAA. You'll realize soon enough we throw formality out the window."

She pulls at the curtains and jerks it around until it surrounds her bed. My lips curl into a smile.

"You know it's not soundproof, right?"

Déjà vu.

Kit Kat rips the curtain open.

"What's your problem?" she says to me.

"You're spun kind of tight aren't you kid?"

"You think cancer is a joke?" I feel the heated anger coming from her.

"Here's one for you Kit Kat: I was diagnosed with leukemia. Months later I was all better. Now I'm back. Guess why? Never mind, I'll tell you. My cancer is no longer in remission. How's that for a joke?" She says nothing. "How long have you had AML?"

"I found out three days ago," she says her voice rising.

"Wow. I bet you don't have a hair left on your head. Oh look, still intact."

"Why don't you leave me alone?"

"The last thing you need Kit Kat is a pity party."

"I didn't ask for you to be here."

"Too late. You might as well get with the program roomie."

"What's your problem?"

"I've been where you are kid. You can spend the time you have on this earth whining and complaining or you can live. Trust me when I say your life is far from finished. I want you to imagine two lines ten feet apart. Now I want you to imagine there's a frog on one of the lines. The frog hops towards the other line. With each hop that frog covers half the distance. Will the frog reach the opposite line?"

Samantha's mind is sharp, much sharper than mine. I can see the mental calculations she makes.

"No."

"That's right. Do you know what this means?"

"I don't have a clue." From her blank expression, I believe her.

I walk over to her bed and stand there until she moves over. I sidle in next to her.

"That's okay Kit Kat," I say staring at the mural, "we've got a lifetime in front of us."

AT MID-AFTERNOON, I walk back to the room having completed my second story time for the day. My feet move, but do not maneuver at the speed they once did. When I arrive at the room Mom has arrived She's sitting on a chair with her feet up with Abbie asleep in the stroller.

"Hey Mom," I say approaching the bed. Mom stands to help me.

"I've got this," she says pulling the sheet and blanket back for me. "How are you today Allie?"

When Mom asks that question nowadays, I know better than to give an automated answer. Since the return of the leukemia, we've no time for unnecessary superficial conversation. Things are very real between us now, in a good way.

"I'm more tired today than yesterday. Each day forward I'll deteriorate a little more, but I'll deal with the challenges as they come."

"We'll walk through them together," Mom says. She tucks the sheet and blanket around my body. "You're a brave girl," she says, kissing me on the cheek. "I don't think I could soldier on the way you do."

"You'd be surprised at your capabilities. Daddy said everything that comes my way goes through God first. So, I figure if God's allows it, then why do I need to worry?"

"Jack and I are very proud of you."

"Where is Daddy?" I ask only now realizing he's not here.

"He went up to the lake to clear his head."

"Is everything ok?"

"He needs time to think," she adds as an apology. "He's the strongest man I know Allie. Your sickness has taken him to a deep place."

EXCEPT FOR THE occasional walk to the restroom I'm confined to my bed. On good days, the nurses will wheel me to the story room where I do my best to entertain the young at heart with tantalizing tales of cissy love and adventure.

As my body slowly yields to more pain, my medication increases to compensate. Enough to manage the discomfort not obliterate it. When it gets too bad, I will take my trips away to unknown worlds. Sometimes Teresa joins me on these excursions. I enjoy having her with me.

Today, I wake with a contradiction of emotions. I'm going home which means leaving my kids. Who will tell them stories when I'm gone.? I regret that I did not groom a person to take over for me, I will make note of this in my diary for future reference.

Daddy arrives with Mom and Abbie. It won't be long till she starts crawling. They carry several large duffle bags with them. I've accumulated quite a bit of stuff in my time at the hospital. While they pack, I use the motorized scooter Daddy and Mom bought me and say my last goodbye to each one of my children.

It is by far the hardest thing I have ever done. I cannot bear the idea of never seeing them again. Tears wait at the borders of my eyes for me to give them permission to fall. They unleash themselves without my will. I call on God's strength for each moment.

Death is a morbid enemy; one I cannot seem to overpower with strength or will. In his quest to take me, he is not particular who he wounds in the process. Everyone near me will suffer injury. In his lust to see me dead, none is spared.

My greatest resistance to leaving the hospital is knowing that the doctors can no longer help me. They are letting me depart to comfortable surroundings to prepare for death's arrival.

Dark settles in, a faint hue remains in the sky. I watch as clouds race toward me stifling the remnant of light. In seconds, darkness reigns. A cold breeze replaces the warmth and soon turns bitter.

I'm lost and can't remember how I got to this place.

In the pitch dark, I imagine the clouds above swirling until they surround me completely. Eerie sounds accompany the supernatural display around me. It sounds as if a metal ball and chain is being dragged my direction.

Faint rays of orange swirling light appear in the distance. As the light grows stronger so does the heat that accompanies it. The tornado is real and leaping flames envelop me. No matter which way I turn escape is impossible.

"You're afraid of me." I tremble at the voice that echoes a thousand earthquakes and fall to my knees. "You should be."

Fire shoots out at me from the spinning flames. The heat is unable to singe my skin. I swivel to find the source of the voice forced to content myself within the churning flames. I stay in a humble posture.

"Because very soon you will be mine."

I follow the one-sided conversation comprehending Death's visit. This foe who's done everything he could to make me fear him these last months

On my knees, it feels as if I'm worshiping something that has no place in my life. "What do you want?" I say standing to my feet.

"I have what I want or should I say, 'I soon will.'"

"Then why are you tormenting me?"

"Because I can." Thunderous sounds from his deep voice echo from the flames. His words are pure evil. I long to be anywhere else.

"Leave her." Another voice whispers out of the darkness. The voice is small and still. Had I not been listening I might have missed it. "Leave her," the voice repeats for a second time with even less volume.

Mad flames swirl around me even faster now. They are close enough that if I were reach out my hands, I'd be incinerated by the ferocious heat. The fiery tornado rises above me and I watch it descend into the blackness.

I do not notice the change, yet in an instant, serene light fills the space around me. My surroundings are familiar. The blue ocean is before me. My horse which has been grazing in the meadow nuzzles its head in my side. I scratch his mane.

There is joy inside me I can't describe.

"You're here," I say.

"Yes Allie, I created this home for you. We'll always be together. Remember nothing can bother you here."

"My friends?"

"They will live their own lives."

"And Ian?"

"My child, he'll enjoy an incredible life as a doctor and painter. You will forever be his inspiration."

"And what about Mom and Abbie? Will they be okay?"

"They will live long productive lives."

I pause. The words stick in my throat, and I can't speak them.

"You want to know about your dad?"

I nod with my eyes shut.

"Because of you Allie, Jack will impact the lives of many during his lifetime." I pause out of selfishness. "None of them will ever forget you Allie."

"Will I ever see them again?"

"Yes."

"One more question, please?"

"You know you can ask me anything Allie." His voice lingers soft. My ears no longer strain to hear. He stands next to me.

"Will you please give me the time and the strength to say goodbye?"

"Of course, my child."

Chapter Fifty

Extended naps are part of my *forte* these days. Too weak to argue or fight exhaustion, a persistent and unrelenting taskmaster, I submit to these recurrent moments of slumber. Following one of those snoozes, I awaken to discover Ian sitting across from me. He's stares into my fluttering eyes rising from the lounge chair to come closer. A toothy smile touches me long before he reaches the bed.

His hands, strong and warm, reach for mine. I offer weak and pale hands to the man I've come to love a great deal. Ian's daily visits add peace and joy to my day. The day I learned the cancer had returned I called Ian to let him know. Though six weeks into classes at the University of Washington, and upon hearing the dire forecast for my health, Ian took a leave of absence to spend the rest of my life with me. At first, I let him have it for doing something so irresponsible. I imagined an eruption of fireworks took place at home when Ian's parents learned of his decision to defer schooling. He stood there, grinned, then leaned over and kissed me. We never discussed the subject again.

That day, at Karla's insistence, when Ian spoke with Daddy to ask for permission to date me, my life exploded with unimaginable feelings. Three months of bliss we've spent together before he left for college and then the tragic news I was no longer in remission. Our days are purposeful, and I split my time as evenly as I can with Ian, Mom, Abbie, and Daddy.

Knowledge of my looming death doesn't make living easier. In fact, it's quite the opposite. Each person in my inner circle has me concerned. Assurance from God they'd be okay doesn't stem my soul's anxiety. Yesterday, and the day before, I spoke to Abbie, and Mom, respectively.

Abbie babbled, giggled, and slobbered. She pulled on my clothes and mountain-climbed my body. By the time I finished telling her the things in life to avoid, and the right choices to make, we laughed together and even more when I started tickling her.

My talk with Mom ended with us both in tears. I did my best to affirm Mom of her worth to the family and the fullness of life I might have missed had she not returned to Brescade. We hugged and cried, mostly cried. Daddy is a more difficult proposition. Each time I try to speak with him words stick in my throat promising to choke me if I go forward. For the time being, I've tabled our final conversation until the right opportunity arises. That leaves Ian.

"I hope my sneezing didn't wake you," Ian says.

"What time is it?"

Ian reaches for the phone in his pants pocket. "Two-thirty."

"Tell me you haven't been sitting there since lunch?" His sheepish grin confirms my suspicions. "Ian," I'm forced to suck in another breath. "I've told you, you need to get out more. You can't be cooped up in the house with me the entire time. When's the last time you saw or spoke with your parents?"

"While you slept, I called them."

"Oh, that's nice. How are they?"

"They're my parents. I can't expect them to change their ways right away. On a positive note, they've accepted your dad's invitation to dinner tonight."

"I didn't see that coming." I say surprised.

"Neither did I. They're changing Allie. In these last few months, they've learned their parenting technique contained flaws and have come to the realization that our family is laden with imperfections. It's a good thing."

"It'll be nice to see them again. What's Daddy cooking for dinner?"

"Costela de porco, Brazilian-styled rice, and *Pão de queijo*."

274

"Sounds yummy."

"Let me help you to the lounge."

"Thanks," I reply in haste motivated to get out of bed, knowing it will take time and energy to make that happen.

Ian pulls back the comforter till it rests above my knees. He turns and waits for me to adjust my gown. Careful to retain my dignity while preserving my independence, I slide off the bed. I grip Ian's extended arm loosely with both hands. My feet slip from underneath me, but Ian's hold keeps me from falling. He walks with me to the lounge his arm firm around my waist.

A long sigh leaves my lips after I'm situated on the couch.

"You alright?" he asks.

"Fine," I answer having to take in multiple quick breaths before I can speak.

"No time for dishonesty, remember?"

"I know, I know." The big breath I take gets stuck in my throat and comes out as two hiccup burps. "Sorry," I say.

"What's on your mind AAA?" Referring to me by my nickname carries on the legacy left by Teresa—no sourness in his voice as he says it.

"If this sounds morbid, I apologize. You know I don't have many days left."

"I know." His hand closes over mine. Two tears, one from the corner of Ian's right eye, and the other from my left, drip onto the back of his hand trickling into the crevices of his fingers sealing our hands together.

Words corralled by my terse thoughts refuse to leave my mouth. I try a second time. My mouth opens to speak. Nothing. I struggle to take in another breath.

"What's wrong Allie?"

Not the question you ask a dying woman. My answer rings with the pleas of a human spirit that wants to stay on earth for many years. And yet, I know better.

"I want you to promise me something," I say suffocating the other thoughts that parade around inside my mind.

"Depends on what you ask."

His abrupt out-of-leftfield answer stuns me.

"Are you refusing to grant a dying girl her final wishes?" I gasp.

"If you're going to ask me to find a nice lady, settle down, and have kids then yes consider this a refusal. Plus, it's a promise I'm not sure I can fulfill. You know Allie Adonia Alexander I love you. I can't imagine loving another woman as much as I love you. I've loved you since the third grade, I'm not going to stop now."

Ian's right. Though he preempted my speech, I should never have tried to tell him to do something that counteracted his prerogatives. You would have thought I'd learned this lesson by now. Ian's allowed to love whomever he wants even if it's a dying woman. Peace settles solidly into my heart at the inflexibility of his words.

"I'm sorry." Ian lifts his arm. I slide in next to him feeling the warmth of his body. My heart races out of control, and for the umpteenth time I struggle to find a breath. "When I'm gone—"

"Allie—"

"Ian, let me finish." I speak unhurried. "When I'm gone, I don't want you to stop living." Primed tears hold back their assault. "Unquestionably, you will change the world. You're going to make many awe-inspiring achievements. When I consider the possibilities, excitement overflows within me."

"You really believe that?"

"I have it on good authority."

"What do you mean?"

"Nothing, except when it comes to art and medicine, promise me you won't get sidetracked, refuse to settle for second best. Reach your goals." A gasp, not from my words, but from my struggle to breathe, catches in my throat. "Ian, I beg you, use those gifts God's given you to help others

276

in this world. Nothing is more important. You have all the time you need." Now the tears flow at will. "I'm so proud of you Ian," I say blinded by the salty waterfall.

Overcome with emotion, Ian can't respond right away. Reality wallops his soul as he realizes the truth of my near departure.

"Allie," the pause is pregnant with introspection and solemnness, "in another life, would you marry me?"

I laugh through the sparkling river of tears. "Oh, Ian. I can think of nothing more wonderful or fulfilling then to live the rest of my days with you in this or any other life."

He pulls me closer. While in his arms, I drift off to sleep to the thoughts of a small wedding: Daddy, Mom, Abbie, Ian's parents, my children from the hospital as well as the nursing staff are in attendance. I walk down the aisle with my arm inside Daddy's. My dress is plain and white. Smiles and joy abound. Live music underscores my short journey to the front where the man of my dreams, Ian McPhetridge, awaits. Petals fall from above covering everyone in attendance as heaven partakes in the celebration.

"ALLIE. ALLIE." A familiar voice penetrates my pondering. Daddy stands in front of me dressed in a black tuxedo with a large white linen napkin draped over his arm and carrying a covered tray.

He sets it on the adjustable table that slides underneath my bed. I push the button to raise the head of my bed and when I am situated, he slides the table toward me.

"For lunch today mademoiselle, we serve your favorite, *farine d'avoine*." He removes the lid.

"Oatmeal," I say delighted.

"And don't forget the side of toast." He procures another small plate from behind his back and sets it on the table. "*Bon appétit mademoiselle.*"

"Thanks daddy."

"Nothing but the best for you Princess."

As I try to ingest the steaming porridge Daddy paces the room. At last he sits on the bed and puts his feet up on the spread.

"You're not wearing shoes. What kind of waiter are you?"

His laugh soon turns solemn.

"It can't be easy for you and Mom."

"Allie, we take it one day at a time. Some days are better than others."

I nod my head.

"I don't want the remaining days of my life filled with sadness. That's not how I want to make my exit. There should be joy and celebration, parties and get-togethers. Events where we laugh and joke together. Don't you agree?"

I can tell he's conflicted by my comments.

"Allie, you came into my life seventeen years ago. You've been a major part of it. To lose you is to lose myself." Tears drip onto his tux. "It isn't easy knowing what we know. I might die or Karla or Abbie could die at any moment. It would be a shock and awful. Knowing the day you're going to die is right around the corner is, well, it's different. It snatches the joy right out of your life."

In my preparedness to die, I realize I've stopped short of thinking it through. Those left behind are the ones with the difficult times ahead of them.

"We'll do our best to stay positive and hopeful. Understand Allie, we'll face days when the mountain crushes us."

"I'm sorry Daddy." My arm reaches out to touch him. "I wish I could block the pain from reaching you."

"And I wish to God He'd answer my prayer and let me take your place."

"Daddy!" I'm aghast at his statement. "You raised me to believe God has a plan for each of us."

"That's right Princess."

"Why mess up what God wants to do in your life? Mom needs you and Abbie needs you not to mention the other lives you are going to touch in your lifetime." He looks as if I've prophesied something profound about his life. "You have an incredible life to live."

More tears flow. He kisses me on the forehead before leaving. I tell him I love him. He doesn't hear. My voice has caught in my throat.

Exhale

The cloudiness has disappeared from my eyes. The veil holding back my lucidity has been lifted. I have total clarity. Its briefness becomes evident as the momentary light disappears followed by darkness. What I hoped for at the end as I transition from this place to the next has come to be. I have run the race, and by God, I have won.

My eyes squint and my heart skips a beat though I imagine it leaping through the ceiling. Daddy is still here. With him are Mom, Abbie, and Ian. I love them all. I want Daddy's image to be the final one my eyes rest upon in this world. I memorize his face for eternity.

I notice the sadness in his eyes and detect a stream of uncertainty. A single tear releases from the damned up well of tears. More will follow. I refuse to let him go until his unrestrained thoughts find calm. His eyes penetrate mine. I leave them open as he watches a movie montage of my life play before him. Only milliseconds pass, but Daddy's eyes brighten.

Enclosed within daddy's firm grip, my thin anemic fingers twitch, but not from the enclosure. His eyes lower from their hold on my face as if seeking a final message—the last communication I will make on this side of eternity. And he's right. Daddy releases his hold keeping his hands cupped underneath mine. For my contentment and desire, one final time, I need to confirm his understanding of my life. With mere moments remaining, I have but one message: my life has been fuller than I deserve. The sparkle from my engagement ring, I imagine, matches the twinkle in his tear-filled eyes. At last I know he's, if not at peace, comforted by the knowledge I lived a complete life.

"I'm sorry I doubted Allie."

His smile is reassuring. With my voice out of commission, I cannot make known to him how much I love him. No words remain unspoken between us. Notwithstanding, a lifetime of I love yous' we want to shower on one another. I communicated to him the other day through my failing scribble. *"No goodbyes,"* I wrote. He nodded.

When I am positive Daddy understands everything, I close my eyes.

My first breath, I'm told, came when the doctor held me upside down and smacked me on the bottom. The nerve. I gasped from the pain sucking oxygen into my lungs for the first time. I continued to cry unhappy over the doctor's actions. When he left the room, I quieted. He returned twice more to the room. Each time I let him know I didn't approve of his birthing ritual.

I remember none of that.

Let me tell you what I do remember: nearly missing the opportunity to live a full life and impacting the lives of those around me. I remember how love is supposed to feel as it brushes over your heart as if someone is tickling it with a feather. I'm unable to forget the power of forgiveness between mother and daughter. Lives once lived apart now joined in family and spirit because of a conscious choice to love. I can't forget the refreshment that occurred when reconciling with a friend who loves you as much as you love him. Or seeing a roommate carry on your legacy with the children you left behind. One more thing: I will never fail to remember how the everlasting love of a father shaped and reshaped my life.

This time, no spasm attacks my body and I slip away, the quiet after a song has concluded milliseconds before the applause begins. He tightens his arms around me and grips me with all his strength. He is not powerful enough to keep me from leaving this time. *"Thank you, Daddy, you were right. Infinity exists between the lines. It prevails within a single breath."*

"I love you sweetheart," he whispers in my ear for the final time. "Save a spot for me in the kitchen. I'm making your favorite."

I exhale.

About the Author

Richard C. McClain II, is one of five children who at an early age grew up in the world of imagination. His exposure to children's records and books inspired Richard to pursue music, theatre and writing.

Richard later became a pastor where from the pulpit he used his story telling abilities to bring the word to life in the hearts of the congregation.

Richard is husband of Sharon, and father of Nicholas, Nicola, Nathan, Natalie, and Nadia. He has had the privilege of honing his storytelling craft and understands the balance between imagination, fantasy, and real life.

Author of The Coterie – Declaration, and Perfect Imperfection released in Spring of 2017, and My Last Breath – The Space Between the Lines released in January of 2018, Richard's newest work, Singed Dreams – The Quintessential Dancer will be released in the Spring of 2018

With family living on two continents, Richard splits his time between America and Australia.